# SPIRIT MAN

by

George Mendoza
and
James Nathan Post

D0731445

Postscript Publishing Company
Albuquerque NM

# Spirit Man

Copyright © 2008 by
George Mendoza and James Nathan Post

All Rights Reserved

This book is entirely fictional. No character is intended to represent any real person, nor is any action the description of an actual event.

Cover paintings by George Mendoza.

No part of this book maybe reproduced or transmitted in any form or by any means, graphic, electronic, or mechanical without the written permission of the publisher.

Postscript Publishing Company
813 Valencia Dr NE
Albuquerque NM 87108

www.postpubco.com
www.georgemendoza.com

## DEDICATION

To the Universe, and its Creator, for providing me with a complicated, funny, crazy, difficult, and rewarding life to write about;

To my mother Cindi, the best mom and dad a son could ever have;

To my friends and family (in no special order) who have encouraged me to pursue my dreams: Bobby Cook, Judy Fein, Hal Fore, Emroy Shannon, Dave Harris, Paul Vachal, Alan Sachs, Estella Mayorga, Bill Buchanan, James McConnell, Neal Hidalgo, Felix Serna, Clyde Montoya, Pancho Castillo, Ernie Barge, Sonny Irizzarry, Dennis G. Carmen, Mark Medoff, Robert Duvall, Rob Carliner, Dick Guttman, and Jane Seymour;

To my children Michael and Lou. Let the Spirit shine in you always;

To Bethany Ball, and to John Prats, for their creative contributions to the original story concept;

And for his unending encouragement, years of creative collaboration, and magical enhancement of each visit to "the other side of the gate," my long-time conspirator and word wizard, James Nathan Post.

*George Mendoza, Jr.*

## PREFACE

When I first met Olympic blind runner George Mendoza in 1983 in Santa Fe, New Mexico, I was amazed with his unbreakable spirit.  His determination and persistence are inspirational to me and to many others who know him.

I had the honor to host "The George Mendoza Story" which was aired on the Public Broadcasting System (PBS-TV).  I also enjoyed reading his biography, "Running Toward The Light," by award winning author William J. Buchanan.

George told me years ago of his plan to write a novel based on a strange experience he had while on a long-distance run in the desert of southern New Mexico. He described running through a gate in the air into a strange magical world. That run and the incredible events that followed played a big part in the creation of this delightful book.

SPIRIT MAN is George's unique vision, and I personally found it filled with vivid imagery and concepts I have never thought of before, told with the lyric intensity of the best work of novelist James Nathan Post.

This is one of the best books I have read in a very long time. I could not put it down.

*Robert Duvall*

## PROLOG

"Speed is power! Speed is power! Mine, mine, mine, mine!" Michael Seymour chanted as he drove himself up the path. He leapt and pranced, the power of his youth making him feel invincible. As he reached the crest, he hooted and crowed, "Top of the world! Mine!"

Behind him a few yards, his friend Mark Serna pressed to sprint the last few steps to catch up. "Come on, hurry up. It's great up here," Michael called.

Sweat dripped down Mark's deep tanned face, and matted the thick black hair hanging long on his forehead. At the top of the path, the runners rested against a boulder overlooking the Mesilla Valley. From their vantage high in the granite crags of New Mexico's Organ Mountains, they looked out over a desert landscape of stunning beauty. Below them to the west lay the green band of the great river valley, the Rio Grande, and to the north the sweeping rust-red panorama of the Jornada del Muerte, the journey of death, where so many pioneers had died trying to reach the life-saving water of the river. Ninety miles away, the forested massifs of the Gila Wilderness lay heavy and dark on the horizon. A storm rose high above the distant mountain peaks, and the late afternoon sun pierced the towering piles of cumulus clouds with shafts of light that glowed crimson and gold on the valley below. The river wandered south, weaving its thread of green through the strange lunar blackness of lava flows, toward mysterious distant peaks in Mexico.

"Know what I feel like?" Michael asked. "Like this moment is the frontier of creation, and everything is beginning from right here. All that world down there, and all those people, are suspended in time, just waiting for me to come back down from the mountain."

Above them in the jagged dogtooth crags of the ridge, a single column of thunderclouds boiled up, and began to grumble. As the runners felt the first drops of the afternoon rain falling from it, Michael began to prance again on his toes. "I'll race you back," he challenged.

"How about we just run back?" Mark suggested. "I don't want to make you feel bad."

"Oh, that's funny," Michael scoffed. "Maybe there's something you haven't noticed. I have always been faster than you, and that's the way it will always be. It doesn't take a prophet to tell you where I'm going. I'm the best this school has ever seen, and you're looking at solid Gold in the next Olympics."

Without another word, Michael turned and set a driving pace down the path. With a sigh at his friend's hubris, Mark started after him. He knew Michael was not without some justification in his boast. Over six feet tall, the fleet young athlete looked like a wild creature of the plains, sunset glowing in warm colors from his fair complexion, emerald fire in his bright green eyes, thin but muscular limbs giving him a bounding grace — a perfect running machine.

The storm hovered over the runners, and a gust of wind blew down the trail behind them, carrying with it the fresh smell of rain. When Mark came around a bend in the winding pathway, he found Michael waiting for him, a taunting grin on his face. "That's funny, I don't feel bad at all," Michael said sarcastically. "You look like you are about ready to die."

"OK, hotshot," Mark said with a friendly but wry smile, "you just keep looking over your left shoulder, you hear?"

A short drive from the end of the runners' trail was Michael's house, which had once been some distance out of Las Cruces, but was now along its outskirts. It was a lovely old adobe hacienda, surrounded by giant cottonwood trees. Their ancient branches spread from gnarled trunks five feet thick, creating a sheltering space like a thousand hands webbed and cupped.

The two-story house featured a vaulted living room with a large stone fireplace. On the ceiling, a sunroof allowed light to spread throughout the house. The thick adobe walls kept it cool in the summer and warm in the winter.

The runners ducked into the house just in time to escape the pursuing storm. Michael headed into the kitchen, then reappeared with two cans of beer. "Ah!" agreed Mark, popping one open.

"Don't you guys have a race tomorrow?" asked Michael's mother Linda Seymour, as she stepped into the room.

Michael jumped back startled. "Mom! You scared the hell out of me."

"I was just wondering if that was going to affect your performance," she said.

"One beer isn't going to kill us," he scoffed. "That's tomorrow, and I'm not going to lose. This is the best I've ever felt before a race."

In her late forties, she carried herself as if twenty. Her delicate features and slim figure still provided her with admiring glances. She was devoted to her work as a surgical nurse, and spent countless hours giving the best care possible to her patients, her family, friends, and often as not, their pets, lost desert tortoises, and busted-wing birds.

"Lock the house if you leave before your Dad gets home," she said. Then she stopped, as though surprised. "Oh, how could I have forgotten? Your coach called and said there has been a change. Buddy Dunlap fell off his horse, and he won't be able to run tomorrow. Mark, he said you are going to replace him in the 1500 meter race."

Michael looked more astonished than Mark did. "What, is he crazy?" he blurted. "Mark is only a sophomore. Buddy was our best shot at taking second place."

Mark frowned, but held his tongue, and Linda gave him an apologetic little shrug. "Well, you wanted me to race," he said to Michael. "I guess you got your wish."

When she left for work, there was a moment of uncomfortable silence. Then they toasted with their beers, and made their way upstairs to Michael's room. It was immaculate, as though kept clean by a professional. Actually, it was. A large new stereo sound system rested on a built-in shelf, and like everything else in the room it was the best that money could buy.

"My man, I just can't help envying the life you've got," said Mark.

"Only the best for the best," said Michael.

"It must be nice to have rich parents."

"You mean like winning all those races for me, or just the wealth and social station?" Michael asked, sucking beer.

"No, but I just think, if my father was a lawyer and my mother was a nurse, I just think I wouldn't be like you. I'll tell you that," said Mark.

Michael chuckled and said, "You got that right. If you had what I have, you still wouldn't be like me. The reason why you are what you are is because you don't see yourself worth any more than what you've got."

"You don't know how it is in my life," Mark objected. "You have it easy, a free-ride, and you don't even know it."

"Hey, I'm sorry, but yeah, winning does come easy for me," said Michael.

Pressing their friendship as Michael had pressed him running, Mark went on, "You know, you are the most egotistical individual I have ever known. I don't know how...what is her name? Does that girl thing you hang on your arm have a name? Wendy, isn't it? I don't know how Wendy can put up with you. You keep her around like one of your trophies, to take down and polish up when you want to show off."

"Hey, what kind of crap is this?" asked Michael. "You get a chance to even get into a race with me, and you're giving me a bad time now?"

"Think, Dumb B'nee! How many friends do you have?" Mark pointed to his own chest. "One, right? And I still don't know why."

"Are you kidding? Everybody wants to be my friend, Marcus. I just don't have the time to put up with them," said Michael.

"They are not your friends," Mark persisted. "When your glory is gone, they are gone, and you know it. The truth hurts, and if it doesn't hurt now, it will hurt later, you hear me?"

"Well, passing glory is one thing I don't have to worry about. I'm the greatest ever, remember?" said Michael.

"Only a man with no spirit can go around acting as if he were the best thing that has ever happened to this earth," Mark told him. "You're so busy appreciating yourself, you don't even see the important things in life."

"Right, and what might those be? I think you're just so jealous you've started peeing green," said Michael.

"Jealous of you? Hey, you've got a lot of nice stuff, but I'm sure not jealous of somebody who has no friends, who treats people like dirt. You're all attitude and no spirit, Michael. Me jealous? Give me a break."

"What are you talking about, spirit?" asked Michael. "Are you recruiting for some kind of church thing?"

"Naw, I mean spirit, knowing who you are, not having to feel superior to someone to feel good about yourself. Come on, Michael, it's not just about sharing what you have, the material things, but what you are, all of you."

"They don't give the glory to losers, Mark, and I win the races. You can respect that, or you can envy it, but you can't share it. There is only enough room at the top for one, and I've got the trophies to prove that belongs to me."

Mark shook his head, feeling more sorry for his friend than envious or angry. He looked into Michael's eyes and said, "The top is a lonely place, if you think it means you're better than the rest of us."

There was a long moment of silence as Michael thought back on his experiences as though to see if his friend could possibly be right, and not merely expressing his own pique. For as long as he could remember, in everything he did, he had been better than all those around him. "No, Mark," he said. "People are not born equal. I really am better than all of you suckers. That has not been an easy fact to face, but I have faced it, and sooner or later, all of you will have to face it too. I was the one who brought victory to our high school again and again," Michael persisted. "You were there. You saw it. How can you say I have no spirit?"

"Just because you're the star, that doesn't mean you have spirit. OK, you were born good at sports. Is that supposed to mean something?" Mark crushed the beer can and tossed it in a wastebasket.

"It isn't just sports," said Michael, uncomprehending. "It's everything we've done together. I have always done it better, school, girls, everything. If that isn't spirit, what would it take?"

Mark spread his hands. "OK, pal," he said, "you're right. You win...again."

"Things comes easy for me because I have spirit," said Michael, as though in simple summation of a self-evident case.

Mark looked at his watch and said, "It's time to work. I have to make a living. I don't know what you'd think if you ever had a real job."

"A year from now people will be throwing money at me just to hear me say the name of the shoes they sell," Michael said. "All you mean by 'a real job' is mindless work for no pay. That's why you will always be a nobody, and I will always be somebody."

"Whatever you say, Spirit Man," said Mark. He picked up his shirt and left.

Michael opened the balcony doors and stepped outside. The fresh air was brisk on his face, and he inhaled deeply, taking in the earthy smell of rain on the desert. From the second story bedroom, he could see water running down the driveway. He watched Mark hurry to his car, skipping over puddles and then ducking quickly into the little VW bug. In a minute the ancient machine crawled down the driveway, spitting smoke from its exhaust, and was soon out of sight.

He stared at the trophy case on his bedroom wall, a glass monument filled with the memories of countless victories, engraved in brass and silver. On top of that, his academic success had been exceptional as well. He planned to receive degrees in Civil Engineering and Political Science. After an illustrious career as an athlete, he reasoned, he would move into government, and become a man of influence. His dreams were coming true and all he wished for was almost a reality, just one little moment away.

"Spirit Man, huh," he scoffed. "All right, I'll show him. I'll show them all."

The tournament was a set-up for glory. The right pro scouts were there, and the big media from the city. A dedicated crowd cheered with fervent school spirit, and the name of Michael Seymour was on everyone's lips. As the underdog school, they were ready for a miracle, and ready for him to bring it to them. The team had come through, and held the line on points. Then as his main event came up, the coach told him, "Michael, we're down to the wire. You are our shot at the championship. It all depends on you!" Sure, that's how it was supposed to be. Then there'd be no question about it — they all would see.

Michael was breathing deep, stretching, prancing, trying to focus all of himself on the race, while at the same time putting on a good show for the fans and their cameras. He looked around the track, and in his mind he pictured how he would win. He would fall in the middle and keep a steady stride, letting those go who wanted to try getting an early lead on him. He would pace himself to conserve energy, then at the right moment he would give it all and speed past the tiring quick-starters. Then he would take the advice he sometimes gave not quite jokingly to other runners: "Get out in front, and stay there until the crowd starts screaming." Michael focused his mind on seeing his fans cheering in admiration as he brought his school to glory. There were his Mother and Father, with tears of pride in their eyes. There was the coach, cheering, "You're the one, champ!" There were the girls, the cheerleaders, the new sorority pledges, every one of them wanting him more than any other, even if only for one night.

"Oh, Michael!" called a voice from across the track. Wendy ran toward him, arms wide and a smile of rapture on her face. She threw her arms around his neck and kicked up her feet. For a moment he was caught off-guard, and the thought struck him that she was embarrassing him by making a big show of him being her possession. Then Michael could feel her warm body press against his. Her golden blonde hair carried a wonderful fragrance, making her all the more beautiful. Her blue eyes sparkled in the sunlight, and he wanted her, and in the confusion of emotions for a few seconds Michael forgot about the race.

Trying to hold both of those reactions at the same time, and a bit frightened of both, he abruptly jumped back, pushing Wendy away. "Wendy, come on," he said. "I'm trying to concentrate here."

"I just wanted to wish you luck," she said, crestfallen. "I love you."

"I don't need luck, and I don't need this now!"

Wendy's eyes widened. "Michael, what do you mean?" she cried. "What are you talking about?"

"Will you get off the track!" he snapped at her. "This is no time for some kind of big relationship thing. I'm supposed to look like a hero here, not your pet horse. This is important!"

Devastated by his incomprehensible attack, she broke into tears and fled the track.

"What the hell was that about?" Mark asked him as they took their places to enter the track. "What the hell did you say to her?"

"Don't worry about it," Michael said sternly. "You just get yourself in my draft, and try to stay close enough to take second place. We need the points, even with my win."

# SPIRIT MAN

The loudspeaker announced the 1500-meter race. "Let's go, you two," called the coach. "Let's see something out there, all right?"

Michael positioned himself on the line, set his feet on the starting blocks, and waited for the starting gun. The sound seemed to drop to nothing as his mind focused on the moment, and he knew that he was going to win this race.

His body tingled with the rush of adrenalin as the gun fired and his legs hurled him forward like the elastic tendons of a slingshot. In two steps the wind was rushing by him, and he could feel the cool bite of it against his sweat-glistening skin. Other runners took the lead in front of him as he positioned himself in the pack. He calculated each breath, reserving his strength to give it his all on the last lap. His body felt great, as though each muscle were inflated with some pulsating form of vibrant energy. Absolute confidence swept over him, and he began to laugh, and to stalk each of the runners ahead, planning the moments he would overtake each of them, and then taking them, one after another, until there was no one in front of him, and only one lap to go. The crowds were on their feet, cheering, "Michael! Michael!"

An instant from abandoning himself already to victory, something caught his attention. A part of his mental training he sometimes thought of as his "tail gunner" was a habit he had developed, to be very conscious of the sounds coming up behind him. To his surprise, he heard someone close behind him, closing on him. He pressed a little harder, and realized he was running flat out, and still he could hear the crisp aggressive chop of the runner's feet on the track, not thumping, but grabbing at the cinder. He could hear the runner breathing, not the gasping of someone's last try, but the strident hiss of someone pumping up a head of new steam, an instant from letting it loose to accelerate like a locomotive into the last sprint.

He knew better than to look back, of course. He couldn't afford even the tenth of a second it might cost him to snap his head around, much less the half second he could lose by breaking stride. But his astonishment that someone might actually be passing him got the best of him. He had to look. When he did, his astonishment turned to shock. It was Mark Serna.

For an instant, they were eye to eye, and what Michael saw in Mark's eyes sent a jolt through him that seemed to stop time. For an instant, his body moved while his mind did not. Then he felt a hot stab up his leg, and he felt his knee collapse, his ankle turn, and his toe catch his heel. In a horrid instant, he saw his arm swing out as he wrenched around and tumbled toward the lane beside him.

His knee scraped against the asphalt of the track, and then his elbows and his palms, and then his face, and his shoulder. He saw Mark's alarm as he tried to leap over him. Then Mark's foot caught him in the stomach, and Mark tumbled through the sky, it seemed like over and over before crashing to the ground.

The roar of the crowd was suddenly distant, like the ringing of your ears in the bottom of a cave. The runners dashed past, and then he just lay there. "Michael! Michael, are you all right? Can you hear me?" he heard the coach calling to him.

"Get me up, coach, I can still make it," he tried to say, but he felt unable to move.

"Get the medics over here," he heard the coach yell. He was hanging on the edge as the realization flooded his mind that he had lost. He had lost the race. He had lost the tournament. He had lost the Olympics. He had lost everything.

The crowd was stunned, and began to mutter. "There went our championship," he heard someone grumble. "What the hell was he thinking about out there? What a putz."

He wanted to block out the horrible things he was hearing, and thinking, but he couldn't. He felt nausea wave over him as he realized he agreed with the things he heard coming from the disappointed fans. He would forever be the one who could have given them the championship, but did not. He was the loser who had cost them everything. He could hear Mark's words coming back to him. "When your glory is gone, they are gone."

"What happened to you out there?" asked the Coach. "You were steaming, and then..."

"My leg just gave out, and I tripped," said Michael, putting his hands over his face, and then taking them away when he remembered the fans in the stands.

"Oh, you'll be all right," said Mark darkly, as he limped by nursing a skinned and bruised knee.

The paramedics checked Michael over and decided everything seemed normal, and with his parents close by they helped Michael off the track. There was a polite wave of the traditional applause for an injured athlete, but he could tell it was only half-hearted.

"That isn't normal," said the coach. "I want you to go to the campus hospital and get yourself checked. It could have been just a cramp, but lets not take any chances." He put his hand on Michael's shoulder. "And Michael, don't let this blow your mind, OK? There are still other races to win."

It was not until he was in the car with his family that he remembered something else that had happened. His own voice came back to him. "Who do you think you are, Wendy? I don't need luck, and I don't need you." His own words stunned him. What could possibly have made him say that to her? He loved Wendy, didn't he? "I don't need you! Get off the track!"

"I've got to find Wendy," he mumbled.

It was almost evening when Michael drove up to Wendy's driveway, jumped out of the Jeep and started walking toward the door. He saw a window curtain move to reveal a peeking eye, then to his surprise Wendy's mother opened the door and met him outside the house, wearing an angry and very determined look.

"Hi, is Wendy here?" he asked, trying to sound youthful and polite. "I'd sure like to talk to her."

"She doesn't want to see you right now, Michael," the woman said.

"Look, I just want to talk to her," he began to plead.

"Would you just leave?" she demanded, raising her voice.

He started to protest, then found himself embarrassed living out a cliché scene he had seen so many times in kid-romance movies. He shook his head and turned away, and started to walk back to his Jeep when she spoke again. Michael stopped to listen, but didn't turn around.

"Who do you think you are, Michael?" she said to his back. "You hurt the people that love you the most. You have no heart."

He hesitated a moment, then turned to face her, ready to apologize, repent, to promise anything. But she had already gone, leaving him on the walkway alone.

Night fell on the little town as a harsh wind blew across the valley. A haze of dust filled the air, making the sunset dark and ruddy, not like live fire, but like old blood. The dust settled on the surroundings, making them seem even drearier, and making him feel desolate and barren.

He started toward his favorite bar, El Patio, in the old-town part of the valley known as Old Mesilla, the little Mexican village that had been the capital of the entire territory back in the time of Billy The Kid. Then he winced at the thought of having to face the usual crowd from campus out there, and he decided to go down the valley toward Mexico to find a bar where he would not be recognized. That took him a block past Mark's house.

Mark would be mad at him. He knew that was for sure. He would probably even blame him for costing him second place, and costing the school the win. Michael shook his head, knowing it would be no fun to put himself through that, but if he didn't go over and talk to him, Mark would think he was avoiding him because he was feeling guilty. If Mark was so small as to want to make a big show of being mad at him, well, Michael was big enough to forgive him. So he made the turn, and pulled up into Mark's driveway.

It was a small house in an older part of town, but a pleasant neighborhood. Mark had once pointed out to him when he referred to the area as "low-rent" that it was more accurately "low-buy." Many of the residents were owners, proud they could own their own homes even if at the bottom of the economic scale.

Answering the man's call to come on in when he rang the bell, he found Mark's father sitting on his favorite recliner, watching television, working on getting drunk on beer and old movies. "Hey, Mikey, how you been? I haven't seen you in a while," he said.

"It's been a day from hell," Michael admitted.

"I heard what happened. I'm really sorry."

"I guess shit happens," said Michael with a philosophical shrug and a brave grin.

He found Mark in his bedroom, a cinderblock cell decorated in early Thrift Store motif. An acoustic guitar on the bed gave it a comfortable touch, and an old but functional stereo set rested on a bookshelf of boards and patio blocks.

"I don't want to talk about it," was the first thing Mark said.

"Me neither," said Michael. "I just want to go out and get shitfaced drunk and forget about it."

"You sure?" asked Mark. "I don't know if that's such a good idea, if you've got some kind of rare nerve disease or something..."

"Hey, come on, I'm not sick. The coach was just covering his ass," Michael protested. "I just tripped, that's all. Come on, let's go down the valley to Fat Manny's."

"I don't want to go out tonight, Michael. Let's just stay here and watch the tube and drink my dad's beer, OK?" Mark suggested. "I just don't want something else to go wrong today."

"Don't give me that," Michael said, taking the offensive. "If we start living like we were afraid of everything that might go wrong, we're already beaten. Come on, we've got a life to get on with."

They took a back road to reach Fat Manny's Cantina, a small bar in San Manuel, one of the tiny old Mexican villages in the valley south of Las Cruces. The route took them past the huge orchards of America's largest pecan farm, long rows of ghostly trees, perfectly aligned like the identical tombstones of a vast cemetery. The moon's reflection glimmered eerily in the puddles of irrigation water, and between the branches of the trees, as though it were bounding along through the trees beside them. The cool evening wind blew leaves across the road, and Mark shuddered to note they looked like thousands of insects scuttling along the ground in the baleful light.

When Michael turned off the Jeep in front of Fat Manny's, they could hear the jukebox playing The Doors. Though they had been there before, both felt out of place. No one actually turned to look at them, or changed what they were doing, but the attention in the bar seemed to shift. They took two seats in a corner of the room.

"Let's get started, Mark. I'll buy the first round," said Michael.

"Get what you want, Michael," Mark said. "I don't really want to drink tonight."

"Don't give me that shit either. We didn't drive out here for a Shirley Temple." Michael ordered a pitcher of beer and two shots of tequila, and when Mark refused to drink the potent agave whiskey, Michael shrugged and tossed down both shots, following them with a chunk of lime. He poured two mugs of beer, sucked the foam off the top of one, then sat back and surveyed the room.

Through the haze of cigarette smoke they could see four men playing at the pool table, which stood in the center of the bar. Michael sipped his beer and watched them a few minutes, then said, "I can beat any of those guys."

"Yeah, you probably can," Mark conceded, knowing all too well that the game of pool was another of those things for which Michael just seemed to have a knack, "but I think they'd rather be left alone."

"'Zat right?" said Michael, as though just challenged. He stood up making his chair scrape noisily, then sauntered over and put two quarters down on the table.

"Don't get us in trouble, Michael," Mark said when he

returned. "Give it a break."

"Will you lighten up?" Michael said, slicking back his hair with his hands. "I'll just win a couple of bucks from these bozos, and we'll leave...just enough for the drinks."

"Those guys don't look like the type to hustle," Mark warned him. "Let's just have a beer and get the hell out of here, OK?"

When his turn came up, Michael strolled to the table, making a show of trying to look cool. "Hey, what's happening, man?" he asked. "What are we playing?"

"Cost you five to find out," said the player. The man was a few years older than Michael, with tattoos on his arms. His pocked face was clean-shaven, and he wore his hair in a long ponytail. He powdered his stick and waited for an answer.

Michael pulled a wad of bills from his pocket, peeled out a five, and smoothed it on the edge of the table. "Let's do it."

The man made the break, sinking two, then missed the next. Michael positioned himself, shot and missed. "Man, I thought I had that one cold," he complained. The man shot again, and made four before he missed. Looking agitated, Michael scratched, and the men in the bar laughed.

Ponytail quickly finished the game. Michael handed over the five dollars and turned to leave when the man stopped him. "You can stay in for ten, college boy."

"Oh, the big money now, huh?" Michael said sarcastically with a too-cocky grin. "Ok, you got it."

Michael put a ten on the table, racked the balls, and walked back to drink his beer with Mark.

"Michael, don't try to hustle these guys," said Mark again.

"Have another beer," said Michael with a chuckle. "This isn't going to take long."

The second game, Michael played the same swaggering role, and he was furious when he lost. "Damn. I need another tequila to get focused. Another ten?"

"Cost you fifty bucks this time," he said.

Michael looked surprised. "Fifty bucks?" he asked.

"Come on, hot dog," the player taunted him. "You know you're just having a bad run. What you afraid of?" One of his pals began to chuckle and sneer.

"Not afraid of you. It's just a lot of money," said Michael. "You sure you can afford it?" Michael rolled his stick on the pool table to check its straightness. "I'll tell you what," he said, pulling out the cash, "I'll play you for the fifty if you let me break." With his eyes on Michael's money, the man agreed. On Michael's break he sank two stripes in the corner pockets. "Oh, wow!" he cheered, as though he had never done that before. He lined up an inferior shot, then changed his mind and set up another. The target ball dropped, and the cue rolled smoothly to a stop in front of another. "Hey, it's a duck, but we take what we get, right?" he said as he dunked it with a crisp click. He positioned each ball perfectly and never missed until the last one was gone. "Wow, my first perfect game!" he crowed.

"You hustled me, Slick," said the man, as he handed Michael a fifty dollar bill.

"I'm working my way through college," said Michael with a sneer. He plucked the money from the big player's hand and walked back to the corner where Mark was sitting rigid, nervously watching.

"Are you happy now?" Mark asked. "Let's get out of here before those guys decide not to let us go."

When they got outside the wind was blowing in chilly gusts. The sky was dark and murky, though almost clear except for a few high tattered cirrus clouds like ghostly fingers glowing in the moonlight, clawing at the moon through the murky dust.

"I can't believe what you just did," Mark said.

"At least something went right for me today," said Michael with grim satisfaction.

As they reached the Jeep, another man suddenly confronted them, one they did not recognize from the bar. The stranger flourished a weapon and said, "Give me the money you took inside."

Michael stood astonished and just stared at him, mouth agape. He was large, with scraggly hair, a dark, thick-featured, mean-looking man, difficult to tell what races he might have been mixed of. His weapon was a two-foot hunk of heavyweight rebar, the corrugated iron rod used in concrete construction, its jagged end making it a lethal combination of club and sword. The assailant stepped up close to him, quickly, and put the point of it under Michael's chin. Nose to nose, he stared madly into Michael's eyes.

Suddenly more frightened than he had ever been before, Michael couldn't move. He was astonished to see the hate, and the rage, and also, perhaps most frightening, a kind of predatory hunger in the man's eyes. He reached into his pocket and pulled out the money.

"Calm down, man. Just take the money," said Mark. "It's all right."

"Who asked you?" snarled the stranger with the blazing eyes. He snatched the wad of folded bills, stuffed them into his pocket, and then held Michael away and raised his rebar club to strike him on the head. "Think you're something, do you?" he hissed.

Explosively, with a cry like a Kung Fu movie warrior, Mark leaped forward and tried to grab the man's arm. Like it was nothing, the dark grisly man turned and snapped his jagged weapon back and forth across Mark's face. Each swing made a kind of sodden whopping crunch, nothing like the heroic clash of manly armor so familiar to the fans of matinee swordplay. If he had been one half inch closer, the end of the bar would have struck Mark directly in the temples, first on one side, and then the other, and he would surely have died instantly. With each swing, the jagged bar tore chunks of flesh and bone from the front of Mark's face. With no more than a gasp, he collapsed to the ground, where he lay unmoving, blood gushing from his eyes.

The attacker turned back gripping his deadly weapon to hit Michael. Then he saw some people coming out of the little bar, and he turned and disappeared into the shadows between the old adobe buildings of the dark little village.

Someone called 911, and a small crowd from the bar gathered around and stared as Michael sat beside his stricken friend. "Don't give up on me!" he cried.

Someone in the crowd laughed. "Give him a kiss," a voice jeered.

It took twenty minutes for the ambulance to arrive, and the police cars beat them by ten. Mark lay quiet as though lifeless, and the police stood around looking until the medics announced he was still alive, and put him on a stretcher and drove away.

Among the last to arrive was a stocky shock-haired Hispanic man about forty-five, wearing a baggy brown suit. "I'm Detective Steve Hinojosa," he told Michael. "We'd like to get this guy, if you'll help us. Nobody else saw him."

Michael gave as good a description of the man as he could recall. The officer wrote down the details, gave Michael his card, and said, "We'll get your whole deposition a little later, Michael. Go home to your family. There is nothing else you can do."

"What about Mark's family? Who's going to tell them?" asked Michael, his voice choking up and tears burning his eyes.

"I guess that's my job," Hinojosa replied. "In any case I don't think it would be wise for you to go over there right now." He placed a reassuring hand on Michael's shoulder. "We'll take care of all that can be done," he said.

The wind had come up again, and the streetlamps became glowing brownish globs of light, filled with whirling dust and trash. The wind tossed the Jeep from side to side, making the headlight beams dance crazily back and forth across the street, as though the weather were reflecting the storm in hell going on inside him.

When he arrived at his house, he knocked on his parents' bedroom door. "Mom! Dad!" he bawled. When his mother opened the door, clutching her robe and wearing an expression of deep concern, he reached out to touch her and said, "Mom... it's Mark."

Cecil Seymour got up and turned on his night lamp. In

its light they could see the horror in Michael's face, in the tangled hair, the eyes hot, red, and staring haunted from a face as pale as death. "Mark's hurt, he might be dead!" he wailed, and fell weeping onto her shoulder.

"It was all my fault. I took him out and got him killed!" Michael cried.

"What happened?" asked Michael's father.

Michael slumped and shrugged. "I took a little money from a guy, you know, playing a little pool. I just...I just needed to win something, you understand? Well, we got jumped, and this guy with the... like a sword thing...told me to give him the money, and I gave it to him. I gave it to him! But Mark thought he was going to hit me anyway, so he...he tried to take it away, and...and..."

Linda Seymour's throat constricted, and tears sprang to her eyes, and she wished she could hold her boy in the safety of her arms forever and just cry with him.

After a minute, Michael held back his tears. "I guess I ought to go to bed," he said, leaving the warmth of his mother's arms.

His father hugged him and said, "If you need us to help you, just call us."

Michael stumbled upstairs to his bedroom, locked the door and fell onto his bed. His head rang like a man beaten hard, and the room reeled, and his sides ached from crying. He sat up again, and found himself noting the silence and the stillness of the night, the simple reality of his room and his things. He sat staring into the space in his room, as though waiting for something to happen any second, for the movie to end, for the lights to come back up, and his friend to be at his side. But cutting through it all like a ghostly echo, he could hear Mark's voice saying over and over, "Whatever you say, Spirit Man."

Days went by in a blur of numbness for Michael Seymour. He was given some sedatives which helped him to fall asleep, but he slept only fitfully, and found himself startled awake sweating, as though from some dreadful unremembered dream. He spent his time alone as much as possible, seeking dark places and silence.

One day his father Cecil brought him the news that Mark had fully regained his consciousness, and could have visitors. Mark's mother had called to request that Michael and his family should not go to visit. Michael knew he had to go anyway, if he was ever to be able to speak to Mark again.

He found him sitting up in his bed, with bandages across his face.

"What are you here for?" Mark asked him.

"Well," he stammered, "I just wanted to thank you for trying to stop that guy, and to, well, get the truth all straightened out between us."

"The truth?" Mark snorted in disgust. "That part is easy. You know the truth, Michael. You saw it, and so did I, eye to eye. You were running flat out, all you had, and you knew it, and you knew I knew it. I had you, buddy. I'd have flamed your ass."

"Hey, I was surprised you were there, I admit that," Michael protested, "but I tripped. I tripped, and I blew it for everybody, OK? I'm sorry, all right?"

"No, you didn't trip, you son of a bitch," Mark said bitterly. "You took a dive. You took a dive, and you took me out with you, and you took the whole team out with you, because you would rather see everybody lose, than to come in second place to me. And that is exactly what was going to happen, and you knew it."

"Aw come on..." Michael began.

"No, you come on," Mark spat. "Then you had to come over with this big lets-go-get-a-beer-buddy bullshit trying to suck up to me anyway so I'd tell you I forgave you, and you could slink off feeling like you got away with it. Then you had to go jerk yourself off with those guys at the bar, still trying to make yourself feel like a winner. Let me tell you something, Michael See-more. You see less than anybody else I know. Even less than me!"

"What do you mean by that?" Michael asked, sensing a terrible bitterness.

"Oh, didn't they tell you?" Mark said, acid sarcasm,

anguish, and rage bubbling up madly in his voice. "I'm blind, Michael, totally and permanently blind. He tore my eyes out. I'll never see anything again, never, thanks to you. With friends like you, who needs enemies? Who needs bad luck? Who needs curses and crossed stars? You've got all the strikes against you, mister, in spades! The one consolation I have is I'm never going to have to see you again. Now get the hell out of here."

The words struck Michael with the breath-stopping shock of jumping into ice water. He rose up as though to spit out angry words, or pleading words, or reasonable words, but he had nothing to say, no point to make, no disarming bit of wit, no cutting trump line. There was nothing to do but leave. He walked numbly out of the hospital. It was beautiful outside. The sky sparkled above him, a balmy breeze stroked him, birds twittered and sang, a roadrunner scurried through the yucca plants, people laughed, and music played. It was as though the whole world had become some kind of surreal dream created just to mock him. He numbly drove toward the mountains to his beautiful family home. He numbly staggered to the kitchen, looked into the refrigerator, saw nothing he wanted, and numbly climbed the stairs to his room.

He caught sight of his own reflection in the glass of his trophy case — a man humiliated, hunched over in shame, eyes red and staring, the eyes of a haunted man. Behind the glass, the glory of his most wonderful moments enshrined before his eyes: faster than Mark, higher than Mark, stronger, farther, better, better, better than Mark! All he could not find a way to say burst up from deep within him like vomiting magma. He howled his frustration like a tortured man, then lunged to snatch up his ivory-and-silver inlaid pool cue. Grabbing it by the narrow end, he swung it against the case, shattering the glass. "God damn you!" he cried, not just as angry words, but a bitter prayer, a curse. "God damn you!"

"Michael, stop!" Linda Seymour cried out. Michael looked up to see his mother standing in the door crying in horror, and he was stricken to see she was afraid of him. His shame doubled, he pushed past her, ran down the stairs and out of the house, and took the path that led out into the desert, and toward the mountains.

<u>Chapter One</u>

Michael ran across the sands of the desert. He ran until his sides hurt, until his vision lost its color, until his spit was so thick he couldn't spit at all, and he prayed he would run himself into exhaustion, into oblivion. But his flesh began to burn itself, and its power drove him so he could not stop. The mountains rose up higher and higher over him as he approached them, and he began to hear voices coming from them like echoes.

"You have no spirit!"

"You can't run from your problems. "

"Wishing never helps."

"The truth hurts doesn't it?"

"You hurt the people that love you the most!"

The slope steepened as he drove himself onward, and he reached the first high outcropping of free rock. He had climbed the face a hundred times, and he hurled himself up the rock forty feet before pausing. He looked up at the sky, where a small hawk circled overhead, gliding over the tree tops and stony crags, waiting for its prey to emerge from hiding. "It is a death bird," he thought, horrified to think he believed it. "It has come for me." Suddenly he was afraid. He matched his hands and feet to the rock and started to climb, but it was an alien stone he found, like hostile flesh that recoiled from his touch and gave him neither foothold nor grasp. With sickening inevitability, his body slid, scraped down the side of the rock, then fell. There was a shock of impact, and then a metal-tasting ball of light exploded in the back of his head, and he found the unconsciousness he had been seeking.

When Michael awoke, he was already sitting up with his feet crossed in front of him and his arms resting on his knees. His eyes were open, and he was watching blood trickle from his head into a pool between his legs.

Jolted by a wave of nausea, he jerked his head up, and began to recoil from the ringing pain in his head, but was so surprised by what he saw that he forgot himself for a moment. There on the mountainside before him was an ancient gate. Michael forced himself to get to his feet. It was heavy and thick, and deeply carved. With massive wrought-iron hinges it was fastened to a white-plastered adobe wall—which extended only six feet from each side. It was weathered by centuries, and Michael was absolutely certain it had never been there before. He took a step toward it, limping as he discovered new injuries, and then slowly raised the hand-wrought latch. When he gave the old door a push, it creaked, but swung smoothly open.

When he looked through it, the door led to the other side of the mountain path. Michael laughed, as though he had for a moment let himself believe he had expected to see something different. With a bit of his old boyhood bravado, he took three swaggering steps through the door, then turned around and looked back. His legs went to water, and he staggered and fell to his knees. The door was gone. With a cry of renewed anguish, he scrabbled on his torn hands and bruised knees to turn again and look at the place he had come into.

He was standing in a desert, a barren, desolate, and waterless land, strangely unreal. It bore no resemblance at all to the place where he had last stood. The sky was a blaze of flashing colors, in swirling motion as though hurtling through a rush of atmospheric mood swings. The sun was not a warm yellow-gold, but crystal blue-white.

Michael looked around to see if he might spot the gate, but he knew he wouldn't find it. In all directions he could see only rolling hills and dunes, with nothing in particular to give him any reference point. Whenever he looked back at a place, he had the uncanny feeling the hills had all moved, like slow swells in a sea of sand. The glaring sun beat down on the reddish dunes, and Michael began to notice the heat. He reached up to pull off his tie, and was surprised to notice for the first time that he was still wearing the clothes he had put on for the funeral. The sea of dunes stretched in every direction, and he decided since his coming through the gate was...well, somewhat unusual, he could probably expect something was already in store for him, so he might as well just sit down and wait for it. Michael took his tie off and buried it halfway in the sand, as a marker. He sat beside it for a long time, and eventually the sun settled toward the horizon. Feeling like a lost soul in Limbo, he stood and started walking toward the setting sun. Eventually there seemed to be a path, and then a trail. With no idea of where he was going, he began to follow it, looking ahead to pick it up in the fading light.

Chapter Two

The rocky dunes rolled like an endless red ocean. The sand was loosely packed, and walking was difficult. A harsh wind came up and blew sand into Michael's eyes, and into his ears, and down the collar of his dirty white shirt. The spray showered against his face like tiny needles not quite piercing his skin. Through the dunes he could see that the path remained curiously intact, as though the shifting flow of the sand chose to avoid it. Shadows played in the canyons and valleys as the brilliant colors in the swirling sky changed from crimson and chartreuse to purple and deep murky green. The temperature was dropping quickly and at first it felt good to get a break from the heat.

Darkness came, and stars lit up the sky, along with a glowing corona of shifting bands of color, a pulsing nebula extending out into the depths of space as though to embrace the brilliant arc-light jewels of the stars.

The temperature dropped even lower, and Michael began to feel the cold. Realizing he had drunk nothing since leaving the world he knew, he noticed his mouth was as dry as sand and grit grated his teeth. His feet ached, and when he sat down in the twilight and took off his shoes to rub them, he noticed that he had almost destroyed his dress shoes walking through the sand, climbing in the rocks, and running...how many miles had it been? He shook his head and wished he had his good running shoes. How many miles. How many miles was he away from the place on the other side of the adobe gate? Was "here" any place at all?

As he walked, he began to picture the blowing sand slowly carving away his body, like eroding a statue. If he fell, he feared, the sand would simply drain away his life like water, and his bones would crumble into sand and nothing would be left. He was suddenly afraid that he would die alone in this unknown place. Then another thought jarred him. He put his hand to his head and it was still sore to the touch, though he had not felt it for some time. Had he been killed in the fall? Was this his life after death?

Though an alien landscape, the trail and the dunes

seemed as real as any other reality he had ever known. The sand was real as he kicked it with his shoes, and so were the outcroppings of rock which he began to notice around him. Then he was surprised to find a strange vegetation blocking the path. When he brushed up against it in the sky lit gloom, he jumped back in pain. The plants had thick thorns, coarse and vicious, which stuck to his legs like hooks. Sitting down on a rock, Michael closed his eyes and pulled out the thorns one by one. "If this is death," he thought, "it sure isn't freedom from pain."

As he walked through the night, he began to stagger from side to side, wanting to embrace the sand and fall asleep. "Poison in the thorns?" he wondered groggily. He worried that when (if?) the sun came out in the morning, it would bring a scorching, searing heat. If he didn't find water tonight, would he die?

As though summoned by his desire, a pond appeared in front of him, the baleful firefly-green light of the night sky reflecting from its surface. As he approached it, he could see the dark needle-bearing shrubbery surrounded it. It took a long time, perhaps an hour or so, for him to carefully pick his way through the clumps of thistles to reach the water. He dropped to his knees and reached out his cupped hands to the water, then recoiled from the fetid stench. Moss and slime lay on the surface of the stagnant puddle, and bubbles belched up occasionally to release dank swamp gas. Even so, he filled his hands and made himself drink. The water made him gag, but he forced it down.

Michael stood, surveyed his surroundings in the murky half-light, and was suddenly alarmed to see footprints around the waterhole. He sank to a half-crouch and looked around quickly as though expecting to be pounced upon any second. Then feeling totally foolish—but still not standing up straight—he followed the footprints through a gap in the thorn bushes and discovered they led in two directions. One trail of prints led toward the path he had just traveled, and the other led up the nearest hillside. He followed them, and when he crested the hill, he was astonished to discover a city in the distance. In the same manner as the pond—as though it wanted to protect itself against intruders—it was walled with the thorn bushes, surrounded by a forest of the greasy-green tangled limbs with the steel-hard needles. The city appeared to be made of high mud-brick walls, like an ancient pueblo.

He sat down with his hands tight against his sides, trying to warm them. On the horizon, the dark mud-wall structures of the city seemed forbidding. The cold was numbing and he wished he could make a fire. He sat down and waited for something to happen.

A falling star streaked across the ebony sky, and he made a wish. He wanted to go home. He wondered what his parents were doing right then. Were they searching for him, worried? Or was he still lying at the foot of the rock face, having fallen only a second ago?

The silence was intense. He could hear his own breathing, and his heart pounding in his temples. Cold and exhausted, Michael lay down on the ground and pulled himself into a ball and tried to drift off to sleep. He curled down into the sand, trying to hold a little warmth, and he prayed he would dream of home.

He awoke to the sound of horses and men screaming in the distance. A cloud of dust rose in the air, and he saw a group of riders on horseback heading toward him. In sudden fear, he ran toward the brambles and worked his way under them, ignoring the spines poking into him as he squirmed.

The riders came into the center of the basin. It was hard for Michael to make out what was happening in the dark, but he watched as one of the riders dismounted. He looked around the area cautiously, then led his horse around the thickets. He stopped, knelt on the ground, and caressed the sand with his hands. He motioned the other riders to come to where he was standing. Michael could see they were dressed in metal body armor, and carried long swords, like Bedouin conquistadors.

Then suddenly one of the riders spotted him. "There!" he shouted, pointing to the thicket where Michael hid. With the needles tearing at him, catching his clothes, trying to hold him, he rolled and scrabbled along the ground until he could get to his feet. He started to run, a hunted animal with nowhere to hide, hoping his speed would save him from the hunter.

"Get him!" yelled the rider, as he unsheathed his sword.

Michael staggered and fell on the sandy ground, crawling on all fours, trying desperately to get away. Five horses surrounded him, rearing and neighing, their riders laughing and hooting with savage glee. He felt a net fall on top of him, and he fell to the ground and rolled into a ball, expecting any second to be speared or clubbed to death.

"Look what we have here! This will bring us a handsome reward," Michael heard one of them say, with the excited hungry laughter of a successful hunter. He cringed in fear as the rider dismounted and approached him. In the gloomy light, he couldn't see his face as he stepped purposefully over to Michael, spit copiously on his head, then pulled out his sword and put the point of it against Michael's neck.

"Please don't!" Michael cried out, to the amusement of the group. Then even through the numbness of his fear, he was astonished at the stench of the men, as though they were already corpses, or raptors crusted with the rotting flesh of their prey.

"Take him to Gahenna!" commanded the dismounted one, who seemed to be the leader. He stomped on Michael, then again, and kicked him in the back. The other riders dismounted, hooting and cheering. They removed the net that restrained him, then joined together to kick and beat him. He was both relieved and horrified to observe through the shock of the blows that they were all holding back their power to avoid damaging him, but were enjoying striking him hard enough to hurt and bruise. After the beating, a rider held him down, his knee pressing on the back of Michael's neck while he tied his hands behind his back. Another rider roughly tied a rope around his neck, got onto his horse, looped the other end around the saddle horn, and began to drag him. Michael struggled to get up and run behind the horse, the rope chafing and choking him.

As they approached the city, he could see it was ringed with fire, and smoke was spewing from buildings along its perimeter. He wondered if the city might be at war. The path changed to cobblestones. They walked over a wooden drawbridge, and through an arched opening in a crumbling stone wall. It seemed to Michael that the city had the elements of a great ancient civilization that had fallen into decay. There was little evidence of industrial technology, and people seemed to live in a kind of farm-town squalor. Stagnant fingers of wispy fog oppressed the air, doing nothing to clean the stink of sewage and animal filth. The streets were wet, and gutters and alleys were fouled with piles of human waste and garbage.

Great statues of warriors lay toppled over. Water fountains, once beautiful and masterful in their artistry, stood as shallow puddles of fetid sludge. Beautiful buildings, geometric marvels, architectural wonders now lay in ruins, burned, vandalized, or razed.

The soldiers led him past a courtyard, and to new horrors. The smell of slaughter assaulted his nostrils. Bodies hung from the walls, and dead men, women, and children lay covered in black-crusted blood. Swarms of flies and their maggots buzzed and wriggled, eating death.

Then they pulled him down a dark alley where people scurried about like rats, peering from the darkness. In their eyes he could see only the mindless hollow blackness of the devil's soul, full of hate, and hunger. One of the scurrying wretches burst from the shadows and attacked one of the riders, trying to grab the reins. The soldier swung his sword at the man, clipping cleanly through the front half of his neck. He fell to ground, a hideous gurgling gasping coming from his throat as he drowned in his own blood.

They came upon a courtyard that seemed to be the center of the city, stopped, dismounted, untied the rope around his neck, and led him by kicking him through a long corridor to a dank chamber where only the light of torches broke the all-encompassing darkness.

He could hear screams echoing. The stench of rotting bodies nauseated him. Sweat poured down his forehead, and he trembled with shame when he could not keep his own urine from running down his leg. He held on to the bars of a cell, and vomited, horrified by the waves of weakness which swept over his body with each wretched heave.

A skeleton of a man with pus-scabbed grimy cheeks and rotten teeth pushed his face through the bars and screamed, "Maggot! You're dead, maggot!"

Another man growled and hissed at Michael, then stuck out his tongue and chewed it grunting savagely, until a piece fell off. His captors pulled him down the hallway, opened a cell door, and threw Michael in. They slammed the door shut and closed him in darkness. "Back for you later!" a soldier called to him, laughing.

The smell of urine filled his nostrils. He could hear the sounds of something scampering along the sides of the walls, looking for someone's remains to prey on. Groping in the dark, he could hear the sounds of his movements echoing. He trembled, and though he tried to cry out, or to speak into the darkness, he could not make himself utter a sound.

In his silence, Michael could hear other sounds, some muffled, others distant, as though amplified by some strange acoustic quirk of this hellish, subterranean world. The sounds he could hear were the shrieks and moans of pain, as though he were in the burial ground of the living.

The soldiers came again. They dragged Michael out of the cell, and pulled him along roughly, remaining silent. As he was being led, he could hear the screams of a crowd, an angry crowd, loud and boisterous.

They threw him into another cell where three other men cowered in the corners. Then he heard where the noise was coming from. He could see two gates leading to an arena, and from behind them came waves of curses and cheers. He walked slowly to one of the gates, and peered through the iron bars, astonished. He could see thousands of spectators sitting in rows, filling a great stone structure. It was a huge coliseum, like Rome's greatest, and seemed to be the only building in Gahenna that was not in ruins.

A balcony projected out over the arena, where sat what looked to Michael like a judge and a jury. In the center of the arena stood a large cross. Chains hung down, swinging slowly from each end of the cross pole. Two guards dragged a screaming man out through a gateway on the opposite side of the arena. They shackled him to the cross, striking and kicking him as he strained and pulled at the chains, trying to break free.

Guards came to Michael's cell and seized one of the men, then took him to stand before the jury, who screamed and made gestures at the man. Michael couldn't hear what they were saying, but it appeared to be a trial. At one point the jurors all sat back as though in silent expectation while the man at the podium shouted some orders. One of the guards gave him a large knife, which he threw in a long arc to stick in the sandy floor of the arena at the foot of the cross. The man who had been taken from Michael's cell walked to the knife and picked it up. He lifted the blade into the air, and then presented it to the crowd, as though in salute. The crowd went wild, cheering hoarsely in deep-throated approval. He walked around the trapped victim, taunting him with the blade. The one in chains thrashed wildly as the man with the knife lunged at him. Astonished, Michael watched the bloody knife slash and mutilate. When the man could no longer raise the knife for another thrust, he walked to face the judge and the crowd, who cheered. He was brought a cape to put around his shoulders, and led up to become one of the crowd.

Then the guards opened the prison door and grabbed Michael by the arms. He cringed as he was led toward the cross where the ragged body of the last victim was being cut down from the chains. He feared they were going to put him in the shackles, but instead he was led to stand before the jury. The crowd waited.

The judge, a huge man dressed in black and wearing a tall pointed hat, signaled the crowd to become silent. "Michael!" the judge called down to him in a deep voice. "It's time for your revenge! Behold!"

He pointed toward a door, which swung open to reveal a man being dragged out. The guards led him to the cross, and clamped the shackles to him. Michael looked into the man's eyes, and a cry of rage choked his throat. He remembered those eyes, so full of hate, and with the hunger of one who kills for the lust of blood. It was Mark's killer. The memory suddenly flooded upon him, clear as morning, of that same man wearing a sombrero, and holding a flashing scimitar, and then striking Mark right through the heart with it.

"Kill him! Kill him! He murdered your friend!" screamed a juror.

The judge spoke, his voice a taunting roar. "Remember what he said to you? 'Come here and try it, rich boy!' This is your chance, Michael. This is your day!"

"Kill him! Kill him!" chanted the jury, and the mob took up the chant, screaming, "Kill him! Kill him!"

Michael looked at the killer hanging like a sacrifice before him, and his anger swelled within him, and he knew the answer to all he had suffered. Revenge! The crowd sensed his mood, and they began to roar, bull-throated, a sound that he could feel deep in his gut. He wanted to revel in it, to rage! To hate! To destroy!

The judge threw him a sword, which swished through the air to stick with a thud into the sand in front of the chained killer. He lunged for it. The rage and hatred rose up in his throat like vomit, and he lifted the sword to chop and stab. He was ready and the crowd knew it, and his victim hung in his chains, trembling, a meaningless plea for his life babbling inanely from his drooling lips.

Then in the corner of Michael's eye, something caught his attention. In the gateway from which the victims had come, he noticed another prisoner being readied for the shackled cross. In his mindless abandonment to the killing thrill, it might seem nothing could have shocked him, but he saw it was Mark! His sword hand dropped to his side, and he turned in sudden new anger to face the judge. "What is he doing here?" he demanded.

"Who made you a defender?" the judge roared back. "This place is for revenge. Somebody hates him, and has come here to strike for revenge, like you."

"He is a Jew," yelled someone in the crowd in the costume of a Nazi. "He is a long-hair, a faggot, a hippie freak. Kill him!"

"He Whitey," yelled another. "We gonna kill that honky white devil!"

Michael turned back and looked at the man who had killed his friend, a dark-skinned, rheumy-eyed wretch, body ruined from years of bad food, booze, drugs, and violence.

"Michael! Michael!" the crowd roared. "Kill the dirty nigger! Kill the murdering gutter scum!"

"No! I won't!" His voice rang out loud and clear, absolutely astounding himself. Every watcher drew in a gasp, and in an instant the huge coliseum fell into breathless silence.

The judge snatched the hood from his head and stared down at Michael. "What?" he howled. When Michael threw the sword on the ground, the crowd leaped to their feet, and in one voice roared out their loathing. "No revenge, no justice!"

"Coward! Appeaser!" they howled, and they began to throw handfuls of refuse at him.

"Get this abomination out of my sight!" yelled the judge, ripping his cloak apart. The ground beneath him trembled and lurched, and Michael staggered to keep his balance. He turned around and saw the cross and its prisoner had vanished, and so had Mark. At the back of the coliseum, a huge gate began to creak open, making a sound that cut through the rumbling waves of hate and rage made by the crowd. The coliseum which had seemed so Roman to him he now saw had the thick adobe walls of a Spanish mission, and as the heavy carved doors of the gate swung open, he saw it led to the path through the dunes.

"Get out! Get out!" screamed the crowd, hurling animal dung and rotten fruit at him. Without a second of hesitation, he turned and strode purposefully out of the arena. With a ponderous booming sound, the huge doors slammed shut behind him.

The sun was rising and he could still hear the angry crowd in the coliseum, their mumble of dissatisfaction. He sighed deeply, and felt a wave of sadness pass over him. He recognized he did not cry for himself or for Mark, but for the vengeful, trapped in their bitter self-justifying cycles of hate and violence.

As the sun broke over the horizon, it was not the icy blue-white he had last seen, but an electric pink. He looked ahead and could see only the rust-red dunes and rocks, and the thinning fields of thistles leading out into the nowhere of the desert. It was still the same barren and lost place he had entered the day before, but somehow he felt much better about being there.

## Chapter Three

The city of Gahenna was now behind Michael and he trudged along resolutely, casting a grim eye from time to time toward the gathering flock of vultures which circled overhead, waiting for that moment when he no longer showed a sign of life, and could fairly be claimed.

He still had not eaten. The water from the stagnant pool had been his only nourishment, and his body was letting him know of its distress. Trusting that his being there was for some purpose, he kept moving, waiting for whatever was going to answer his prayer before he collapsed to answer the buzzards' prayers.

Across the dunes, five men on camels appeared, wearing robes that covered their bodies from the desert sun. They were dusty, and they clopped and flapped along as though driven by the dry wind, but in his mind Michael could see only sparkling clearness, and he could taste only cool wetness, and hear gurgling and lapping. "Water!" he croaked. Suddenly filled with energy, he began to run toward them, running as he had never run before. But the camels were moving too fast. As though the sand were clutching his feet, Michael ran slower and slower through the desert screaming, "Wait! Wait!"

Just as Michael thought he had been abandoned, one rider in the rear of the Caravan looked back and then stopped. The other riders continued, as Michael fell to the ground exhausted. In a moment, he looked up to see the rider standing over him. The man appeared to be an Arab, with his face dark and burned from the sun.

"What are you doing out here without water?" the man asked him. "Why are you walking across the desert?"

"Water?" begged Michael, with his hands cupped in supplication.

The nomad dug into his pack and pulled out a leather pouch, which he tossed to Michael. Michael removed the cork and drank the water in big gulps.

"Don't drink too fast. It will make you sick," said the man.

"Thank you. I thought I was going to die," Michael said, making himself take the water in little sips.

"It was a good thing we were passing through here or you would have," the man said, taking the pouch from Michael's hand. "What are you doing here?"

"I'm just trying to get out of this desert," said Michael, shielding his eyes from the sun with his hands.

"Where are you coming from?"

Michael hesitated a second, then said, "Gahenna."

"Gahenna?" the man repeated, astonished. "That is a forbidden place. I have never known anyone to return from there. You must be an uncommon man."

"All I want is to go home," said Michael. He tried to wipe the sweat from his neck, and found it covered with a gritty plaster.

"Where is your home?" asked the nomad.

" America," answered Michael, and then in reply to his blank look, added, "You know, where never is heard a discouraging word, and the skies are not cloudy all day."

"I have never heard of that place," said the man, trying to sound sympathetic. The camel on which he sat gave a whuffling snuffle that sounded all too much like mocking laughter to Michael.

Michael nodded silently, and took a fresh look around. He looked up and noticed that the vultures were gone.

The man on the camel chuckled and said, "You will not be their meal today. Come with me. I am on a pilgrimage to a very sacred place. Perhaps you may find what you seek there."

"Thank you," said Michael. "Where do we go? And who are you, sir, to whom I owe my life?"

"I am Ahmed Yamani, and we are going to the Holy Mountain that holds the Cup of All Good Things. We are half a day's ride away." The man looked toward the horizon and saw that the other riders were out of sight. "I am on a pilgrimage to wish for the Cup of All Good Things to be righted," he told Michael. As though invited to prayer, the camel dropped to its knees. With a swing of his leg, the rider jumped down from the high camel saddle. "What happened to you?" he asked. "How did your clothes get so torn?"

Ahmed dug into his pack and took out a clean cloth and a corked ceramic bottle of ointment. He told Michael to take off his clothing so he could clean his wounds. Michael was hesitant, but he had decided he had no option other than trusting Ahmed, so he dropped his ragged clothing and stood as Ahmed gently cleaned his sores with the salve. Then he took out a long robe and a pair of sandals, which Michael put on, leaving his old clothing on the sand. "I don't know how I can repay you for your kindness," Michael said.

Ahmed swung himself back up onto the camel and extended his hand to Michael. "Living is its own reward," he said. "Come with me, and if you wish, you can continue on your journey after we get to the Holy Mountain."

Michael climbed onto the camel's back awkwardly and with obvious apprehension, to Ahmed's delight. "You have never ridden a camel before, I see!""

"I have never even met one before," said Michael, struggling for balance. The camel grunted, stood up, and started to move, its long lumbering stride causing Michael to lurch and sway. "I don't know how I can thank you," said Michael as he began to learn to sway to the camel's walk.

"There is no need to thank me," Ahmed reassured him. "I welcome anyone who comes to wish for a better world."

Michael thought any place would be better than where he was, but he didn't say anything.

"What do they call you?" asked Ahmed.

"Michael. Michael Seymour."

"Mikelseemore," Ahmed repeated, trying the unfamiliar sounds on his tongue. "Strange. Of the many people that come to this land to wish, I have never heard such a name." With a bemused expression, he rode along stroking his beard.

They rode for long hours until the sun began to settle

ponderously on the horizon. In the distance ahead of them, a range of high mountains touched the sky, a dark purple band against the red of the sunset. Michael imagined they were forested mountains, and he wished he could be there, so he could relax under cool sighing pines, bathe in a cold mountain stream, and remove forever the crust of desert sand from his body. Then as they crested a small hill, Michael was astonished to look down on a valley where long lines and masses of men and women could be seen walking across the desert in the glow of sunset. With a sweeping motion of his arm Ahmed spoke, "See these people. They come from every part of this great land to visit the Altar."

"What is the Altar," asked Michael "and why is it so important?"

"In the days of my forefathers there was great prosperity," Ahmed told him. "The Cup of All Good Things was the center of our lives. Our fields were lush and fertile and gave us all we needed. Then a great wind came, and The Cup of All Good Things fell. Its contents spilled and our land became unproductive. Droughts, floods, and famine tormented our lives. All of these people come here to wish for it to be righted, so things will return to the way they used to be."

"How can a cup be the center of all good things?" asked Michael.

"Because the falling of the Cup is a curse upon us. When the cup is righted again, all the problems that are plaguing our people will be no more."

Michael was quite certain he believed that curses can only hurt people if they believe in their power, but he had already seen that things were not quite normal in this strange world, so again he said nothing.

As they made their way down into the valley, Michael could see a large hill that thrust up out of the plains. Masses of people were gathered at its base, all moving slowly. And at the very top he could see there was a great stone altar. A long procession of people was climbing up the path, which zigzagged across the mountain to where the altar stood.

"That is the Holy Mountain," Ahmed told him. Then he began to hear the noise coming from the hill. The thousands of pilgrims kneeling at the bottom of the hill were chanting, their voices rising to a crescendo and then falling off like a receding wave as they repeated the chant over and over. The volume of the sound alone was awesome to Michael, and the physical effect of it against his body was thrilling, like being close to a huge waterfall. What could be so important about the Cup, he wondered, to create such a huge and moving reaction in all these people.

Half a mile or so from the great altar, Ahmed reined his Camel to a grumbling stop, ordered it to its knees, and then helped Michael down. As though the throngs around them did not even exist, he went through the moves of setting up his simple camp. At the foot of the Holy Mountain itself, he lay out a carpet, set up a goat-hide lean-to, and started a small fire with some dried camel dung he carried in a leather bag. Though he was not asked to help, Michael tried to make himself useful to Ahmed, and was very grateful when the smiling nomad finally invited him to sit beside him on the carpet by the fire. Ahmed produced yet another pouch from his camel pack, and took from it half a loaf of dark rich bread. Chuckling to see how Michael could not take his eyes from the hearty food, he tore off a fist-sized chunk and handed it to the hungry young man. Though he had to swallow twice just so he could speak, Michael controlled his ravenousness and waited until Ahmed had torn a chunk for himself. "Thank you, Ahmed," he said humbly.

"Thank the One who feeds us all," said Ahmed, bowing and touching his forehead. Then they both addressed their meals with great eagerness, chewing and savoring every bite of the heavy many-grain bread, and washing it down with great draughts of the sweet water from Ahmed's leather flask.

After they finished, Ahmed gazed at the Holy Mountain, and Michael could not help but notice the way the man's eyes seemed to glaze over, and to burn with a fervent hope. It seemed as though he were watching intently, waiting every instant for the Mountain to speak to him. "I have traveled for days," he said, not so much to Michael as to the Mountain. "I am ready." Then he turned to Michael and took hold of his robe, and pleaded with an intensity that surprised Michael, "Follow me to the Altar. Come and wish with me!"

Michael looked at the throngs, seeing them differently in the light of their torches. These were people who had come from everywhere, from different lands, from every region and valley, to wish for the curse to be lifted, and for the Cup to be righted once again. In the glare and the dust of the day, they had been pilgrims. In the mystical glow of a thousand smoking torches, they became supplicants, dedicated souls.

Though the throngs pressed around them, Michael and Ahmed were able to proceed as quickly as they could climb the lava stone steps that led to the summit. As Michael got closer to the top, he found the view more and more breathtaking. Looking down at the valley below, he could see processions coming from all directions, looking like strings of glowing golden beads thrown across a black velvet desert. Michael could hear the people chanting as they approached the Temple in the Sky.

When Michael and Ahmed arrived at the Altar, they found people on their knees wishing with all their hearts for the Cup to be righted, tears coursing from their eyes, pleading for their souls to became one with the Mountain so its spirit would move the earth to right the Cup and end the curse. Some brought offerings, in the form of flowers, fruit, the carcasses of small animals, symbols engraved in gold, stone, and wood, carvings of various body parts, and a nose-wrenching variety of smoldering incense. Some read aloud from ancient scrolls, and others ate strange seeds and leaped and howled madly, wishing, pleading, cajoling, entreating, begging and promising all if only the Cup would be righted.

The Cup, which looked to Michael exactly like a big teacup from an amusement park ride, seemed to be made of solid gold. It appeared to reflect the wealth and prosperity of a bygone time, a relic from a world long past. It lay on its side, resting against its ornately curved handle.

Michael looked around at the supplicants, and was at first moved by their passion, but the more they seemed to him to be utterly sincere in their wishes for the Cup to be righted, the more he was irritated by their apparent ignoring of the obvious. Beside him, Ahmed dropped to his knees and began to wish with emotions so intense that Michael could feel them like heat. "For the people," he wished, tears springing to his eyes. "For the land, and the forest, oh, how I wish the Cup were righted!"

The hair stood up on the back of Michael's neck and his breath caught in a gasp in his throat as he realized what he was going to do. Without a word, he walked straight up to the Cup. When he grasped the rim and squatted down to get his legs beneath him, the noise of the congregation suddenly dropped to nothing. He drew in a deep breath, then pulled upward on the rim with all his strength. The people stood frozen as they watched Michael slowly raise the rim until he could push it over to land with a thud, once again sitting upright.

There was a numbed silence for a long, long moment, until one man fell to his knees and cried out, "The Great Prophet has come!"

"The Messiah!" proclaimed another, falling prostrate before Michael.

The word spread down through the masses, which responded with a cheer that rose to a roar that rose to a thunder that made the Holy Mountain itself tremble. Michael did not know what to do or say. He stood there frozen like an idol, helplessly watching as the people began to worship him fervently.

"He was a stranger lost in the desert," Ahmed cried out to them. "I gave him water, and shared my bread with him, and now he has fulfilled all our wishes!"

The crowd lifted Michael up and carried him, passing him from hand to hand so he seemed like a man riding on the seas of the masses to the bottom of the hill. They sat him down on pillows and began to serve him, bringing rich carpets and clothing, and all kinds of fine food. Big fires were built, and in the tents and temples where rituals of wishing had been conducted, rituals of gratitude were being written. As the piles of food grew, people began to bring long tables, and soon a great feast was laid out for all, and everywhere men and woman danced in celebration. The sounds of bleating and bawling cut through the din of the people as animals were sacrificed and skewered on roasting spits. The aroma of spice-basted meat cooking over pungent, smoking fires made Michael's mouth water and his stomach growl with anticipation. The people rejoiced and sang songs that had been all but forgotten, and Michael let himself go with the festive mood and began to laugh with them.

With Ahmed sitting on a pillow beside him, he let himself be served, and fussed over, and fed, and entertained. He ate until he couldn't even open his mouth, and he laughed until his face hurt. It was clear the people had all immediately accepted Ahmed as his first disciple, and they knelt before him as well. Michael tried to accept without distress the astonishing notion that just hours before he had been walking alone in the wilderness near death, and now he was being worshiped as a prophet.

As the hour grew late, and everyone had eaten all he could, and danced and sung, they began to gather around Michael's fire—thousands of them.

"Mikelseemore, they want you to speak to them," said Ahmed. "They desire to hear your words of wisdom. They want you to prophesy and to lead them!"

"Ahmed, I don't know what to tell them," Michael protested. "I can't lead them."

"What are you saying?" Ahmed said, astonished. "The people need a leader. You have righted the Cup. You have restored their hope. Do you want to take that away from them?"

Michael pressed his hands to his forehead and squeezed his eyes shut, trying to make himself remember

47

where he had come from, and who he was...or had been. "I...I have a curse of my own, Ahmed," he confessed. "I tried to wish it away. Maybe I'm still trying to wish it away, but I know wishing won't work, no matter how much you wish it would."

"What are you saying?" asked Ahmed again.

"I can't give them hope, Ahmed. All I did was raise the Cup. They must find their hope within themselves." He looked into the perplexed face of his new friend. "Do you understand?"

Ahmed stood and looked at the people around him, who all had been laughing and singing, and who now stood waiting anxiously. It seemed to him that hope filled the air for the first time in years. "I couldn't bear to watch my people fall again," he said resolutely. "Look at them, Mikelseemore. They are not afraid of life anymore. They are free of their curse. They have been saved, and now they need direction. They need a leader!"

"I am no leader, believe me," Michael told him. "I can hardly keep myself together!"

"Then what do you plan to do?" Ahmed demanded. "Abandon them? Destroy the hopes of thousands of people?"

"You have to understand, please. You're the only one here I can talk to," begged Michael. When Ahmed turned his back on him, Michael retreated into the privacy of a tent which had been set up for him, to try to think out what he was going to do. When the people saw he was not going to speak to them, they went back to celebrating for a short while, then soon all went to their own fires and quiet settled over the camped throngs.

After a while Ahmed Yamani came to his side again and asked, "What are we going to do, Mikelseemore?"

Michael drew a deep breath, and told him, "Tonight I will fix the mistake I made. I must go back to the Holy Mountain alone."

Ahmed said nothing, but nodded, and Michael stood and began to walk up the path to the altar. When he got to the top of the mountain, he looked down at people below him and he was even more certain what he had to do. He walked up to the Altar and held the great golden chalice by the rim, then with a single resolute heave, he pulled the Cup back over onto its side. As it fell, it made a deep booming sound like a bell, and for a moment Michael feared that the people would awaken, rise up and see what he had done, and decide to call him a false prophet and crucify him, or skewer him on one of the sacrificial roasting spits.

The first light of morning was beginning to tint the sky, and he could see just the outlines of the high mountains beyond the valley. The path from the altar on the Holy Mountain led up into the higher hills, and then on to the lofty crags, and ice-chiseled canyons. He set out walking and did not stop until he reached the first rocky ledge that overlooked the Holy Mountain. It was still close enough for him to see what was happening, and to hear what the reaction of the people would be.

In the subtle light, he could see people gathering around their morning fires, and beginning to move up the paths to the altar. Then a cry began to rise and to swell as the word was passed, "The Cup has fallen! The Cup has fallen!"

The valley came to life and he could see people swarming up the Holy Mountain, falling on their faces before the Altar, wailing and praying for the Cup to be lifted. He shook his head and tch-tched to see them right back where they had been the day before. Then to his surprise, he saw the crowds part to make way for a man slowly climbing up the stairs to the altar. Without hesitation, the man lifted the cup and once again it stood upright. Instead of cheering, however, there was only silence. Then someone began to clap, and another picked up the rhythm, and soon the whole mass was applauding together. Michael could not see who it was that had lifted the Cup, but he knew that man was Ahmed Yamani.

He smiled to himself, knowing in his heart that Ahmed would treat his people well, and would lead them to create their own salvation. Ahmed, and with him, his people, had begun to learn that misfortune should never be looked upon as an end, but as a beginning, and the road to inner strength. Then the grin turned wry as he found himself wondering if it was a lesson he was learning as well.

Michael turned away from the Holy Mountain and looked toward the peaks, which were glowing pink and gold as the sunrise struck their icy crests. As though they had moved miles closer since last time he looked at them, they dominated and surpassed all other sights, timeless creations filled with mystery, which drew him like the sirens' call to a fate he dared not even imagine.

# SPIRIT MAN

## Chapter Four

As Michael made his way up the winding path toward the high peaks, the barrenness of the desert lay almost forgotten behind him. The artistry of nature seemed most brilliantly expressed in the exquisite lushness of the life that rose to embrace him as he walked. So fluid was the change that it seemed the flowers actually sprouted up and bloomed at his feet as he walked, and the stones and trees parted before him to make a path that was effortless to walk. Michael gazed at a wondrous new valley, where the land laughed with waves of flowers in full bloom. The mountain held in its cradling embrace an expanse of green meadows, where colored birds flew in shimmering clouds over seas of waving grass that trilled like a thousand violins in the wind. He gasped, and then cheered out loud as he was struck by the fragrances greeting him on the cool refreshing breeze. "Wow! Yes, sir, this is more like it!" he cheered, and he began to run.

On the sides of the path, enormous hickory trees soon marked the way, bold statements of the enduring strength of an ancient land. Huge gnarled branches, shaped and intertwined by decades, perhaps centuries of growth, lent a feeling of deep wisdom and serenity to the place. As Michael climbed higher, wisps of mist began to gather in the hollow places, and streams of light cut down through the tousled masses of cloud above to give a cool and moist glow to the scene. With the sun behind him, he marveled at the huge rainbow arched above the valley in a swirling kaleidoscope of colors. He followed the path around a grove of dark green tamarisks and found a grotto among the rocks where a waterfall tumbled down to splash joyfully into a crystal pool.

He was filled with a sense of awe he had never before known as he looked wide-eyed around the grotto. At a glance he could see grapes and fat boysenberries ripening in the morning sun, and limbs bent down under the weight of succulent fruit he could not even identify. "Whoo!" he hooted, and laughed as his voice came back to him in echoes, "Whowoowooo!" He leaped into the air and capered around in a circle, then raised his arms to the waterfall and began to applaud. "Author! Author!" he cheered, as though expecting The Creator Himself to appear any second to take a bow. Then like a rock singer casting himself into his audience from the stage, he ran to the edge of the pool, scampered up to an overhanging ledge and dived into the swirling, bubbling water. Chilled to perfect crystal keenness by its descent from the snow-capped peaks, the water filled him with energy, and he splashed and plunged like an otter.

He drank not just gratefully, not just greedily, but passionately, and seemed to be refreshed as he had never been before. He swam to the side and climbed out onto a smooth expanse of polished rock to bask in the sun. When he was dry and enjoying the cool breeze against his sun-warmed skin, he stood and saw his reflection in the water. He had several days' growth of beard, and his tousled hair seemed much longer than it had been. Michael picked up the robe he had dropped—the robe Ahmed Yamani had given him—and washed it in the water. He laughed to himself, wondering if those people would really change, or just go on endlessly wishing for something that was already theirs. For a moment, Michael forgot that he was lost. Naked in the sun, he ran his fingers through his hair, and he wished he could stay there forever.

A sunset of crimson and gold marked the end of the day, and as the evening began to cool, he put on his robe and sandals. After a meal of berries and fruit, he walked around the grotto looking for some shelter for the night. A little way from the waterfall he found a place shielded from the night mountain breeze by several large boulders, which seemed like stone faces frozen forever in time. As the stars began to fill the sky, he heard an owl begin to sing its lonely chant. Then as a huge golden moon rose up over the valley below, other night voices joined the stealth-winged hunter. Michael slipped into a dry little cleft beneath the stone-faced boulders and listened in delight to the nocturnal chorus.  He was warm and secure there, but even so he wished he could start a little fire, just for the cheerfulness of the light.

As he drifted off to sleep he thought he heard a bell. It was a sweet tone, but he was unable to tell where the sound came from or if it was real at all.  Dawn came and he was awakened by the sound of birds celebrating the new day. Michael rubbed his eyes to clear away the sleep, and then stretched slowly to loosen the knots in his neck and back from sleeping on the ground.  He drank from the sweet crystal pool again, and tried a new kind of fruit he found, then took a look around to see what he might do next.  He was curious to notice that the path he had come on looked as though it had not been walked upon for weeks, and was silently fading back into the native landscape.  On the other hand, the path that led up around the boulders toward the hilltop above the waterfall seemed to be well traveled and well kept.  With a laugh, he turned his back on the pool and started up the path.

When Michael got closer to the summit of the trail, he gasped in wonder.  Nestled among the tall tamarisks and firs was a splendid little pavilion, like a miniature castle. The closer he drew to it, the more the land seemed to take on an aura of magic, as though everything were just a little more real than reality.  The perfectly random artistry of nature gave way to the subtle enhancement of meticulous tending, and then to the surreal perfection of the most gifted landscapist.

As he approached the Chateau, it seemed to grow in size, and its salt-white marble walls shone so brightly in the morning glow that he was sure he could almost hear them. Though the gardens approaching the building were laid out like a maze, he found himself led, rather than obstructed, by their patterns.  A giant clock tower dominated the grounds, a four-sided monolith six stories high, like the main building cut from what seemed to be a single piece of white polished marble. The hands and numbers were made of black wrought iron, in an ornate style reminiscent of the age of Faberge.

Under each one of the clock faces, the word "Paradisa" had been carved deeply into the stone. Though the words were carved in a style much more like old Roman, the incongruous juxtaposition seemed particularly artful to Michael. Everywhere he looked as he wandered the vast grounds, he saw marvels: hedges cut into skillful designs from animals to abstractions; beds of bulb flowers, tulips, irises; carpets of crocuses blossoming in patterns like Persian rugs; and bowers of roses surrounding the Chateau.

Strong lofty walls, ingeniously engineered in stone, reflected the work of superb masons. Arched doorways, domed ceilings, and galleried patios were interconnected by halls decorated with extravagant plasterwork ornamented in gold leaf and inlaid silver. Then he heard the sound of splashing water, and women laughing and giggling on the other side of one of the gardens. Peering through one of the sculptured hedges, he saw a group of women swimming in a pool cut into the marble of a patio. Like the other things he saw, these were certainly the most beautiful women he had ever seen, not just healthy and well-proportioned young women, but utterly flawless, and perfectly graceful.

He saw they all seemed to be rapturously devoted to serving one man, one hideous, grotesquely fat man who was sitting on a throne overlooking the pool. He was smacking up the gobbets of food they held to his great slobbering lips, slurping and slopping wine, which dribbled down his chins and stained the fine satin of his tunic. They massaged the hairy pallid mounds of his blubber-laden back and shoulders, and they laughed delightedly when he belched copiously and lecherously clutched at their flesh with his fat and greasy hands. They giggled and capered like children when he flatulated with a sound like a thunderclap echoing from the marble walls. He greeted their laughter with obscene wagging of his huge hips, which made his thick thighs slop back and forth and slap together as he sat in his throne.

When the fat man saw Michael, he stared at him for a few seconds with a perplexed expression, then struggled to his feet, pushing himself up with his arms. "Out of here!" he snapped, and the women instantly scattered and ran to depart the courtyard, their tanned athletic naked bodies looking like deer scampering for cover in the woods. He motioned Michael forward, and watched him suspiciously as he walked around the swimming pool. The closer he got, the more Michael was astonished to see how the grotesque flaccid body, on the downside of middle age, was decorated in every possible place with elaborate jewelry. "What is this place?" Michael asked him. "Who are you?"

The man slowly sat back down, shaking his head and smiling. He put out his arms and pointed in all directions and said, "Welcome to Paradisa, my fair friend. My name is H. Mortimer Snodgroot-Ralph—Mort to my friends. So what was the best your mama could do?"

"What?" It took Michael a moment to register what he had been asked. "Oh, right. She named me Michael Seymour, Sir."

"Sir? I like that!" said Mortimer, laughing. "And you not even one of mine. So where the hell did you come from?"

Michael had to stop and think a moment. "The Altar of the Cup?" he said, making it a question. To Mortimer's blank look, he added, "The Holy Mountain in the Sky?"

"The Holy Mountain in the Sky? The Altar of the Cup? That sounds like a joke." The fat man laughed, then started popping grapes into his mouth and trying to laugh around them, making the juice squish out of the corners of his mouth. "Have some grapes?" he asked, extending a dripping fat hand. When Michael accepted them and upon tasting a few realized how hungry he was, Mortimer clapped his hands and bellowed like a bull walrus, "Fooood!" In seconds, the group of young women came running back (or was it a new group just as lovely), and they set up a huge spread of food across a long row of tables. "Eat!" said his host.

Michael had no trouble getting into the mood of the place. He pulled a leg off a turkey that was still steaming as though only seconds from the oven. By it were mounds of mashed potatoes, fresh and cooked veggies, pies,

Thanksgiving dinner, Christmas breakfast, a Hawaiian luau, enchiladas, a Polish wedding feast—anything he could think of seemed to be right there on the next table. "What, no kidney pie?" he joked around a mouthful of the turkey.

"Right there behind the leg of lamb," one of the women pointed out.

As though he had not eaten in days, he capered from table to table, stuffing his mouth with one delicacy after another. When he finally could hold no more, he waddled over to plop himself down onto a thick pillow beside Mortimer. The fat man snapped his fingers and one of the women came at his command with a small golden box full of fresh cigars. She pulled one out, put it in his mouth, and lit it. White smoke puffed upward as the man exhaled. "Had enough already? Anything you could possibly want is here," Mortimer declared.

"I think I made a pig of myself and I apologize," said Michael wiping his face with an embroidered napkin.

"Michael, my man, you don't have to apologize about anything here!" Mortimer informed him grandly. "You will find Paradisa will fulfill your every wish. This place is mine, created to my order. I can give you a few pointers on how to get your own thing going."

"Actually, Mort, I was just looking for a way to get back home," Michael told him. "Can you tell me how to get out of here?"

"Out? Look around you. Why would you ever want to leave Paradisa?" Mortimer took another drag of his cigar and held up his hand. "Wait," he said. "Come let me show you my beautiful home. Do you like my women? There are as many as you want." Again he hooted a loud command, "Riiide!" and immediately a sedan chair appeared from around the side of the building, carried by four huge rippling-muscled bald-headed identical black quadruplets dressed in leather loincloths and rubbed to gleaming with oil. "Meet the Cadillac brothers," he said. He snapped his fingers again and the four silent giants lifted him off the ground and placed him into the chair.

As Michael followed, jogging along beside the sedan chair, Mortimer led him on an endlessly-bragging tour of the palace. "Do you see all these rooms? Each one will see to your every wish!"

"What do you mean, my every wish?"

"Your. Every. Wish! Which word don't you understand? Look in here." Michael's eyes widened even more to see a room where precious stones and jewelry encrusted all the furniture and walls. A single window made of hundreds of panels of crystal glass brought in the sunlight to make every stone shine as though with a light of its own.

In another room he found sculptures, each one like a live woman plated in gold, or turned to sugar crystal.

"This is fantastic!" exclaimed Michael.

"This is nothing," answered Mortimer nonchalantly.

It began to occur to Michael that he had seen a surprising number of clocks in the palace and on the grounds. In one hallway, a remarkable grandfather clock—some nine feet high, with a massive pendulum swinging slowly—caught Michael's eye. It seemed incredibly old, as though it had been taken from an ancient Egyptian tomb. He reached out a hand to touch it.

"Don't touch the clocks!" Mortimer snapped at him with a sudden intensity and anxiety that surprised Michael. "That's the only thing I ask," he added, much softer.

Michael backed away and said, "I'm sorry. I didn't know."

"I told you there is no need for apologies here. Just look around and make yourself at home. By tomorrow, I'm sure you'll figure out what you are going to do."

A gong sounded somewhere, and the four coachmen opened another door and stood at attention by the chair, then quickly moved to pick up Mortimer when he signaled he was ready. "Wait," said Michael. "Where are you going?"

"Not your concern," Mortimer grunted. "Meet me back at the pool in the morning." Without a further word, he pulled a short whip out from beneath his cushions and began to beat the two men on the front of his chair. Moving at a fast trot, they quickly disappeared.

The chamber was silent. Michael looked around in wonder, staring at the beauty of the white Chateau. From where he stood, hallways beckoned and staircases wound upward to the second and third floors. The largest hallway seemed to lead to a hundred different rooms. With a shrug, he opened the first door he came to. He turned the golden knob and walked into a gallery filled with exquisite paintings.

There were stunning original works which he was sure must have been painted by the greats themselves. He recognized the styles of Van Gogh, Da Vinci, Rockwell, Parrish, Picasso, and Pollock, the engineered grotesques of Giger and Escher, and even a matte painting on glass which no one could have done but master Harryhausen himself. Hundreds of other painters all had their spot on the walls.

Strangely, three clocks of different kinds were placed through the room, each clock exactly synchronized to the others, all ticking softly at exactly the same time, in exactly the same rhythm. An easel holding an empty canvas stood in the middle of the room. A palette had been freshly loaded with paints, and brushes were lying on a little table just waiting to be used. He picked one up and dipped it into a small container of paint, then almost absently started to stroke the empty canvas. The painting quickly took him away, as in his mind he found he had a perfect vision of an idea that came to life as he brushed the colors against the white surface. He laughed to see the image appear as if by magic at his touch, a portrait of a man gazing at a landscape. As he viewed the painting, it was as if he were looking though a three dimensional window. It was alive! It was obvious to him that his own work was far greater and far more deeply inspired than all the other paintings in the room. He marveled to imagine if Dali or Michelangelo had been able to touch the fountain of creativity he was experiencing what they might have created.

He had never painted before at all, yet in that place it was possible. He left the gallery and studio actually feeling

proud of himself and swaggered to the next door of the
hallway. Inside he found a giant library, where the greatest
words ever put to paper were shelved along the walls, with
the cover of each volume named in gold leaf: Shakespeare,
Hawthorne, Heinlein, Defoe, Kozinski, Rand, Zelazny, Poe.
He picked up a volume of Dante and found he could read it as
fast as he could turn the pages. He sped with delight
through volume after volume, until the chiming of a dozen
clocks distracted him. He glanced at his wrist for a watch
that wasn't there, then saw all the other clocks were reading
six o'clock.

On a table in the middle of the room an elegant new
computer sat humming softly, as though just waiting to be
used. Still flushed with excitement by the power of the
painting he had just created, Michael sat down before the
computer, set his fingers gently on the keys, and started to
type. A tantalizing first line laid itself across the screen so
casually, but when he read it, his breath caught in the back
of his throat. Already it was a story no one could put down.
As Michael wrote, the hours passed swiftly. Each paragraph
was so eloquently designed, the drama so intense, that he
found himself in tears again and again. As though he had
entered yet another world, he was obsessed with an
intensity he was sure no drug could match. His own adrenalin
flowed through his veins like high-voltage power as he typed
madly on, unable to free himself from the compelling story.

At last he fell back exhausted, finished, and he
realized he had created a literary masterpiece above all
other writers! Not the scholars of Oxford, the masters of
Rome, nor the scribes of Osiris had ever created such a
work. As though he knew he would find it, and exactly
where, he ran through the stacks to the shelf where he
pulled out a handsome volume, bound in fine leather and gold:
"Spirit Man" by Michael Seymour. He had never written an
original word before, but then and there in Paradisa, he was
immortalized. In a daze, he walked to the next room down
the hallway.

The giant gymnasium was prepared for an Olympiad,

with trampoline, vaulting horse, parallel bars, rings, and all the other equipment necessary for world class competition. Though literary creation was new to him, he had long been an athlete, and knew all the events well. He stepped eagerly to the parallel bars, stood between the bars and lifted himself up. At first his body felt stiff, then as he swung back and forth he started to loosen up until every muscle in his body felt agile. Coordination and complete control developed, as strength poured through him. He felt indestructible, able to do acrobatic feats as if he had been practicing for years. His body was able to endure the most extreme stress as he flew back and forth on the bar. He performed a crisp double-twisting-fliffus dismount and landed precisely on the pad. Vowing he would return to defy the laws of gravity and the limits of art in motion, he left the room, filled with energy and strength.

He opened the door and found a bright sunlit conservatory. Under its high glass panes, an array of musical instruments lay on tables and stands. Though something about the ornately-carved harpsichord strangely drew him, Michael picked up a gleaming white Gibson electric-acoustic guitar. He had long wished he knew how to play the instrument, and when he sat down on the floor and placed the guitar on his lap, it seemed naturally familiar. His hands fit easily, and he quickly found he could intuitively feel just where he should put his fingers to form the chords. He softly stroked the strings, and then plucked them with increasing confidence, and the sound of music filled the chamber, reverberating with the classical touch of a professional. As he played Michael laughed to recall Mortimer's words, "Each room will see to your every wish."

The music took him away. He knew what it meant to be a genius and a master, able to evoke from the instrument any song he could hear in his mind. His hands simply coaxed or struck the most sublime of voices from the strings. Tears rolled down his cheeks and for the first time he felt he really knew what music was and he was emotionally overwhelmed by his perfect understanding of its profound depth. The music seemed to come from heaven, as though it was not his body's senses that heard it, but the senses of his very soul.

On sudden impulse, he put down the guitar and actually ran the ten steps to the huge grand piano, which dominated the room. His hands leapt to the keys and he started to play. The piano came alive at his touch and his mind and his heart fell deeper into the music. Then, when he thought there could be no greater sound, a curtain swept back from one entire wall, revealing a high proscenium behind which sat a full symphonic orchestra. Its full chords filled the room with sounds of acoustic perfection as the musicians picked up the theme he had created, and wove a rhapsody around his brilliant statements, his eloquent counterpoint. Like a man in the throes of deepest passion he played, and then after a crescendo to a coda like the rising of Asgard from the flames, he collapsed onto the keyboard, exhausted. Then he heard the roar of an audience, the deep-throated cheering and screaming of people taken to heights beyond themselves. "Bravo! Bravo!" they cried out their approval, tears streaming down their cheeks.

Their presence startled him, and suddenly embarrassed, he held up his hands and called out to them, "Look, I really don't know how to do this. I've never touched a piano before." In an instant, the curtains swept across the wall, and the crowd and the orchestra disappeared and Michael was alone in the silent chamber. He sat a moment catching his breath, then thought he heard someone moving close by. "Is anybody there?" he called out softly. He heard no reply, nothing but the soft ticking of a lonely clock. "Hello?" he called again.

"Yes, Michael?" asked a sweet voice behind him. He turned to see a lovely young woman standing at the doorway. She was dressed, to his surprise and amusement, in a college cheerleader's outfit. "We girls would sure like to relax you, Michael," she said sincerely, and though his mind tried to remind him she was probably just like the paints and the piano, he was attracted. Seeing his interest, she brightened eagerly and said, "We've got this really nice hot tub, and a steam room, and you won't believe what we've been learning to do in massage classes."

"OK," he nodded with a grin. "All right, I guess I'm up for this too. Lead me to it."

As daybreak's light filtered into his bed chamber, Michael rubbed his face to wipe off the morning. He was alone. He got up from bed and gazed out a window that looked upon the high mountain range. He ran his fingers through his cleaned and stylishly cut hair, stroked his smoothly shaven face, then asked himself, "All right, Spirit Man, what wonders are you going to perform today?" He was a bit disturbed to hear the sarcasm in his own voice. "Well, I can perform wonders here. Doesn't that count for something?" he retorted.

Then he heard a chime, and bells, and then from everywhere the sound of clocks chiming the hour, and he began to suspect there was an unwelcome truth awaiting him. New clothes hung on a bedside valet, and a pair of tennis shoes stood beside the bed, waiting to be worn. They were exactly the kind he liked best.

He walked down the hallway to a central court, where he found Mortimer sitting on his throne, smoking a cigar. As the corpulent glutton saw him approaching, he leered and asked, "What would your mommy say this morning, you naughty boy? Or are you a man now?"

Ignoring Mortimer's lewd insinuations, he sat down on a small stool beside him and helped himself to a Bavarian-cream-loaded Bismark. "It was incredible! I have just finished making love to the most beautiful women I have ever seen, just played the guitar and piano better than the pros, wrote a masterpiece, and a dozen other things I had only dreamed of." He turned to look squarely at the fat man. "I only have one question for you. What are you doing here, Mortimer?"

The corpulent hedonist frowned in disappointment and said, "Have a cup of coffee." Michael nodded, and accepted a porcelain cup of the finest and freshest coffee he had ever tasted. "Paradisa is here to satisfy me, to take care of me," said Mortimer, lighting another cigar.

Michael shook his head and said, "What good is a place where everything you want can be easily attained? Where every wish and thought can come true simply by thinking about it?"

"Isn't that what everybody says they live their lives for? So they can die and come here? There is no disease, no pain, no suffering," said Mortimer, taking a sip of his coffee.

"No goals, no hope, no success," Michael countered. "How can you stay here?"

"How can you think of leaving?" asked Mortimer.

"Your world is without substance, without striving, without meaning!"

"I am a god here!" Mortimer declared. "I am the meaning. I am the substance. I rule this world."

Michael blew on his coffee, took a small sip. " A god of what, Mort?" he asked. "An imperfect man ruling artificial perfection? You're just a slave who is entertained instead of beaten."

Mortimer said nothing for a moment, and when Michael glanced up and looked into his eyes, he saw the man's pain. "People have made fun of me, abused me, tried to cheat me, ignored me, thought I was stupid. No matter how I have tried to be a good man, women have never been able to see beyond their disgust at my appearance. I started hating everyone, including myself." He shook his head sadly, swinging his flabby jowls back and forth. "Don't you see? Here no one makes fun of me. No one abuses me. No one ignores me and my women love me!"

Michael nodded. "Yeah," he said, "but you are still alone." When Mortimer did not answer, Michael went on, "Thanks for the coffee, Mort. I've got to try to find my way back home."

"Wait!" said Mortimer, reaching out to grasp Michael's arm. "There is still one thing that I want to show you. It's the best part of Paradisa."

"I really need to get going," Michael protested.

"Just one more thing," Mortimer whined. "Come on, you've got to see this."

Michael looked towards the mountain and took a deep sigh. "Ok. Show me what you want to show me," he said.

Mortimer got up from the table and Michael followed him to an arched doorway, which led into the base of the tall marble clock tower. He pulled the doors open wide, revealing a winding staircase leading upward.

"What are you going to show me?" asked Michael.

"The truth, Michael—what this place is really all about," said Mortimer in a voice that ran a chill down Michael's spine. As they slowly made their way up the stair case, hundreds of pigeons flew from perches around the inside of the tower, as though frightened by the echoing footsteps. Fluttering and screeching, they flung themselves along the walls, struggling to escape through a small opening at the very top of the building.

When Michael and the wheezing Mortimer finally reached the top, they entered the clock room through a large door barred by a heavy beam. Michael was immediately delighted and impressed by the antique timepiece. It seemed as though it might have been the oldest mechanical clock in the world, each piece, each cogwheel, ratchet, and lever bearing the marks of hand filing, preening, and polishing. Each cogwheel from the largest to the tiniest turned rhythmically second by second, driven by chained weights and a long pendulum tipped with a polished sphere a foot across.

Mortimer stood by the door watching him, and then said, "You are right, Michael. Even in my own paradise I am alone. The longing for real companionship here, someone real to share this wonderful place, has always evaded me. That's why I can't let you go!"

"What do you mean, can't let me go? Why don't you come with me?" said Michael.

"Oh, dear, I hoped you would understand," cried Mortimer plaintively. "This place is everything to me, and it could be everything to you too. But everyone else who has ever come here has ended up leaving—and why? Why, to seek dissatisfaction when they could have fulfillment, to pursue things they cannot have when they could have everything. But me? I can never leave!" With a surprisingly fast movement, Mortimer stepped back, swung the heavy door shut, and dropped the bar into place with a booming thud. "You'll change your mind after you think about it a while," came his voice through the thick panel of the door.

"Mortimer, wait!" Michael called after him. After a few minutes, the heavy footsteps were gone, and Michael sat in the quiet room, listening to the cooing of the pigeons as they found their way back to their perches, and to the interminable, implacable chik-kachung, chik-kachung of the clock. Unstoppable! Michael stared at the relentless mechanism and he understood Mortimer's misery. If there is such a place as Heaven, he thought, it must surely be eternal, but there, even in the illusion of paradise, time was still running out. And even though every form of human accomplishment seemed to be possible there, it was still in some very important sense, wasted time.

He then heard Mortimer Snodgroot-Ralph's voice calling from far below. "Michael! Michael!" Though he had not noticed them from below, there were several slit windows in the stone tower, and when he looked out through one, he could see the fat man pulling a woman by the arm.

"Look Michael! Can you do this in your world and still be loved?" yelled Mortimer. With the back of his ham like hand, he struck her across the face, splattering blood from her nose. Recovering her balance, she turned to him, apologizing for his anger, begging to make him feel better. "Do you see? She still loves me! What do you say about your world now, Michael?" he raged. He slapped her again, laughing, and ordered, "Kiss my feet!"

"Oh, thank you, Mortie," she wept gratefully, falling on her face before him.

"It's Paradisa, that's all!" Mortimer yelled to Michael, and started walking back to the chateau, leaving the woman behind. She got up and stepped lightly away, disappearing like a genie whose task was finished.

Michael turned his attention back the building, to the clock mechanism. Michael remembered Mortimer's anxiety when he had said, "Don't touch the clocks! That's all I ask."

Small gears and cogwheels turned to the seconds, medium sprockets turned to the minutes, and the ponderous pendulum slowly swung back and forth, measuring each chik-kachung of the escape wheel. Michael found a length of heavy iron bar lying near one wall, and he tried to pry it into the teeth of the sprockets, but no matter how he levered the bar, he could not stop or even slow down the clock.

Then he noticed that the pendulum had an adjustment device on it, a screw-like thread on which the sphere could be turned to move it up and down on its long shaft. Michael remembered learning that a pendulum's period, the time it takes to swing back and forth, is not determined by how far back and forth it swings, but by how long the pendulum is. This one had been turned all the way down to the bottom, so it was measuring time as slowly as it could. By twirling the sphere as it swung back and forth, he could make it move up the shaft, and the clock began to run faster and faster.

He twirled the ball again and again, and the clock tower came alive. The large cogwheel spun and the giant apparatus started to churn like a metallic monster. It was quickly apparent that, as he had suspected, every clock in Paradisa was linked to every other. Hours began to chime almost constantly, and he was sure he could smell lubricating oil heating up as the gears moved faster and faster.

He looked out the window, and laughed like a manic child to see that everything was moving forward faster. The sun traveled across the sky in a great fluid arc, followed shortly by the moon. He stepped to the slit window and shouted out into the flickering light of day-night-day-night, "How much time do you have left, Mortimer?"

Then he heard the man's anguished voice cry back, "Put it back! Please, put the clock back!" In a few short minute-hours, the fat man flung open the tower door, his face pale and white. "Please! Stop!" pleaded Mortimer, shuddering to catch his breath.

Michael stood glaring at him a moment, then turned to the clock and spun the pendulum's weight back down to the bottom. "You are the only one here, because that's how you want it to be, Mort," Michael told him.

"You are free to leave," said Mortimer, resigned. "It was a desperate move, I admit it."

"Why do you stay in this place? Look at what you have become."

He nodded in resignation. "Everybody else has left, but I can't. I hate being lonely, but I would rather be lonely than face the humiliation of my life." Mortimer sank to the floor, covering his face with his hands, and he began to blubber and bawl.

"Let me tell you something," Michael said. "Lots of people who happen to be fat are very happy and loved by many friends and family. And so do people who are skinny, or disfigured with scars, or have weird names, or... or who have diseases nobody can cure." He put his hand on Mortimer's shoulder as he stepped around him to get to the door. "I hope you find the courage to get out of this candy-covered hell," he said.

He walked down the staircase to the bottom of the tower, flung open the door, and looked around to find the path. As he expected, he discovered he could see it leading into the woods away from the white marble chateau. He didn't look back, as the bells of the Clock Tower chimed. "I would rather have one more day of honest challenge, than a hundred years in Paradisa," he said to no one in particular, and he laughed to hear the forest rustle as though the mountain were applauding him. Then he was struck by a memory he had not remembered for a long time. Was it not his fleeing from the anguish of losing his High School "paradisa" which had brought him to this world? He looked around himself, then shook his head and muttered, "I'm still here, so I guess I haven't finished the course. What's next?"

Before him, the path beckoned.

## Chapter Five

Having put Paradisa behind him, Michael struck out walking confidently, certain he would shortly be returned to the trials and challenges of his real-world life, and things would be back to normal again. He didn't really think about what those challenges might be, but the fact that he had willingly accepted them made him feel pretty good about himself.

Overhead, low menacing clouds began to gather, and he heard the low rumbling of thunder echoing from the hills as lightening flashes lit the forest. Then the clouds turned darker gray and rushed along like lost souls, growing more and more restless, more and more tattered.

The sky became yet darker as the sounds of thunder grew louder, and he could see ragged sheets of rain falling on the mountainside not far away. As the first drops began to splatter the path around him, he came to a large crevice in the rock. "How convenient," he chuckled, and entered the chamber to seek shelter from the advancing storm. Inside, the cave widened, allowing more than enough room for his body, but it was clearly not a comfortable place. The light coming in through the crevice was meager, and beyond where he stood, the cave was plunged into blackness. Rocks dangled in awkward, unbalanced positions, ready to collapse.

With a sound like the mountain itself splitting apart, claps of thunder rang out. White-hot flashes of lightening stabbed through the little cleft, bright enough they almost hurt, making the shadows even darker. The wind blew past the cleft as over the aperture of a whistle, making the inside of the cave vibrate in a deep booming roar. For a moment he was frightened that the sound would actually bring down the precariously perched rocks above him.

Fascinated in spite of his fear by the storm's violence, he crept close to the edge of the opening so he could peer out. The valley had come to life like the dangerous waters of a storm-swept sea. The rain was not constant, but fell in wind-torn ragged sheets, so he could see a surprisingly long way. The trees swayed and rippled like waves, and leaves were stripped from them to fly like foam. Michael watched as the hollows in the rocks—huecos, he would have called them back home—filled with water. Streams of muddy water started flowing from all directions, running together, and cutting dark and widening channels through the soil in their tumbling rush to reach the canyon below. He saw the streams begin to trickle around the boulders where he hid, and to flow between his feet into the mouth of the cave.

He retreated deeper into the cave, and in the strobe-flashes of the lightening he could see that water was filling the lower portion of the chamber, and clearly was getting deeper by the second. Clearly, if the rain didn't stop soon, he would be forced to leave his sanctuary. The horrifying choice he faced was to go deeper into the dark cave or return outside to face the storm.

When the water reached his knees, it began to rush down some unseen crack, and the increased flow eroded a deeper cut through the mud at the entrance of the cave, and the flow increased more. "This is happening for a reason," he said to himself, feeling like a little boy whistling in the dark. "I am not abandoned."

Michael braced himself against the rocks and climbed out of the cave. The fierce rain struck him like whirling fists, stinging and numbing his face, and then his whole body as his light clothing quickly soaked and stuck to his skin, offering no more protection than nakedness. The noise was terrifying just by itself, and he knew if he screamed even he himself would not hear it. He crouched against the rock, clinging to a tiny crumbling crack to keep from being swept away by the wind. As he watched, trees and shrubbery were bent, broken, uprooted, and swept away. Then suddenly the wind shifted around to the other side and plucked him from the rock like a doll, and sent him tumbling and sliding in the slick mud toward the largest of the rushing channels of surging water. Just as he thought he was inescapably doomed, the wind slammed him against the trunk of a splintered tree. He grabbed the stump with both arms and pulled himself up to wrap his legs around it also. By grasping his own ankles, he was sure he could hold on, and the stump seemed to be secure, so he took hope and resolved to stay right there as long as it took. Then a rumble coming from the higher part of the mountain made him look up. His stomach plunged, and he felt himself lose control of his water as he faced a six-foot wall of mud rushing down the hillside toward him. Again, he faced his choice of horrors and finally let go of the stump and flung himself into the rushing water.

Sucked under the dark swirling mass, he clutched for anything, felt a boulder go by, grabbed a limb that was rushing along as fast as he was. Then, sure it was all over, he felt himself suddenly falling free, and knew he had been spit out over the edge of a cliff. Having long since forgotten about the "real world" back home, he submitted himself to the inevitable death he knew would be coming when he reached the bottom of whatever it was he had fallen from. He took one last deep breath as he fell through the air and water, and he waited for the end.

He awoke to find himself spitting out a mouthful of mud. A wave of deep nausea swept over him, and he retched up another gush of muddy water, then lay there on the edge of consciousness waiting for the spinning to stop. The sounds of thunder drifted off as though gone to torment some other valley, and sunlight warmed his back. From a distance away, he thought he could hear a waterfall, and he wondered if that was where he had fallen. Then to his surprise he heard voices. "Over here," someone said near to him. "He is alive!" With great effort, he opened one eye and looked up to see four men in full Egyptian attire and armor staring at him.

One of the men prodded him roughly with a sandaled toe, and another drew his sword. "We will take him to En-Ausar Simbel." When they grasped him by the shoulders and hauled him to his feet, he was surprised to discover he was completely naked. As though they were accustomed to finding people lying beside the river, they whipped him with short little quirts they carried, and soon got him staggering along. They followed a winding path through dunes and past fields of grain and rows of date palm trees, then came again to the wide slow-moving river.

They took him to a long, low building made of mud brick, barracks of some kind, he guessed, not unlike the adobe workers' quarters he knew back in New Mexico. Inside the walled compound, he saw hundreds of workers—slaves, by the way they were treated—being herded about by a cadre of dark men in loincloths and trapezoidal headgear. One among them was clearly the master of all. He wore a robe embroidered with gold thread, and had several well-oiled servants and jeweled handmaidens clustered about waiting for his word. Michael's captors cast him headlong upon his face in the dust before that eminence. "We found this by the river, beneath Cheron's Fall, Lord Simbel," the leader said.

With a disdainful twitch, Simbel fastened a gimlet eye on Michael. "What god do you serve?" he asked.

Michael frowned and stammered, "I...I guess I don't serve any particular god."

"A man with no god? Then you are not from here. What are you called?"

"I am Michael Spirit Man," he said wearily. "I have come from...from Paradisa, on the other side of the mountains. There was a storm..."

"We saw the storm," the tall, arrogant-looking nobleman said loftily. "It was very unusual. In fact, it has not rained here in the valley of the river Ciceron for centuries." He turned to address the leader of the patrol. "There is something very important about this slave, and I must consult the oracles to discover just what that may be. You will take him to the monastery at my quarters and see that he is properly prepared for my audience."

"Just a minute," Michael said, holding up his hand. "If this is ancient Egypt, how come you're speaking English?"

"Hmff!" the gold-robed noble snorted. "I don't know what you think you are hearing, but we are speaking

Aegyptian. And no, this is not ancient Egypt, but the most modern and forward-looking Aegypt, thanks to the vision and will of the Most High Pharaoh Cheron-Rey-Neteru, Destroyer of Death."

Michael was taken to his new quarters, a clean and simple room with a bed in one wing of the great temple palace of Cheron, on the bank of Ciceron, the mother of rivers. He was cleaned, fed, and quickly taught a daily routine. Every day he was awakened by silent monks and taken to the roof to greet Rey at sunrise, then exercised, fed, and taken to Simbel for tutoring.

Near Ciceron, Michael was taught, the great empire of Aegypt had been founded on the belief that the survival of all could best be ensured by absolute social order, and that was best achieved by making Pharaoh a god, and all worshippers in His temple. Cheron, the great Pharaoh, had a lifelong obsession. As his father Ankh-Marcus lay dying, a vision had come to Cheron. The best way to ensure the survival of all would be to conquer Death. Therefore, he would devote his life and use all of his power to become the Destroyer of Death.

He called upon all the oracles, and all the seers in the temples, and set them searching for his answer. Submitting himself completely to the fanatical belief his cause was just (and also possible), he set out to create a nation that would attain immortality. A man of great intellect and passion, he inspired his people to believe in his cause. His obsession had directed the nation's course. It became a war machine, conquering other nations and enslaving their peoples to provide the manpower necessary to pursue the courses of action called for by the oracles and the engineers. The more ambitious his attempts became, the more he believed he could find the answer to Death and destroy it if he could rule the world.

His greatest project was a quarry as wide as an hour's march, which was being dug by tens of thousands of slaves. This immense hole in the desert was shaped like a steep funnel, with a road that spiraled to the bottom along its sides. Even with the ant-like hordes of dust-caked slaves working day and night, the work had already taken decades. To feed them, Ciceron herself had been re-routed by dams and canals, and made to serve Pharaoh by watering crops tended by thousands more slaves. The purpose of the project was to uncover the Abode of Death, which the oracles had told him was to be found in the bowels of the earth beneath a certain spot.

Cheron Pharaoh had proclaimed his cause as most vital to the country's existence, and therefore justifying any expedient whatsoever. His use of power was without limit or mercy, driven by one simple ethic: anyone who refused to be part of Cheron's plan was a defender of Death, and therefore an enemy of Cheron, and immediately eliminated.

In the years since he came to power, the people were on the whole much happier than they had been before, Simbel assured Michael. The country had endured great hardships before Cheron, because everyone was pursuing his own interest for his own gain. Cheron had brought a common dream to all the people, to conquer the world, and to defeat Death. "By giving His people belief in the possibility that we might all enjoy immortality," Simbel said, "our great Pharaoh Cheron-Rey has given meaning to the lives of his people."

One afternoon, Michael was taken by two of the silent monks through a long underground corridor to the main building of The Great Temple. He was escorted through halls of increasing splendor, and then made to wait just outside the Central Chamber of Cheron Pharaoh. Though he could not see into the room, Michael could clearly hear what was being said. "My dreams tell me I am close to finding Death," said a voice he immediately knew was Pharaoh's. "What my dreams do not tell me is how I am to kill it."

Then another voice spoke, which he recognized as Simbel's. "It is in the Scriptures, Radiant Eminence. The Sacred Scrolls tell us:

> Out of Ciceron will come
> A man to go before the Sun.

# SPIRIT MAN

From Death's Abode he shall return
The answer to the seeking one."

"Anh! I know that scripture as well as you," the
Pharaoh snapped, throwing his wine goblet to clang on the
floor. "Riddles! Do the Scriptures tell you when this man
will be here?"

En-Ausar Simbel, Scribe of Osiris, High Priest of the
Temple, and Pharaoh's closest advisor simpered. Michael
recalled hearing him say if you had the job of interpreting a
man's dreams, you could rule him. "The Scriptures also say:

When the moon closes its eye
The journey will be finished.
The end a new beginning,
The beginning a new end.

The astronomers tell us there will be an eclipse of the
moon tonight. I feel that you will have your answer then."

Cheron raised his hand in the air and the advisers
stood motionless. "Tonight!" he said, his voice hushed with
awe. His powerful steps echoing in the chamber, Cheron
walked to the wide shuttered windows that overlooked the
teeming warrens of the laborers' city. The guards
immediately pulled open the heavy shields and bowed before
him. "Can you hear it?" he asked. "The screams of Death
dying, crying in anguish, the ultimate victory for our nation!
Can you hear it?"

Simbel spoke with great reverence and sincerity,
"Mighty Pharaoh, only you are great enough to hear it. We
humble servants must rely on the words you give us. It is as
the Scriptures say:

The Great Ruler will bend
Ciceron to his will.
In the bowels of the earth
will he find Death's Abode."

"Yes, yes?" Pharaoh barked. "We all know that is why we are digging the pit to the Abode. Why do you stop there?"

"Now attend this, Radiance," Simbel went on. "This is why I have come before you today:

> Out of Ciceron shall come
> A man whose god is not any one.
> Traveled through the healing earth,
> He goes before the mirrored truth
> To share Death's secret with the Sun."

There was a moment's pause, and then Cheron spoke in a hushed voice. "Have you found him, Simbel?"

"I have found a man," Simbel said. "He was discovered lying in the mud of Ciceron, and he told me he had been washed from the high mountains by the rains which heal our valley each year. He said he worshipped no one god, and are you not the Sun? If he precedes you where you must seek, will he not bring back your prize?"

"Bring him to me!" Pharaoh ordered, and in seconds, Michael was on his knees before the mighty Cheron-Rey-Neteru, Pharaoh of Aegypt, God of The Temple, and would-be Destroyer of Death.

Placing his hand on Simbel's shoulder and speaking as if to a friend, Cheron Pharaoh said, "Simbel, I am close to fulfilling my dream. My thanks to you are eternal, I promise."

Suddenly, a commotion could be heard spreading throughout the temple, "Great Pharaoh! Great Pharaoh!" Ushered at a run by a phalanx of guards, a man Michael recognized as Commander of the Pitslaves rushed into the room and threw himself on his face. "It is there, Radiant One!" he cried out. "Just as you said it would be. We have found the Abode of Death!" Tears of joy gushing from his eyes, he continued, "It is a great stone dome, and when it is struck, it rings like a bell. The slaves are clearing a passage for Your Radiance right now!"

"The world is mine!" Cheron laughed, "And eternity will be mine! Bring the horses and light the way with torches. Make the night day so I may see that which I have sought for so long. Go!"

The news of the discovery spread quickly throughout the city. People awoke from their sleep and lined the street that led to the pit. The court yard of the Great Temple was a chaos of men yelling orders, horses screaming as they were pulled and whipped into their places, and people running in all directions. Women carrying jars of oil ran forward to permit the torch slaves to dip their torches in preparation for the descent into the deep dark pit.

As the sun set, Cheron Pharaoh and his advisors mounted their sedan chairs and their horses and began the parade through the city. Michael was placed in a chariot-like cart and driven along beside Cheron and Simbel. The people screamed out their praises and their prayers to their leader as he passed among them, and they threw thousands of little funnels made of woven papyrus reeds before him as he proceeded. Overhead a brilliant full moon seemed twice as large as ever before. Then their screams increased to a mad howl, and their hopes and fears drove them to groveling tears as the sky began to darken.

As thrilled as any of his people, Cheron thrust his arm up to point at the moon. One side had begun to darken, as though the orb was evaporating away. "Just as the Scriptures read. When the moon closes its eye the journey will be finished."

"It is written!" declared Simbel.

Torches were blazing in the pit, illuminating the long winding road to the bottom with a ghastly flickering light. Each time they hurried round and round, the sky above became darker and darker, and by the time they reached the bottom, the moon was in full eclipse. The torchlight revealed a half-excavated smooth dome of polished rock. The Commander of Pitslaves had a phalanx of armed men keeping the diggers on their knees a little way off, and it was clear they would run away in fear if not restrained. One of them leaped up and ran past the guards toward Cheron. "Pharaoh, Pharaoh! Spare us! Let us flee!" he screamed. "I heard voices, screaming in pain! We have discovered the gates of Hell!"

Cheron glared at the man with loathing and shouted, "We shall harbor no fear! Kill him!" A soldier immediately stepped forward and cut the man's throat.

Cheron stepped down from his sedan chair and walked boldly to the structure. It stood the height of three men and was about forty paces in circumference, a sealed dome of polished granite. He walked around the structure feeling and looking for seams, and found none. He placed his ear to the dome and listened, but felt only the coolness of the stone against his face. The silence hung in breathless suspense as the people waited for their Pharaoh's command. After what seemed like a very long time, Cheron motioned to one of the guards to bring him a heavy worker's pick. He took the handle in his hands and swung the head against the dome. Beneath their feet, the ground shook as the dome rang like a bell tuned to the lowest possible note a man can hear.

"Make a hole big enough for a man to walk through, here," said Cheron, pointing to a spot in the dome. In seconds, the slaves were driven forward, and their tools began to ring on the stone again and again. The noise of metal against rock reverberated in the still air at the bottom of the pit. As soon as one slave grew too tired to respond to the task, another took his place. Inch by inch the rock surrendered to their relentless assault, until a chisel penetrated to the other side. With a sound like a dying scream, the dome seemed to exhale. The slaves closest to the puncture howled in terror, dropped their tools and backed away. They were whipped, clubbed, and slashed with swords, and replaced with fresh labor.

"Keep working!" screamed the guards, their own fear only just kept in control by whipping the slaves. In a few minutes, the doorway was completed.

Cheron stepped close to it and peered in, but no

matter how many torches were brought, the darkness inside swallowed up the light, and nothing at all could be seen. "It is time to fulfill my destiny," he said. He drew his own sword and stepped toward the gaping doorway.

"Wait, Great Pharaoh!" said Simbel, grasping the ruler's forearm. "Send another man in first. Let him tell you what he finds." Cheron turned to look at him sharply, and Simbel added, "It is only for your safety, Pharaoh. We your people cannot live without you."

Cheron put his sword back into his scabbard and pointed to a slave. "Send him in," he said.

The man shook, and though he knew there was no appeal, he fell to his knees. "Please, have mercy!" he wept.

Cheron kicked dirt at the whimpering man. "Here is your mercy. Kill him!" The guard was swift, cutting the man's throat. Cheron pointed to another slave. "Over there! Send him in!"

The man closed his eyes, whispered a prayer, and walked courageously into the entrance, where he was instantly swallowed by the blackness. They waited. No one moved, until suddenly a tortured voice cried out from the dome. "No! No!!" The slave stumbled out, his hands covering his eyes, and collapsed at Cheron Pharaoh's feet.

The Pharaoh snatched the slave's head up by his hair and demanded, "What did you see?"

Unable to answer, the slave looked into his Pharaoh's eyes. Even in battle Cheron had never seen a man so filled with terror. Cheron drew his sword and raised it to kill him, when Simbel stopped him. "Why use a cowardly slave to do the job of a brave volunteer?"

"You are right, Simbel," Cheron agreed. "Which of my faithful will not fail me?" he called out. "Who will go into the dome in my name?"

After a moment's pause, one of the guard officers stepped forward. "I will serve," he said. And after a few minutes, he too staggered from the dome, babbling incoherently and shuddering with unnamable dread.

Cheron shook his head sadly, then turned to Simbel.

"Well, High Priest?" he demanded.

Simbel turned to his guards and said, "Bring forward the one who has been taken from Ciceron, the one who has no name of god, and let him go before Cheron-Rey into the Abode of Death." In seconds, Michael was brought to stand before the gaping blackness.

"You have come from Ciceron, you claim the name of no god, and you have come through the mountains whose rains heal our land. Are you the man who has come to bring me the secret I seek?" the Pharaoh asked Michael.

Michael could only answer with the truth. "I am a man looking for my way home. I have traveled through Gahenna, The Mountain in the Sky, and Paradisa. When your soldiers found me, I had survived the river and now, I stand before you."

"Enter!" Pharaoh commanded.

"What if the answer I find is not the Pharaoh's answer?" Michael asked him.

The Pharaoh was silent. He turned, looked at the dome and looked back at Michael. Simbel broke the silence, "Oh Great One, do not fear the answer. The Scriptures say, 'The Answer he will share with the seeking One who seeks.' His words will be the truth!"

Again Pharaoh ordered Michael, "Go!"

He entered the darkness, and immediately a white light blinded him. When his eyes adjusted, he saw he was surrounded by mirrors. From every angle his reflection looked back at him. The images began to metamorphose and in the eyes and expression and the flesh he saw in the mirrors, his own insecurity, his fears, hatred, jealousy, and greed came to life. His vision of himself crumbled before his eyes as he saw what a vain, selfish, and despicable person he had been, and his shame overwhelmed him. All his faults were displayed in graphic detail, tangible, vivid, real. He had to close his eyes. Even with his eyes closed, he could see as clearly as if they were open, and the truth was too much to bear. He wept as he tried to control the urge to flee, and he hated himself for his cowardice.

Suddenly to his left Mark's killer appeared to him again, taunting him. "Come on, rich boy! What are you afraid of!"

Michael stared at him and his visit to Gahenna ran like a movie through his head. "You want me to hate you? I don't hate you. I feel sorry for you." The mirror shattered and disappeared. In another mirror, Michael saw his mother crying and he saw her fear of him. "Mother, I'm so sorry," he cried out. "I didn't know what I was doing!" The mirror shattered.

A more horrifying image appeared in front of him, not one from his past, but from his future. He was sitting in a wheelchair, his body and his mind destroyed by the ravages of disease. The image sat motionless, uncaring, unfeeling, dead while alive. Repulsed, Michael turned away from the image, his guts reeling and mind crying out in denial, "No! No!" Then he remembered what he had learned on the Mountain of the Altar of the Cup of all Good Things, and the mindless utopia of Paradisa and he screamed at the pitiful creature in the mirror, "Smile, you fool! Cry! Live, damn it! It's the only life you have!" The reflection shattered.

A thousand faults came to life in the mirrors, and as he faced each one, he knew he could deal with more and more. "I can go back and change," he told the last of the mirrors. "I can forgive!"

No more mirrors appeared. All that was left was the silence, and the sound of his blood pounding in his ears. The most extraordinary peace came over Michael. He had faced Death the Unforgiving, and had forgiven him, and in so doing had forgiven himself.

He walked out of the dome and faced Cheron, who was astonished to see deep calm instead of fear in his eyes. "Well? What have you seen?" the Pharaoh asked in a hushed voice.

"We must speak alone," said Michael.

Cheron looked at the moon and saw that the eclipse was in its last phase, and the orb was becoming brighter by the second. He could still lose it all. "Everybody leave!"

Cheron commanded.

"I cannot leave you, my Pharaoh," Simbel protested.

"There is nothing you can do," Michael informed him quietly.

Cheron nodded, and the dig came to life as the swarm of men began to leave the quarry. They watched the thousands follow the spiral path to the top like an army retreating apprehensively, leaving their leader behind.

When even Simbel had moved a few tiers up on the spiral path, Michael turned to speak to Cheron. "What you will find in the Abode of Death is the Mirror Of Truth. What the Mirror has to teach us is that we should not fear to die, but to have not lived. To live, we must not flee from the world, but face it, and to do that, we must be able to forgive. To forgive ourselves, we must see the truth. I cannot tell you what you will meet in the dome, Cheron Pharaoh, but if you seek to know the truth, you have your chance tonight."

His voice trembling like a frightened servant, Cheron said, "I have created the greatest army that has ever walked the earth. I have conquered other nations and I am sworn to destroy Death. If this dome holds the truth, I will find it. If I cannot accept it, I am not worthy of leading this nation. If I come out screaming, I am less than a slave, and I beg you to kill me!" He removed his armor and threw his sword upon the ground, then entered the dome without a step of hesitation.

Michael sat down on the fresh-turned earth to wait, and on the tiers of the spiral road above him, the thousands of watchers sat down also. Silently, the long hours passed. Then, just as the Great Radiance Rey broke over the eastern horizon, Cheron Pharaoh stepped out of the dome into the clear golden light of the dawn. He seemed even taller and more handsome and impressive than he ever had, and he looked at Michael with deep suffering and compassion in his eyes.

"I have been a fool," he said. "I have followed a nightmare instead of a dream. Michael the Spirit Man, whoever you are, I promise you—and myself—that these blood-stained hands will never take another man's life again."

Michael stepped close to Cheron and put his arms around the Pharaoh and embraced him as a friend. "You have time," he said. "You can heal the wounds."

At the same time, both of them remembered the throngs who were watching them. "What are you going to tell them?" asked Michael.

Cheron looked up at the thousands waiting in breathless silence. "I will tell them Death is what makes us human, and we are not to defeat it, but to accept it so we can fulfill our lives. Today the Conqueror of Death has died within the dome. I will begin my new life by spending my vast wealth to pay these people to fill this pit, and to construct over it a great pyramid to remind us of Death's finality."

Cheron Pharaoh raised both his arms as though in triumph to his people, and a mighty cheer made the deep pit shake. "Come with me, Michael Seymour, and we shall get to work," he shouted over the roar. "I shall begin by freeing all the slaves, and offering them all good wages to stay here and work."

A single horseman came galloping down the path towards them, leaving a cloud of dust behind him. He reined the horse violently, making it slide to a stop on its rear hooves, leaped from its back, and fell prostrate before Cheron. It was Simbel.

"Oh Great One!" he howled, groveling and crawling backwards to stay in front of Pharaoh. "What have you to proclaim to us? We await upon your word with all our lives! Speak to us, Mighty..."

"Oh, shut up, Simbel," Cheron said. "I have seen the truth about myself, which has made it very easy for me to see the truth about others. I see clearly that you are a self-serving toady who has cunningly manipulated my pride to your own advantage."

Simbel began to squeal like a cornered pig, and a dark wet splotch began to spread down his garment. The Pharaoh went on, "But I also see that you are basically a good person, trying to do the best you can with your situation. Get up now and stop making a fool of yourself, my old friend. We have a future to create!" Simbel staggered to his feet, his eyes wide and round as the Sumerians' painted on the Temple walls. He began to scurry along ahead of Cheron and Michael.

"Now what about you, Spirit Man?" the Pharaoh asked. "You know you can have anything you want in my kingdom, including Simbel's job."

"Thank you, Pharaoh," Michael said, "but what I really want is to find my way home."

Pharaoh Cheron called to Simbel, "When we get to the top of this ridiculous hole, I want you to get Michael a suit of our best light armor, a fresh horse, as much food and water as it will carry, and two soldiers to accompany 'The Man from Ciceron' wherever he wishes to go. He is free."

Simbel bowed before Pharaoh and galloped his horse back up the path, yelling out instructions for the chair bearers to hurry to Cheron. As they approached at a run, Cheron waved them off, and continued the long walk with Michael at his side. As they passed the people, they fell in line behind him, so when Michael and Cheron finally reached the top, the new day was radiant. The sky was blue and the smell of honeysuckle filled the air, and a procession of thousands followed them.

Michael remained one more day and night to share the celebration hosted by Cheron Pharaoh following his announcement that every man and woman in his kingdom was thereafter a free citizen of Aegypt. In the morning, Michael dressed himself in the simple and comfortable attire of an Aegyptian light cavalryman, mounted the horse Cheron had given him, bade a sincere farewell to Pharaoh and Simbel, and departed the Temple. He permitted the escort to accompany him to the edge of the desert, thanked them for their help and told them to return to their homes. Then he swung himself down from the horse, slapped its rump to send it after the soldiers, and turned to face the barren sands.  As he looked, he noticed he could see a path before him, not well traveled, but still recognizable, leading away toward the most desolate part of the desert.  Taking a deep breath and calling up all of his resolve, he struck out on the path.

# SPIRIT MAN
## Chapter Six

The land seemed more familiar the farther Michael traveled, though it became even more barren and bleak. Red dunes like a sea frozen in high swells stretched in all directions beneath a cloudless indigo sky. He heard no sound at all except for the abrasive wind and his own soft footsteps. For a moment his mind was clouded by the fear that he had made the wrong decision—perhaps he should have stayed in Aegypt, or at least kept the horse Cheron gave to him. Here he was meaningless, a wandering soul trekking through the desert, part of some demented artist's sketch in an endless sea of air and space. He felt empty, hollow, and lonely, dominated by the sand, the wind and the sky. Rainless clouds the color of the sand piled up above him, and he felt as though buried alive beneath an ocean that had not seen water in millions of years.

Mirages played in his mind, visions of fertile valleys, flowing streams and serene rivers with green slopes and lush pastures. It was springtime and the fields were full of tall blue grass. Then in the waves of grass, he saw a single bright red blossom. He stared at it, shook his head, and was surprised to see the little swatch of red remained when he returned to the world of sand. Excited, he began to run, and in a few minutes he stood panting with his own tie in his hand, the same tie he had buried so long before. He had been traveling in a circle!

He looked up and in front of him stood the adobe gate, the oracle, the doorway he had been seeking. Michael walked to the gate, dropped the tie in the sand and put his hands against the door. It was vibrating softly, like the purring of a sleeping cat. He put his hand on the ancient crystal knob and swung open the portal. A giant vacuum, like a tunnel from one universe to the other, sucked him from his feet and sent him tumbling through the gate. Static electricity enveloped his body and his hair stood out in all directions. A swirl of wind stripped his curass and tunic from his body and sent him spinning to the edge of consciousness.

The door slammed behind him with a mighty booming sound, and an all-encompassing darkness surrounded him. Then a beam of light cut through the blackness, creating a fissure in the void through which he could see.

Through that small crack in the shadows he saw a hideous looking man curled in a fetal position on the ground, his skin ashen, his body scratched and bruised, his head and shoulders splattered with blood. The pathetic creature crawled on the ground, crying and whimpering, "God, let me die! Please, end my suffering!" The pitiful figure looked up and Michael was astonished to see that the man was himself.

Shaking his head with patient sympathy, he knelt and looked himself straight in the eyes. "Let me help you," he said. He reached out his hand, and when his cowering self saw, and accepted, and reached up to grasp it, he drew him up into his arms.

"Who are you?" the suffering Michael asked.

The new triumphant Michael answered, "I am Spirit Man!"

In an instant the world burst into a shower of light. He fell through space, through constellations, stars, planets, clouds of nebulae and galaxies. The kaleidoscope of colors exploded, blinding him, and he spun dizzily.

Then when the dizziness cleared he looked around, and was astonished to recognize he was back on the mountain path, overlooking the fertile valley of the Rio Grande. The Organ Mountains towered above him, and the voices of friends and family seemed to echo from the rocks. Michael was home!

He touched his head and found it gashed and very painful to touch, but he didn't mind. He checked himself over and found he had no other injuries, and he jumped to his feet. "Spirit Man! Spirit Man!" he shouted, and when the rocks called it back to him, he laughed happily and began the walk back home.

# SPIRIT MAN

## Chapter Seven

Michael felt like a new man as he bounded down the side of the mountain toward the hollow nook in a sandstone cliff arroyo where his home nestled beside the beautiful Rio Grande. He was thrilled to see once again the sweeping lawns and manicured gardens of his one hundred twenty three acre estate, famous throughout all the world as Spiritland.

How wonderful it was again to sit gazing at his backyard, which was covered in a sea of brilliant autumn colors, orange, and red under a blazing yellow sun. Most of the leaves had already fallen from the trees onto the ground. The leaves were very dry and brittle, and a gentle but blustery wind swirled around the yard, picking them up and sweeping them to another place, clearing a patch of the earth, and then covering it again like surf in a tide pool.

Fall was the favorite time of the year for Michael. He loved it because the weather was perfect, not too hot and not too cold. It was mid November in The Land of Enchantment and still quite pleasant for this time of the year. In fact, it had been an unusually warm season until then. Maybe all those weird predications from the scientists in The Los Alamos Labs in northern New Mexico were right after all, Michael mused. They claimed that the world was going to warm up at least five to ten degrees from the greenhouse effect, and that was going to cause the human race many problems for the future of our planet— maybe even destroy life as we know it. Even Hey Jude in Santa Fe said that there was no snow this year for the skiing buffs and there was going to be a big-time water shortage throughout the state.

It seemed to Michael that his life was like The Beatles' song, The Long and Winding Road. While he was walking upon that road, so many different kinds of wonderful things, and yet so many different kinds of terrible things had happened to him all at once. He was thinking about how good things happen to bad people, and how bad things happen to good people all the time in this crazy world. Like the saying goes, "The Wicked prosper, and the righteous suffer." In spite of the spiritual experiences he had known, this saying had always made him uncomfortable thinking about God. What in hell was The Creator doing lately to benefit mankind? Was God dead? Was He on some kind of permanent vacation? Did He give up on the human race? Had He forgotten about the planet Earth?

"We lose so many dear and precious things in our lives," Michael thought. "And then, we somehow gain something else just as precious and wonderful that keeps us all going. The wheel of the wicked world keeps on spinning, faster and faster. We are expected to go along for the ride. If we don't hold on tight enough, we will fly off, crash...whatever that might mean."

By far, the best thing that ever happened to Michael was finding the gateway. In his luxuriously appointed executive office, Michael sat leaning back in his dark leather chair, and he wondered if he would ever again find the magical gate, which led him to the four cities on the other side. He wondered if the money had anything to do with it. His great uncle Elmer Spiritman, of international shipping fame, had died and left him hundreds of millions of dollars in a trust fund.

At the moment Michael signed the necessary papers to inherit Uncle Bud's immense fortune, life changed for Michael as he knew it. He had money and lots of it, and he was free to do whatever he wanted to do. He formed a company and became President and CEO of Spirit, Inc., which hired ghostwriters to write books for him about his travels across the universe and back.

It seemed like years had gone by since construction began on the multi-million dollar estate called Spiritland, and he had become wrapped up in one tedious business matter after another. Between running the entire operation of his production company, and building Spiritland, he became so busy and bogged down with the day to day responsibilities and everything else that went with it, that he soon found himself forgetting for long times about all of his travels and great adventures on the other side of the gate. Maybe it was the money, but whenever he found himself with a few moments to stop and think, and he thought about Spirit Man, he became disturbed, and something deep inside of him nagged him in a way he could not understand.

Michael jumped, startled as the telephone rang on his desk. He picked it up. He looked at the Caller's ID plate on his phone and realized that it was coming from the guest house where his companion, housekeeper, and personal assistant John Lohman lived. Michael answered the phone, "What's up, John?"

Lohman reminded Michael that he would pick him up tomorrow morning at seven thirty, as they had planned. They were going to drive down to San Carlos, Mexico, a small but very pleasant resort seaside town. They would spend a few days fishing, and a few nights at Neptune's, where it was their intent to check out some of the most beautiful Mexican women in the whole wide world. Though they could have taken one of the company airplanes, they were planning instead to drive, about eight hours on the road.

"See you in the morning, big guy," Michael said and then hung up the phone. He had given Lohman a job about two and a half years before then, working as a handyman to keep the grounds at Spiritland looking great all the time. Lohman trimmed all the pecan trees in the orchards during the late fall and early winter months. He had planted several different kinds of splendid gardens, including a herb garden, a vegetable garden and flower beds of pansies, petunias, marigolds and rows of beautiful roses that surrounded Michael's three story mansion. He made a point of never asking Lohman about his past, but was pleased that the man took such eager and productive advantage of every opportunity he was given. Michael admired Lohman's green thumb, since he himself had no particular talent for making thing grow. In fact, Michael admired Lohman a lot. The two of them had become good friends and they traveled together whenever they could get away on a well deserved vacation.

# SPIRIT MAN

The late afternoon sun was swiftly moving in the western sky. Michael knew he had to get ready and pack for his trip. He got up from his chair and walked out of his plush office down the long hallway toward his master chamber, a large room with a balcony overlooking the eastern portion of Spiritland. He had a perfect view of the Organ Mountains, the last chain of the easternmost of the Rockies stretching all the way down from Colorado. He enjoyed a beautiful stone fireplace in his bedroom and along one wall was a long work area, with several pieces of computer equipment, a fax machine, and other high tech devices he used in his writing and his business.

Michael made a few phone calls while sitting on the edge of his bed. He talked to his parents to see how they were doing and to tell them that he was going to San Carlos. He told his mother that he would be gone only for a few days and not to worry. Then he called two of his many women friends, Mercy and Susan, and talked to each one of them for a few minutes. After he hung up the phone, he got up and stretched, and then walked around his room for awhile longer, until he grew very tired and was ready to call it quits for the day. That night, he slept alone in his master suite without a single dream disturbing him.

At the first peep of dawn's early light, Lohman woke up and got dressed in a pair of blue jeans, a muscle shirt, and a denim jacket. He grabbed his favorite worn out suitcase from his hobo days, and then went to the three car garage around the corner of his guest house. He picked out the white Bronco because he figured that it would handle the rough roads much better down in Mexico. He opened the front door and climbed into it, started the engine and let it warm up. Then he slowly pulled into the half-circle driveway leading up to the front of the Spiritman Mansion, on the magnificent estate known world wide as Spiritland.

Lohman was forty-seven years old, almost twice Michael's age. He worked out every day in the local gym, a popular sweatmill called Genesis, and he also ran twenty five to forty miles a week. He was in excellent shape for his age, and always reminded Michael of his dear Uncle Wallace Spiritman who was a lifeguard in California. Lohman's hair was snow white and he wore a long ponytail, which Michael always teased him about looking like a girl. Michael would always say, "When is the old pussy going to get a hair job? You look like a movie starlet."

Lohman would smile and never say much in response. He was an easy going kind of guy and it seemed to Michael that nothing really bothered him much in this world. "Why should it?" Lohman had said when he mentioned it to him, "Long as the chow is good and I'm not being shot at, I just don't sweat the small shit." Michael thought perhaps he had once been a Marine.

Lohman drove the nimble little truck around to the front of the mansion and stopped there, where Michael stood waiting for him next to two Reebok gym bags lying on the grass. Lohman picked them up, opened up the back door to the Bronco, and threw the bags behind the seat. They both hopped in, Lohman started up the engine once again, and they pulled away from the mansion.

"How you feeling, Mike? You ready for this?" asked Lohman, as he made the turn onto the highway west to Arizona, then south to Mexico. Michael turned to look at him, and though only an instant passed, it seemed to him like he sat and studied Lohman's lean, tanned face for a long time, admiring his top physical condition, and the confidence in his gaze and relaxed manner. He made a silent vow to start running regularly once again, maybe this week on the beaches in Mexico.

"Fine, feeling great," he answered as he snapped out of his thoughts. "I am going to nod out for awhile. Wake me up when we get to Arizona, okay?"

"You got it, Chief," Lohman replied.

Michael slept all the way as Lohman drove past Deming and Lordsburg in New Mexico before coming to the Arizona border. A few long hours later, Lohman got off Interstate 10, and turned right on Motel Boulevard, heading into the little town of Benson. He passed by a bank, which had an electronic sign flashing the time and temperature, one after another. It was twelve o'clock on the nose and ninety-nine degrees, which did not seem out of place to him as the leaves swirled around the truck.

"Its hotter than hell out here," Lohman said out loud as he pulled into the parking lot of Cindy's Cafe. He parked the Bronco and nudged Michael. "Benson," he said. Michael sat up straight and shook his head from side to side to wake himself up. Then the two men got out of the vehicle and walked inside the cafe, and  sat down at a table by a big picture window. Lohman could easily see the Bronco and this made him feel at ease and comfortable.

"Hungry?" Lohman asked Michael, as he took a look around the tiny cafe. It was over half full, maybe fifteen people in all sitting down enjoying their lunch. It was not the first time they had eaten there. In fact, Lohman and Michael often came here to eat because the food was good and it was roughly the halfway point between Michael's Spiritland estate and San Carlos in Old Mexico.

"Starving," Michael answered. He looked around the place and noticed a group of college kids, tourists he thought to himself, looking like they were also going down to Mexico to party and have fun. He overheard one of them say, "Hey, Allansworth, kiss my ass," and another respond, "You kiss mine first, Kailey, you dirtbag!"

The waitress who came over to their table was about twenty-five years old and quite attractive. She had dark brown hair and the darkest jet black eyes Michael had ever seen. She was wearing tight blue jeans with a white apron tied around her waist. She caught Lohman's eye right away. He read her name plate just above the out thrusting front pocket on her pink blouse. It read, "Betty Lou."

"Well, hello, Betty Lou!" Lohman said and then added, "How do you do?"

"G'd afternoon, gentlemen—and I say that loosely! No, I am just kidding you!" She laughed with a genuine smile, and asked them what they wanted to drink while they read the menu. Lohman ordered an ice tea with a slice of lemon and

Michael ordered a coke.

Lohman watched Betty Lou leave to go get their drinks. "Nice buns on that little burger plate, huh?" he asked with a chuckle.

"Yeah, real nice," said Michael, watching her walk across the room to the kitchen door. "Now quit drooling before it runs down your face and onto the table. I want to eat my lunch in peace!"

A few moments later, she came back with their drinks. She placed them on the table in front of them and asked, "OK, what would you boys like today?"

"A taste of your honey, sweetheart," said Lohman, with a conspiratorial grin.

"Shut up, give her a break," Michael told Lohman. "Don't mind him, Miss. He's just got no manners."

"Oh, he's not such a tough guy," she said. "Some guys who come here really can get to a girl. They say the nastiest things like... oh, you don't want to hear all that. I should take your order now. You must be starving, you look so huuuungry." She grinned at Lohman.

They each ordered the Cindy's Cafe Special Jumbo Cheeseburger, with fries. She turned around heading back to the kitchen, and Lohman's eyes were popping even farther out of his head and his tongue hanging onto his shirt as she walked away from them.

"I guess you think she likes old men," Michael kidded Lohman.

"Don't you know that I turn-on all the women in the world!" Lohman boasted.

"Keep on dreaming!" Michael scoffed. He grinned, thinking he was not sure if he could put up with any more of Lohman's bull. But the truth was Michael really admired his good friend Lohman, and liked being around him a lot these days. Among the many other things Lohman was in Michael's world, he was certainly comic relief in a hectic world that had become so damn serious.

Then both of them took huge gulps from their drinks. "I was thirsty as hell, and didn't even know it," Lohman said, as he put his ice tea mug down on the table in front of him and wiped his mouth off with his hand.

"Me too," Michael replied.

"That trip across the desert is so damn boring," Lohman stated. "Especially in this kind of weather."

"Yeah, you got that right," Michael agreed.

"What are you complaining about? You slept all the way, amigo! You don't have to do a damn thing but sleep—and maybe eat and take a whiz now and then."

"Hey, who's paying for this trip?" Michael asked with mock seriousness.

"You got me there, boss! Only kidding, just funnin' you!" Lohman replied with equal mockery, knowing Michael was making fun of him.

The fact was Michael had been very generous to him, and Lohman was grateful for all of his kindness and help. It just seemed like yesterday that Lohman was alone, homeless, an unemployed janitor down on his luck, and now he was living at Spiritland. Though of course Lohman knew that Michael was the Spirit Man, they almost never talked about that. Ever since Michael decided Lohman was a genuine friend and took him under his wing, Lohman lived and breathed like a rich man, worked on the estate like a fanatic, and partied like a true son of Bacchus. For John Lohman, life couldn't get any better, that was for sure.

## Chapter Eight

As Michael sat sipping his coke and looking out the window, his eye was caught by a beat-up green and yellow van parked across the street underneath a group of tall cottonwood trees. Looking like it had been painted by a hippie with some left-over house paint, the van was partially hidden by some overgrown salt cedar bushes. Then the sliding door to the van opened up, and a bearded and long-haired man dressed in army fatigues stepped out.

Concealing something against his chest that Michael couldn't quite make out, the bearded man started walking very briskly toward the tiny cafe. Then, to Michael's surprise, he began running full steam, darting between the cars in the parking lot. Michael signaled to Lohman to take a look for himself. Lohman turned to look, then frowned as he saw the bearded man coming toward them.

"Where is your gun?" asked Michael.

"It's in the truck, man," Lohman said. "What do you want to do?"

"I'm not sure yet," Michael said. Betty Lou came to their table carrying two hot plates of good smelling food which filled up the air with rich aroma. As she set down the plates, Lohman put his hand on her arm. She looked at Lohman in surprise, then saw him motion to her to look out of the window.

She looked up and then gasped as she saw the man running across the parking lot, aiming his gun toward the sun.

"Oh my God, it's Joey "who just got his big, fat hairy ass fired" Pachuco!" she screamed. "Big Bob just fired him, and Joey ran out of here swearing he was going to shoot Big Bob and anybody else in the cafe!" Knocking a plate from the table behind her as she backed away, she started to run toward the kitchen.

"Run!" she cried.

"Get down!" Michael shouted to the customers in the tiny cafe. His warning was not needed, though, because at that moment, Joey let the machine gun rip into the tiny cafe. Bullets flew everywhere, tearing up the place. The glass in the windows shattered into millions of pieces. A round flew past Michael's ear, making a mean, gnarled sound like the attack of a scorpion, and he and Lohman hit the floor and began to crawl along it, looking for a place where there might be escape or shelter. A motion—a flick in the mad slow-motion of the event—caught his eye, and Michael looked up exactly at the instant that a bullet struck Betty Lou in the back of her head. She snapped at the waist and pitched forward to the floor, where she lay with her arms sprawling behind her, and her beautiful buns now jutting awkwardly up from a fast-spreading pool of blood.

People dived in all directions as the shattered glass of the big picture windows sprayed through the air. Michael rolled across the floor to lean against the counter aghast as one woman screamed and screamed, clawing at the glass sticking out of her legs and face. Beside him Lohman gasped.

A part of him seemed to be detached from himself, as though he could hear a narrator saying, "As the bullets and the glass flew all around, Michael wondered what it meant to be the Spirit Man at a time like that. What would the Spirit Man do?"

"Stay down!" he said to Lohman. "It's going to be all right!" But it was all too clear to Michael that things were not going to be all right at all. In fact, they were in great danger and that he didn't have a single idea about what to do. Was he going to die?

And again, that ridiculously detached part of himself was saying, "There he sat, remembering every birthday and Christmas that he ever had. In his mind's eye, he could see himself blowing out the candles on his cake and opening up all of his presents on Christmas morning. Would he ever see another Christmas ever again? Would all of these fine people here die together? What about all their families? What about all their dreams going up in smoke? Life seemed so unfair to Michael, so full of defeat and despair. Was this the end?"

Michael didn't want to die. He told himself he was not
afraid to die, because he had learned so much about the
mortal illusion being the Spirit Man. Even so, he cried out in
his heart that he had so much to live for and he was still so
young.

But he knew. He knew everything was about to change
for all these people on that dreadful day in Cindy's Cafe in
Benson, Arizona. He knew as he sat there looking at the
horror in his friend Lohman's face that the only thing left to
find out was how many people were going to get killed, and
who would get to watch the entire bloody event happen all
over again on the evening news.

Then Joey Pachuco kicked the door wide open with his
boot, and he walked inside Cindy's cafe. He began to fire,
not madly spraying bullets everywhere inside the place like
hail in a windstorm, but in tight savage little bursts, bursts
that snarled with vicious immediacy, punctuating the
screams and crashes of the people who pushed and knocked
each other down trying to protect themselves from the
deadly sprays. He yelled, "Yah! Yah!" as he chopped down
each in turn. Then he held the trigger down and sprayed a
pile of six people, a family out for lunch together. Six
seconds, seven seconds, eight seconds. Two of the college
kids leaped to their feet and tried to run away, but Joey
Pachuco, Joey the loser, Joey who just got fired from his
glorious job as a dish washer at a dinky nowhere-town cafe,
cut them down. Like he was stabbing them with a pike, he
thrust a spray of bullets through their backs. "Yah!
Yaaaaaah!" Allansworth and Kailey scrabbled and crawled
across the floor, then jerked and sprawled, and lay twitching
their last seconds away.

"Nobody fires Joey Pachuco!" the wild-eyed assassin
cried out loud. "Where are you now, Big Bob with your fat
ass?" Then he fired into the ceiling and laughed. "Oh,
Mister Manager, Mister Massa'. Come out now, wherever you
are! You don't want to miss your turn."

Then Joey stepped over a couple of bodies and
walked around the end of the counter, and there in front of

him sat Michael and Lohman, leaning against the counter, eyes wide like a pair of rabbits caught in a spotlight.

Michael was surprised that he could suddenly smell a strong sour scent coming from Lohman, and he wondered if that was what people meant when they said some animals can smell fear.

"Have you seen that fat stupid bastard that fired me?" Joey asked them, pointing his long assault rifle at them. He tipped up the barrel and then snapped the magazine from the stock. "I'm going to plug that chicken-fried piece of dog liver up with a belly full of bullets." He pulled a full magazine from his belt and snapped it into place and let the bolt slam forward with a crisp clank.

Michael opened up his mouth to speak, to say anything that might distract Joey, but he wasn't able to say anything at all. Nothing would come out, not even a gargle or a croak.

Then Michael was taken by complete surprise when Lohman lunged to his feet.

"Bastard!" Lohman snarled as he dived at Joey.

"No!" Michael cried out, but it was too late. With a contemptuous one-handed burst from the rifle, Joey plugged Lohman's belly full of bullet holes. Lohman fell to his knees, clenching his blood soaked muscle shirt, his face a study in pain. Gasping his last breath of air, he fell to the floor, and his head hit with a peculiar hollow sound. In three seconds, he lay face down in a pool of blood and broken glass.

"Lohman was dead," said the journalistic narrator who kept speaking in Michael's head. "He was a goner, never had a chance. Just like that, Michael's best friend was gone, Lohman the only one who really knew who Michael was, the Spirit Man himself."

"Wanna be next, amigo?" Joey asked Michael, "Wanna be next?" In slow motion, he waved the rifle at Michael, and grinned. "Wanna be next?"

Michael looked into the eyes of Joey Pachuco, the mass murderer, the killing machine, and the strangest sensation came over him at that moment. He was suddenly not afraid, but instead moved with grief for the loss of his friend whom he witnessed being killed in cold blood. With a calmness and sureness he had not felt for a long time, he took a deep breath and started to stand up.

"I'm going to stand up now, and nothing is going to happen, and no one else is going to get hurt."

Trying very hard not to let his body jerk or twitch, Michael got up. When his foot slipped on the broken glass on the floor, and his arm jerked up to balance himself, Joey went a little berserk and aimed one of his huge pistols point blank at Michael. It was clear he was just about to blow Michael's head off just like the others, but suddenly a strange look came over his face. Michael's eyes locked on Joey's eyes. The finger tightened on the trigger, and he hesitated. His jaw clenched, and again he squeezed on the trigger, but did not fire.

"I know why you shot all these people, Joey," Michael said, and he took a step toward him. "Down on your luck, aren't you? Just got fired, your wife of thirteen years left you."

"You better shut up," Joey growled.

"She took your three kids too, didn't she Joey?"

Joey's eyes bulged, red veins turning them into blazing balls of fire. "Don't come any closer or I will shoot you!" he screamed. He staggered back a few feet and then he backed up against the counter. "How the hell do you know all that about me? What are you, some kind of psychic?"

Michael just shook his head and stood there in the middle of the tiny cafe, gazing at the anguished Joey Pachuco. All of his clothes and shoes were covered in blood, and when he moved his shoes on the floor, they made a crushing sound.

"Give me the gun," Michael said, not like a request or even a command, but just as a statement of fact.

"No, no way, Jose!" Joey snarled. "I'm going to do you and then myself. You and me are going to die together, amigo! That's how it is going down for both of us, now!" Joey held his sights right on the spot between Michael's eyes, and then suddenly he snapped it up to point at the temple of his own head.

"Naw, don't do that, man!" Michael said, waving in dismissal. "You don't want to stop living, you just want to make things better, don't you really?"

"No. No, I don't," Joey declared. "You see, there is a big difference between you and me. I want to die. I got nothing to live for anymore. My wife left me. She took the kids. I ain't got a job. No money left in the bank account so what is it all for, tell me?"

"I don't have the answers to your personal problems, Joey. I probably couldn't help you even if I wanted to, but I'm sure there is somebody who can. Maybe we can get you some help, someone that understands."

In the distance, a police siren screamed as it raced toward Cindy's Cafe.

"The cops are coming, Joey. Put down the guns, and let them get you some help."

For a wild instant, it looked like Joey was going to put down the guns and let himself be taken away. Then his eyes grew dark, and he said with cold deliberation. "No. I'm not going to let the pigs take me away! I will die first!"

He pointed the pistol again at Michael, and in the instant of tension that followed there was at first a distant sound of wind chimes in the air, suddenly arresting Michael's mind with beautiful music. It became louder and louder until it was almost deafening, a clanging of huge chimes and bells, hurting their ears and jarring their heads with awful piercing sound.

Then in seconds, a desert storm blasted in from nowhere, pouncing on the little cafe like a predatory beast. A huge dark cloud hovered above Cindy's Cafe. Lightning cracked and thunder roared across the sky. They heard a terrible explosion which sounded like it was about a block away, and then the ground continued to shake as though the blast had set off a major earthquake. Then in the form of a dust devil, a tiny fierce tornado, the wind storm came ripping through the small cafe. The windows that had not been shot out by Joey Pachuco all burst and showered the room with glass. Several bolts of lightning exploded on top of the roof above them.

His eyes bulging, Joey staggered backwards in a full circle as he turned all the way around to see what was happening. When he turned back to face Michael, his face was open and astonished, like an infant's. He raised the pistol again, and he shot Michael once, twice in the chest... and then again in the stomach... and then again in the top of the head as he fell forward.

Then with an expression of bewilderment and disbelief, he raised the pistol to his own head and pulled the trigger, shooting himself in the temple. The two men fell to the floor together, in the raging swirl of wind and broken glass and blood and dirt.

A burst of kaleidoscope colors swirled through the cafe as the wind blew off the roof. There were several more explosions on the ground and then balls of light and fire shot up into the sky like the Fourth of July had come late that year. An entire section of a wall was torn apart from the foundation and swept away by the wind. "Holy shit!" yelled a fat faced cop as it landed on his police car in the parking lot of Cindy's cafe.

Then the back door blew completely off its hinges, and a huge cloud of smoke and light rolled out from the deep darkness within the interior of the back room. The cloud of smoke and light swirled into the shape of a human being. It floated along the back wall of the cafe and then hovered over Michael's dead body.

A voice from the spirit cloud said, "Come, run with me, Spirit Man!"

Michael rose up out of his body which was lying on the floor. His spirit stood up straight and hovered over the body, looking exactly like Michael did in his earthly form. At first, the face of his newly formed spirit person looked very pale and without any color, but soon his face flushed pink as though with life and blood. Michael looked down and saw his good friend, Lohman, lying dead on the floor. He also saw Joey's body a few feet away from Lohman's body. "What a waste this has all been," he whispered to himself. "What purpose does it serve?"

Then, as though it were the most natural thing in the world to do, Michael leaped over the counter and headed for the black hole in the back door. He ran through the back door and crossed over to the other side. He could feel the wind rushing against his face as he let the feeling of running soothe him as it always had in his life. It calmed him, enabled him to set aside his emotions and look at himself more clearly. He had to admit deep down inside that he knew he had been granted his wish. He had found the gateway to the other side, even if he wasn't too happy with the circumstances that led up to him finally crossing over. But Michael wasn't going to worry about that now. Instead, he wanted to get to whatever new place he was destined to visit as quickly and safely as possible.

Michael was a man on fire, full of desire and determination, as he ran from one world to another, hopeful this new world would be better than the one he had just left. "Anything would be better than back there," Michael thought, which surprised him, since he had not thought it was so bad at the time. But he knew that there was absolutely no guarantee that this world would be any better than the previous one.

Michael ran with without effort down a long, dark tunnel. At the end of the tunnel, there was a tiny circular shape, a dim light glowing. He ran through the tunnel and toward the light, which grew brighter and brighter until he burst out into an engulfing light. He turned around to look at the tunnel and its dark entrance, and in the blink of an eye, the tunnel vanished forevermore. Michael shuddered at the thought of being stuck there, even though he had no idea at all where he was, and no reason to believe he would ever able to get back home. He had after all, he remembered, been killed.

As Michael's eyes grew used to the light, he could see he was standing in the middle of nowhere. Close to him was a sea of waving grass. In the far distance, he could see rolling hills covered with deep, dark green forests. And way beyond the rolling hills, majestic purple mountains soared straight up into the sky, and the peaks of the mountains disappeared into a thin layer of white misty clouds.

## Chapter Nine

It seemed to Michael he had been walking for several hours in this strange, beautiful, new dream world. In long fluid strides, he walked up and down an endless sea of rolling hills, strides that carried him flowing up and down the swells and swales like a tiny boat. Down the side of a grassy crest he flowed, and before him opened a spacious green valley. Like a giant in a dream of flight, feet touching the ground here, and here, and there, he approached a herd of deer in the middle of the valley, where they stood grazing on the tall grasses that grew along the creek.

He stopped there for awhile, stood a little way off and watched the deer, who didn't seem to mind his presence at all. They stopped eating, looked up at him, and then went back to nibbling on the valley's rich, green bounty. He felt as though he could just stand there forever. He could hear the breeze sighing just gently in the tall heads of the meadow grass, and a murmuring gurgle that told him a little branch of the creek was near. For an instant he thought he could hear a trio of strings, a flute trilling birdsong.

Then the pastoral calm was broken by something that sounded like a rock slide or an explosion echoing in the distance. The deer lifted up their heads and antlers, and then they swiftly ran across the valley, disappearing into the thick forests of the foothills rising to the mountains. Highest of the mountains was a snow-capped peak on the horizon—the eastern horizon, he guessed, as the sun was high in the sky on his right. Since the granite crags of the peak were gray above the timberline before the cap of snow, he estimated that the tall, granite peak was at least twenty miles away—much too far for him to walk to today. Though he did not have a clear picture of his course to his present situation, he found himself getting very tired, feeling certain he had been walking most of the day. It seemed only a moment ago he was curious, eager to explore, and then all he wanted to do was find a nice quiet place to rest for awhile.

As he began to walk up into the hills and out of the wide valley, Michael encountered trees, ancient gnarled cottonwoods, and then pinon and juniper. He found his path led him into a deep canyon, with steep sandstone cliff formations on both sides, like rippled walls of ochre and orange, sculpted by water and wind into bluffs and tall free-standing spindles like sentinels and soldiers. A bubbling little stream tumbled along the boulder-strewn floor of the canyon, and tall solitary pines grew here and there along the edges of the creek, to a small pond of runoff water at the base of the sandstone bluffs. Michael looked at the mountain of rust ochre red rock which was reflected in the shallow blue and green waters of the pond. In the middle of the high cliff wall, in the middle of a rain stain the color of dried blood, there was a huge dark cave, a black hole in the face of the stone.

Michael stood by the stream and stared toward the base of the red cliffs, considering whether to try to climb up to the cave, or to try to make some kind of camp for the night down close to the water. Then he noticed something that surprised him. A part of the hill close to the stream had perfectly cut green grass. It looked like the golf course back home at New Mexico State University—and covered acres. It seemed totally out of place to Michael, and he was surprised to see it in what he had taken to be the middle of nowhere!

"Who cuts the grass out here in the dream world, anyway?" Michael wondered. "I don't even cut my own lawn, if you can call it that, back home!" He laughed out loud, and stood shaking his head. He didn't seem to think it strange that he was surprised he was not alone in this new world. The weariness he had felt came over him again, and his legs began to ache. The more he stood, the more they hurt, and the more terribly he wanted to rest. He decided instead of trying to get to the cave or to build a camp, he would take a short nap on the thick mowed green carpet that he had found in the dream world.

He walked into the middle of the grassy hillside, found

a comfortably curved little hollow beneath a big elm tree, and curled up there to take a short nap. He rolled up to one side and tried to sleep, but he couldn't get any at first. He kept closing his eyes, waiting for sleep, and then opening one eye and peering around, as though he were watching out for danger.

He didn't think of any particular kind of danger, like wild animals or giant mosquitoes, and nothing actually happened to him. Eventually the wind sighing in the high mountain trees and whispering along the edges of the great sandstone walls of the canyon relaxed him and he fell fast asleep.

The sun was low in the sky behind him when Michael gasped and sat up, charged with adrenaline. He shook his head from side to side a couple of times, trying to clear the sleep from his mind. Then he gasped and jumped a second time. Not ten inches from his face was an apparition of the most grotesque nature, a bulbous-nosed, slobber-lipped, scramble-toothed, scrag-moustached, knobby-legged, and sausage-fingered dwarf. Michael was alarmed at first, but then he recognized him as the well-known celebrity Emmitt del Rio—and he was staring at him, right in his face, cheek to cheek, eyeball to eyeball, nose to nose. Michael looked into his big, round-as-the-full-moon watery-blue eyes, and asked him, "Where am I, Emmitt?"

"Y'all in'na Badlands o' Chaos!" the dwarf answered Michael, speaking in a thick heavy Texas drawl which Michael could only barely understand.

The dwarf's big bulbous crooked nose was almost touching Michael's own nose. The dwarf nodded solemnly, and then declared, "We been expecting y'all to come back to us one of these lonely days, Spirit Man."

Michael nodded as if he knew what the little guy was talking about. "I remember crossing over," Michael murmured to himself. "I wonder when that was."

"What the hell you saying?" the dwarf asked, his reeking breath hot and fetid on Michael's face.

"Nothing," Michael answered, crawling backward to

try to get away from the rotten breath of the grotesque little gnome. "I was just thinking about something..."

"Waste ob dime, dat dinking! Get you in a lot of drouble," the dwarf commented, and then he leaned back, took a huge breath, and sneezed, splattering Michael from nose to toes. He took out a crusty red handkerchief, and blew a gurgling blob of snot, sweat flying from his forehead. "Damn shit in 'da air!" he said.

Michael reached to wipe the spittle from his face, and at the first touch decided to let it dry where it was instead. He studied the dwarf and concluded the gross little bastard was harmless and kind of funny. "Who are you? I mean, I know who you are, but what are you? I mean, I know what you are, but I mean..."

The man stood as tall and straight as he could—which happened to be a hunchbacked three foot eight. "Emmitt del Rio, Brigadier Sergeant, my twenty-fifth year in miluhtary service under command of Cap'n Andrew Baylor. I am at youah service, Spirit Man!" he said very proudly, and then saluted. Then he added in a serious tone, "But you try anything funny like the great escape from mah flesh and bones, I will sure as shootin' have mah infantry capture you, torture your young behind, and tie you up in chains of steel and iron bars around your feet. Now git up! Come on, we got a long journey ahead of us!"

"Where are you taking me?" Michael asked Emmitt as he got to his feet. Over six feet tall himself, he stood in front of the mustached and shaggy-haired dwarf looking like the Empire State Building, towering over some rumpled old brick apartment building.

"Fort Huachuca, to go see Captain Baylor," Emmitt replied, peering way up into the sky at Michael. "Damn, you definitely one very tall beast of a man!" He drew a whistle on a braided lanyard from his pocket, and blew a blast on it. "Pee-EET-peetpeet!"

Michael looked beyond Emmitt and saw a group of dwarves begin climbing down several rope ladders that they had thrown down over the face of the steep rocky cliffs, as

though from the dark cave. "These boahs are Del Rio's
Raiders, the best of Captain Baylor's army. S'long as you
cooperate, you will not be gutted and drained like a roasting
goat, or otherwise inconvenienced. Y'all hear, now?"

Michael told him he would certainly cooperate, and
that he wanted very much to meet his commander in chief,
Captain Andrew Baylor.

As though they had been sitting on springs waiting for
the call, a company of about thirty dwarves sprang from
clefts in the rock and began to clamber down rope ladders.
They tumbled and bounced, hooting and yipping like Indians.
The first four of the dwarves landed right on their asses,
and bounced to their feet!  Wearing big name tags reading
Stubblefield, Hailey, Tolbert and Beerbarrel, they landed on
their big, fat round asses, laughing all the way down until
they hit the ground below, with their long Cavalry sabres
clattering.  They hopped up and dusted their butts off,
swatting at each other and themselves with big tassled
gauntlets. Emmitt shook his head as he watched the others
all follow the four leading idiots in falling off the rope
ladders. Michael began to laugh, but at once he saw that this
made Emmitt mad.

"What is so dwarf damn funny?" Emmitt asked
Michael, with a mean looking stare.

"Nothing, nothing, Emmitt," Michael answered him,
struggling to keep a straight face.

"Good. I don't like people to laugh at my soldiers,"
Emmitt snorted, and then he walked around in a tiny circle,
hitting his head with the palm of his hand, over and over
again.  Michael wondered if this was going to give Emmitt a
headache, but he dared not ask him.

Soon all the dwarves gathered around Emmitt and
Michael, staring with rapt intensity at the Spirit Man.

"Hell of a slip and fall!  Right on my ass!" Stubblefield
boomed out loud to Hailey, who was standing right next to
him.

"You mean, you fell on your face! Your ass is your
face!" Hailey hooted and poked his elbow into Stubblefield's
side.

"Shut up, you jerks!" Tolbert brayed at Stubblefield and Hailey. "You are making jackasses out of yourselves."

"Kiss my ass, Jack!" Stubblefield retorted.

"Bend over, Rover! I'll be more than happy to kiss your ass with my boot and ram it in all the way, baby. Yes, siree!" Tolbert replied.

"All raht, now y'all listen up," Emmitt said. He stopped walking around in circles, then took a deep breath and yelled from the bottom of his lungs, "ATTENTION!"

The dwarves all hustled to fall into ranks, banging into each other, pushing each other into place, and in seconds all stood facing front with their arms and hands along their sides at a knobby and gnomish approximation of the position of attention. Emmitt and his soldiers were all dressed in dark blue Cavalry uniforms, with big brass buttons, black hats, red bandannas around their necks, and big tall boots. Though the boots were clearly designed to come up to their knees, most of them had such short legs that there was nothing but boot between their ankles and their asses. Each dwarf carried an enormous sword in a scabbard festooned with braided lanyards, and each had a big six shooter pistol tucked into his belt.

They stood in three ranks of thirteen, with the three on the end being Hailey, Tolbert, and Beerbarrel, each of whom wore two big yellow chevrons on his sleeves. A step in front of the three corporals stood Stubblefield, who wore three chevrons and a bright yellow leaf Michael did not recognize. He raised his sabre high, banged his heels together, and barked, "Yip yip! Ho-oh!"

Emmitt, who wore chevrons all the way up his arm, nodded solemnly and addressed his men. "Y'all oughta know the Spirit Man has come to us from a very far away place. He has crossed over from one world to another to give us some help. Y'all don't have to bind him up as a prisoner. He has agreed to come with us willingly. If he goes against his word and tries to escape, we will track him down, truss him up, and take him to see Cap'n Andrew Baylor. I promised him that I would deliver the Spirit Man to him, and I am a man of my word. Bunk Sergeant Stubblefield, post three road guards."

"Yip yip!" Stubblefield barked. He made sharp facing movements, marched down to the other end of the formation, and ordered the last three troopers (whose nametags read Buster, Weasel, and Shorty) to move out and lead the way up the mountain toward the cave. "Road guards, on the point, at the double, poooost....HUT!"

The three dwarves stepped forward three paces, drew out their swords, raised them above their heads and shouted, "Hail to our Captain! Long may he reign! Yip yip! Ho-oh!"

Stubblefield marched stiff-legged back to his place at the other end of the formation, where he heard Hailey mutter to Tolbert, "Baylor's a drunken bum, a pile of dog shit." Stubblefield kicked Hailey smartly in the back of his knees, making him come crashing down to the ground.

"Whenevah y'all are done grabassin' over there..." Emmitt said.

"Uh, yowsah, uh, yessir, uh, yip yip!" spluttered Stubblefield, as Hailey struggled to his feet. The three road guard dwarves turned around and started toward the red bluff where the cave was. Emmitt motioned to Michael to follow right behind them, then ordered his soldiers to march in line and follow them.

Instead of marching right back to the ropes they had just come down, they went down the canyon, and then up across a part of the mowed area to a place where the trail led smoothly up the side of the sandstone bluff. As the trail became steeper and steeper, Michael noticed there were tiny steps neatly carved into the rock. They zigzagged back and forth, almost as steep as ladders as they led Michael up the mountain to the mouth of the dark cave, which he was surprised to discover was a hand hewn tunnel which quickly disappeared into the side of the cliff.

There was a rather wide, flat area just in front of the cave. Huge slabs of concrete had been poured here on top of this high mountain ledge. Michael looked over the tiny shoulders and heads of the dwarves who ran past him into the opening, and he saw something barely visible, tucked away and hidden deep inside the dark shadows of the cave. He had to squint and shade his eyes to make out what he was looking at—something that looked like a small train, a circus or amusement park train. Then Michael realized that what he was seeing was not a train at all, but a row of ore carts like he had seen in the mines in Silver City back home in New Mexico.

All the dwarves had gathered by then on the high mountain ledge overlooking the green mown grass and the little canyon below. For a moment they were silent, and Michael could hear the chirping of some kind of tiny birds that were flying out of the darkness of the cave and up into the sky above.

The soldiers were quiet, hushed, as though waiting for something. Then he heard another sound, coming from the depths of the cave—a clanking, a whuffing and chuffing, and the clinking of metal wheels on tiny narrow rails. and waited for their orders from Emmitt. All the troops began to cheer, and Emmitt barked an order to get the mining carts ready. "Let's get it on! Fort Huachuca express coming up!"

Then out of the darkness came the beam of a headlight, and soon a miniature steam engine appeared, its cylinders puffing steam like endless rumbling thunder in a raging desert storm. A huge cloud of smoke roiled out of the darkness from inside the cave as the engine drove out into the light onto a big plate of metal like a playground turntable. The troops cheered again, and ran to grab hold of the engine and turn the whole turntable around to point the engine back into the cave. The engineer was a fat jolly dwarf wearing a large hat with a wide nameplate on the front which read Conductor Hal Frisky Jr. He blew the steam warning horn a long shrieking note, and then moved the steam engine forward to the switch where the mining carts could be hooked up.

The dwarves cheered wildly and clapped their stubby sausage-fingered hands together, as the mining carts came rolling out of their dark storage tunnel and into the light of the day. Michael could see the great pillows of black smoke and white steam coming from the locomotive and swirling all around the rusty iron sides of the mining carts. Emmitt lightly punched Michael on his shoulder, and gave him a huge mustachioed grin, making his bulbous nose turn bright red, and revealing the ugliest green teeth Michael had ever seen. Since he could tell that Emmitt was very proud indeed of his mode of transportation, Michael did his best to muster up an enthusiastic smile too.

"Y'all got nothing to worry about, now! Relax," Emmitt assured Michael. He stepped as smartly as his short legs would allow to the train of carts, jerked open a small wooden door on one side of a cart, and said, "Hop right on in there, Spirit o' Man!"

There were just enough carts for the company to all get aboard. Michael climbed into the mining cart, feeling like an oversized kid in a wagon. Emmitt put his fists on his hips and gazed at him, then let out a short and derisive cackle. "I'll be right back, now. I gotta go pre-fright this train." He marched all around, ordering the others to get into the carts. Four to a cart, they packed themselves and their sabres, huge hats and boots into the carts, and banged the doors shut loudly, hooting and yipping as they did. A few unbuckled their wide leather sword belts and took off their dusty blue jackets, folded them up as pillows to sit on and be more comfortable for their trip. Emmitt walked along the side of the train, checking the connections and the sides of the carts. Though the iron sides of the carts were dark with a patina of ancient rust, the wheels were bright and shiny as stainless steel.

Like a dork at a used car lot, Emmitt gave the closest wheel a smart kick. Then he nodded in satisfaction, whistled loudly and sloppily through his teeth, and yelled to Hal Frisky, Jr, "Y'all ready up there, Junior? Ho-oh!"

Emmitt hopped into the cart where Michael was sitting and plunked down on the floor across from Michael as the train began to jolt and move.

"Hold on to your socks, baby! This is gonna be a ride!" Emmitt said as he took hold of both sides of the mining cart's frame.

"Are we going to be safe on this thing?" Michael asked as the cart began to rock back and forth, to lurch and creak as it descended into the darkness.

"Don't worry! Be happy!" Emmitt said. "I never lost man Jack one on this trip in over three hundred years!"

"How old are you?" Michael asked, surprised even in the intensity of the moment.

"Why, heck, I don't guess I rightly know—six, seven hundred years anyhow," Emmitt said. "How old are you, Spirit Man?"

"Well, I, uh, I was... I guess I'm twenty six," Michael answered.

"Well, there you have it. You are one classic young pup, and I am one classic old fart!" The troll-like trooper burst out with a laugh so deep and genuine that Michael could not help but join him, and the two sat laughing their asses off as the train lurched and hurtled madly through the dark tunnel.

Since Michael's cart was at the rear of the train, and he was seated facing back, he could see only where they had been, and not where they were going. He turned around once to look forward, but all he could see were glimpses of jagged rock in the pale glow of the train's little headlight, mostly obscured by the cloud of smoke and steam that stung against his face. Every half mile or so, they passed a widened place where a wick lantern lit up a tiny area. In the eerie flickering light, Michael saw outcroppings of jagged rock and the deep holes of abandoned shafts and pits. Seconds after they passed one of the lanterns, and were back in darkness again, there was a huge explosion and a blinding flash of light. Without a second to brace himself, Michael slammed against the side of the cart and cried out.

"Strikers!" came the cry from the front of the train.

"Action! Let's go! Get hot!" Emmitt shouted to his troops. The dwarves drew their pistols and began blasting away in all directions into the dark Michael couldn't see a damn thing. All he could hear was the deafening sound of gunfire exploding in his ears, and the whine of bullets ricocheting off the rocks and the iron sides of the carts. Then somebody or something jumped on top of him and pinned him forcibly to the floor of the cart. In the glow of a smoky torch someone was carrying he saw what had him. It was a person, enormously fat, with grotesque wattles of flesh hanging from arms and neck. He was wearing tight black elastic pants and a white shirt with poof sleeves, and had a white masquerade-ball mask over his eyes. His lips had globs of red lipstick smeared all over them, and the eyes that peered through the mask were swollen, glaring red, with goo oozing out of them. His black hair was combed back into a ducktail with a slick blob of grease.

Michael screamed like a trapped rabbit as he fought to push the monster off him, but his struggles and blows were just swallowed up in the folds of flesh. The horrid apparition raised himself up to smash his gross fists into Michael's face when the blinding flash and thundering blast of a pistol shot cut the darkness and a bullet smacked right into his fat forehead, knocking him off the train to roll into the shadows.

"Got the fat sumbitch," said Emmitt with satisfaction. "I think we got 'em all."

"What the fuck was that?" Michael gasped as he struggled to get his breath, check to see if all his parts were still with him.

"Don't be rude, now, we don't say fuck in this world," the gnarled little gnome admonished him. "Them big ugly hog people were Strikers. They ain't nothing. More like pests than anything else here in this part of the woods." Emmitt blew the smoke out of the barrel of his pistol which just saved Michael's life. "Hooonh," the tube sang.

"Why do you call them Strikers?" Michael asked.

"This here is the Badlands of Chaos," Emmitt reminded him. "People get crazy out here in the sticks. They get a cause up their ass, they want to strike out save the world from the eve of destruction. Who knows what the

114

hell they think they are doing."

Then Hal Frisky, Jr let out a long blast on his steam whistle, and the train came out from the dark tunnel into daylight. Michael gasped. It was nothing at all like the beautiful green canyon he had just come from. The sky was a dull blue-gray, with strata of dark yellow-brown haze. The sun was hidden behind an indefinable bank of dark clouds, and mists hung in the deepest hollows of the barren landscape. In silhouette against the murky distant horizon, crooked bare branches seemed to grasp and tear the fabric of the gloomy sky.

"Is this your Badlands, Emmitt?" Michael asked, his apprehension raising his voice.

Emmitt nodded his head "yes", but quickly put his stubby, fat finger to his mouth, shushing him with an immediacy Michael did not find reassuring, especially considering that the train was still roaring and chuffing down the rails, carts clattering and wheels clinking. He tried not to imagine what it was that was not supposed to hear him talking. But since Emmitt and all the other dwarves were sitting silent in their carts, eyes wide as a trainload of chickens in coyote country, Michael did not ask why they were all afraid somebody would hear them.

"Whoooot! Who-ooot!" Hal Frisky, Jr tooted on his hooter, as they toodled and trundled through the tundra-like terrain. Then across the desolate scene and in the near distance looming from the mists Michael could see a lonely soldiers' outpost which he guessed was Fort Huachuca. With a thundering grumble the train rumbled over a wooden bridge built just like an old roller coaster, and they crossed over what a sign identified as the West Fork River. As they crossed over the river, the steam engine with all the tiny mining carts behind it made a sweeping left turn around a great puddle of muddy water, and the sun came out from behind the cloud and sparkled from its turbid surface. The dwarves all jumped up in their carts and began cheering wildly as they passed the sign proclaiming the name of the place to be Lake Del Rio.

"Was that lake named after you, Emmitt?" Michael asked.

"No," Brigadier Sergeant Emmitt Del Rio, the famous giant among dwarves, said. "I was named after it."

# SPIRIT MAN
## Chapter Ten

Conductor Hal Frisky Jr. blew the whistle as the steam engine came to a sudden halt at the Fort Huachuca Railroad Station, in front of a fifteen foot high cement platform which had two flights of stairs leading down to ground level.

"Let's go, y'all clear out, now, y'hear?" Emmitt yelled to his troops, who all jumped up and started tumbling out of the carts, tripping over each others' sabres, and falling right on their great round rollicking asses. The mining carts jerked one more time, almost knocking Emmitt clear off his feet. His little stubby arms were waving around in tiny circles as he tried to catch his balance, and all the bright chevrons on his sleeves made him look like a blue and yellow baby bird trying to fly. Michael knew better than to reach out and take hold of him which would make him look bad in front of his troops, but he did manage to brace up against him before he fell on his ass like Stubblefield and Beerbarrel and the rest. Then Buster and Squinty fell out of the last cart and knocked Emmitt spinning like a top out of control. Michael had no choice but to reach out and grab him, whereupon he spun to a heap at Michael's feet, looking dazed. All the dwarves cheered for Michael.

Then he heard another noise, a seething melee, a sound like a mob of manic monkeys and a gaggle of screechey geechie birds, and up the flights of stairs came a crowd of dwarves, dozens of dwarves, a hundred or two hundred, all hopping and shuffling along, chattering, blowing whistles, and twirling clackers around their heads. They rushed forward to greet the forty troopers and all swarmed together hugging, and laughing, and bouncing each other up and down, banging into each other, knocking each other on their fat asses, and pointing and laughing.

After the excitement of such a warm reception began to die down, Emmitt gave crisp spittle-slinging orders to Sutbblefield to form up an escort to take Michael from the platform, down the stairs, across a dirt field, and toward the main gate of Fort Huachuca. All along the way, Michael could hear the whisperings and murmurs among the horde of dwarves, saying, "Is he really Spirit Man?"

Michael overheard one dwarf answer back, "Oh, yes, he must be. Just look, he's so tall."

Then they led Michael up a road with crushed gravel to the thick wooden walls of the fort, and to the wide main gates which were wide open. Emmitt shouted out, "Have no fear, Emmitt is here!" and everyone began to cheer and throw flowers and colored popcorn as the Spirit Man and all the rest of the gang walked into the plaza of the fort.

There was quite a celebration going on as the droves of dwarves were beating on drums and playing frantic magic melodies on flugelhorns and flutes. Horse-drawn wagons bearing barrels of beer were brought round, bungs banged out and taps rapped in, and soon everyone was drinking beer by the bucketful and shooting their pistols into the air.

"It's always like this when I come back with the boys!" Emmitt told Michael. "When you finish suckin' down that beer, I'm going to take you to Cap'n Baylor at Headquarters. Then when y'all get finished, I will take y'both to Fat Eddie's and get you drunk as pootin' coots!"

On the way to Captain Baylor's office, they walked down the middle of main street past a General Store advertising food and guns (and a barber's chair in front), Fat Eddie's Bar and Grill, a silversmith, a medical Clinic, a lawyer advertising cheap divorces and tax assistance, and an undertaker. Then they walked up a couple of old, creaky steps, through two batwing swinging doors, and then into the Headquarters office itself.

Captain Baylor's adjutant, Private Major E.J. Butts, ushered Michael and Emmitt and all the rest of the tagalongs into the center of a large room, where stood a huge, heavy oak table. He got everyone into the room and situated, motioned for everyone to be silent, and then turned to face the table, saluted, and announced that everyone was present.

However, it was quickly evident to Michael that there

was a problem. Captain Andrew Baylor, who was one of the most distinguished and highly decorated soldiers of all time, was drunk! He had been drinking for several days, maybe even weeks, and he had just he passed out ten minutes earlier, right after the little train rolled into the Fort Huachuca Railroad Station.       Michael gazed at the pathetic sight.  The gold-braided and uniformed dwarf was slumped over the old oak table in the middle of the room, with his entire head face down in a bowl of red hot chili stew.  Michael had to admit he found the smell of the stew very delicious, and he wondered if he could have a bowl of it for himself.

Brevet Sub-Colonel Billie Boy Buchanan knew that Captain Baylor very much wanted to talk to Michael whom he truly believed was the great Spirit Man himself, but it was obvious that wasn't going to happen any time soon.  Billie Boy would have to do all the dirty work himself today for his Captain.

"As you can see, Captain Baylor is not feeling well today," Colonel Buchanan said as he put his hand on Captain Baylor's shoulder.  He tipped the captain's head to one side, reached around the puddle of chile stew, and pulled out a letter.  "A little earlier today he composed this letter, and it was his intention to read it to you this afternoon.  If you have no objections, I will undertake to conduct that duty on his behalf, as he is in this incapacitated condition."

Michael just nodded.

The Captain's faithful Brevet Sub-Colonel stood at attention—all four foot two of him— and read the letter.

*"Dear Spirit Man,*

*First of all, let me welcome you to your second adventure in the Mirror World.  I hope your crossover went well for you.  The reason that you have come to us once again is quite simple:  Our Homeland has become the Badlands of Chaos, and we need to fight back!  I believe with all my might and heart that you are truly the great Spirit Man. You are here for one reason and your sole mission is to solve*

*the riddle that has plagued us for so long. Here is the riddle
Spirit Man and see if you can solve it. If you do, the wall
between the dream world and the magic theater that divides
us will come tumbling down. Wouldn't that be neat?
Here is the riddle and good luck to you!*

*What is the name of the man who plays many a cruel
game?*

*Best wishes,
Captain A. Baylor, Cav.*

Billie Boy folded the letter and placed it back in
Captain Baylor's coat pocket, getting only a very little red
chili on it. A hush fell over the room. Michael couldn't think
of a single thing to say, and after a long moment of silence,
Colonel Buchanan dismissed all of them.

Emmitt patted Michael's hand as they all filed out of
the room, and told him not to worry about it. "Maybe later
it will come to you later, huh?" Then the booger-nosed
Brigadier Sergeant turned to the crowd of dwarves waiting
for his report. "Anybody thirsty?"

"Ho-oh! Yip yip!" all the dwarves in the room hooted
back with great enthusiasm.

"Well, what are y'all waiting for? Let's get down!"
Emmitt shouted, and they all turned and swept down the
street like a cloud of manic monkeys toward Fat Eddie's Bar
and Grill.

The sun was setting in what Michael presumed was the
western sky as they walked briskly across the dusty street
to Fat Eddie's. A group of children who looked just like the
pack of Chihuahua bulldog puppies running with them flocked
and gathered around Michael. Dressed in cowboy chaps and
square-dance frocks, they bustled along with him like
ponderosa penguins, each trying to hold his hand or cling to
his faded blue jeans as they walked and skipped along the
street. The tears of joy in their eyes, and the shrill trilling
of their happy songs touched Michael with laughter, and he
found himself swept along with them.

"Y'all party, now y'hear!" Emmitt shouted, and he did a

little dance in the middle of the street, leaping and capering like a fungus-faced troll marionette.

In Fat Eddie's Bar and Grill they met the bartender, an enormous dwarf with a big, bushy red beard. He stuck out a hand that looked like a smooth starfish. "Hope y'all don't mind me place! Needs a little fixin' but its home to me!"

"You're Fat Eddie?" Michael asked.

"Nope. That's just my beard. I had a moustache named Tommy once, but I couldn't keep him out of the gin, so I cut the sumbitch off."

"Oh, then what do we call you," Michael asked.

"Don't call me," the red-whiskered barrel of a dwarf said with a grin almost as wide as he was tall. "Just call the beard, and you'll usually find me following it around. What's your poison, Spirit Man?"

"Uh, Tequila, I guess," Michael told him.

"How about a beer?" the bartender suggested, handing him a mug half the size of Stubblefield's bubble butt. Michael nodded, and took the beer. One swig of the rich foaming brew told him he had been missing out on the good stuff all his life by not hanging out with dwarves before. He chugged about half of the cold malty elixer, banged the mug down on the bar and growled in satisfaction, then joined the laughter of the butt-ugly trooper who stood watching him.

Michael watched Emmitt walk over to the juke box, draw back his foot the foot-and-a-half it would go, and then kick as hard as he could with his lumpy oversized boot. To Michael's surprise, the juke box squawked to a stop, then began to play music he recognized as Don Henley's "All She Wants To Do Is Dance." In seconds, the whole place was rocking and reeling. The music was blasting, the beer overflowing, and Fat Eddie's bartender just kept on serving and smiling away like a fat four-foot fool.

Michael thought it would be a good idea to just sip on the beer, and not get too trashed out, and end up rolling around on the floor like Tolbert and Squinty, not knowing where the hell he was. But by the time he noticed he never asked the beard to refill his mug, he had discovered it never had to be refilled, and he was beginning to feel pretty loose. At that point he remembered he didn't know where he was even if he was sober, and the idea struck him funny enough that he could laugh about it.

Michael danced with all the children, holding their tiny hands and going around and around in circles until he became so dizzy he fell into a pile of drunken dwarves. Then he danced around on his knees, for a moment thinking that he had changed into a dwarf himself.

Then one of the troopers let out a squawk and grabbed his mouth. He sprinted for the door, and let go a great spout of beer puke right in front of the entrance to Fat Eddie's. Then another, and another bent over, rushed to the door, and puked in the puddle.

There was only one fight that night. Good old Sharpie Blades, a rugged cowboy from the good old days, was so drunk that he picked a fight with Stubblefield and Tolbert together. Sharpie Blades swung wildly and missed both of them by a mile. He went flying across the bar, landed rolling, crashed right through the front door of Fat Eddie's Bar and Grill, and landed ears deep in the puddle of puke. Sharpie Blades raised himself up only once, his face all covered in sudsy mud. He let out a croak, and a beer-soaked curse, and then fell back into the pool, where he spent the rest of the night being puked on by the others.

As the rest made their way back into the bar to dance to the music, Emmitt asked Michael if he would stay outside with him to get some fresh air. The moon was almost full and bright enough to see their own shadows.

"Beautiful night," Emmitt remarked.

"Yeah," Michael agreed.

"How are skies back where you come from, Spirit Man?" Emmitt asked.

Michael had to stop an instant to think what he meant by back where he came from. Since he had begun his adventures as the Spirit Man, he had seen many different kinds of sky. "Depends on where you're at," he said.

They stood there for awhile, looking up at the sky. Then finally Emmitt said, "I know the name of the man who plays many a cruel game. At least I reckon I do, but I have been too chicken to say it. If I am wrong, which I don't think I am, I will be killed on the spot. You knew that, didn't you? I can't bring myself to take that chance. But you... you are Spirit Man. It would be all right for you to speak his name out loud, wouldn't it?"

"What are you talking about?" Michael asked. "You mean that you know the name of the man who plays many a cruel game on all your people, and you won't say his name to end the suffering?"

"I've been afraid to," Emmitt said lowering his head in shame, staring at the ground. "If I am wrong, I die. You can understand that, cain't ya?"

"I can understand that, Emmitt. So why don't you give me the name. Then I can tell whoever I am supposed to the name of the man who plays many a cruel game, so we can put an end to all of this bullshit."

Emmitt looked into the blue eyes of the Spirit Man, and he began to tremble. He began to shake and his teeth to chatter, and then the ground at his feet began to shudder, and a cry began to pry itself out between the dwarf's chattering jaws.

"More freakin' Strikers!" Emmitt screamed as a terrible earthquake that shook the ground and made the trees flutter like cardboard cutouts. The buildings along main street began to rattle, and then crackle, and then fall to the ground in dusty piles. Glass windows shattered into shards, and broken glass flew everywhere. The dwarves ran out of the collapsing Bar and Grill, as a huge dark cloud drifted in front of the full moon, and the world became black and blind.

In the Headquarters building, Captain Baylor was still passed out, and the legend thereafter always had it that he slept through the entire ordeal.

The dwarves then ran out of Fat Eddie's, shooting

their guns into the air, into the darkness, and at anything that moved, screaming and shouting, "Strikers! Kill them!"

In the total darkness, someone jumped on top of Michael, throwing him to the ground. A fire burst out in a nearby pile of wreckage, and in the dim light Michael could see the white masked face of another Striker. The Striker had a gun in his hand, and he thrust the barrel into Michael's mouth. Michael tried to take control of himself, to make the right moves to disarm the Striker's deadly intention—relax, cooperate, communicate, and survive.

"You will die now, Spirit Man," the Striker said with calm deliberation, and he pulled the trigger. The bullet went into Michael's mouth, and blew out the back of his head.

In the second instant before Michael died he saw the face of Joey Pachuco in the white mask of the Striker that pulled the trigger. It was only a very short instant, but it was enough. He was sure.

## Chapter Eleven

Michael wondered if he was dead or alive. He seemed to feel like he had expected to be dead, but then it occurred to him that he was wondering, so that must mean he was alive. He decided to risk opening one eye. His face lay in white sand which stretched away before him a long distance. The sun was glaring bright, high in the sky, and a little way off to the side he could see a sparkling blue ribbon of softly rolling surf. Far down the beach, he could see a gleaming white castle towering above bluffs of chalk. White sand dunes stretched forever to the farthest horizon, quite a contrast from the darkened world of Fort Huachuca.

Michael sat up and took off his running shoes. He took off his shirt, and the warm sun felt good on the muscles of his back. He stood up, feeling a bit unsteady, then began to walk barefoot along the beach toward the castle. It didn't appear to be too far away, but it seemed to take him hours to get there. However, when he arrived, it seemed like he had been walking only a minute or two.

When Michael got to the castle, it appeared to be completely abandoned—not a soul around, and it was very still and quiet. The sun was very high in the sky, and when Michael looked up at the castle, he saw it had a pair of twin towers that soared straight up into the sky, and the sun hung between them, bright and glaring like a spark shimmering between two huge electrodes.

The gates were open, so he walked through them into a broad patio paved in red tile. Still he saw or heard no one. There was a huge swimming pool in the middle of the patio, in the shape of the figure eight, and a wooden bridge went over the center portion of the pool, just wide enough for two to pass close together. Though the pool was large enough for a small town, there were only two lawn chairs by the pool side.

"Who could they possibly be for?" he asked himself, "and why are they not here?" He walked over to the lawn chairs by the poolside, walked around them, looked all around the high-vaulted patio, and then sat down in one of them. He almost expected something to happen, and for a moment he lay tense, waiting for it. Then he relaxed, took a deep breath, and stretched his arms and legs out as far as he could. Through the open gates of the castle he could see that he was facing the ocean and he watched the waves roll in, one after another, crashing upon the sands of the beach.

Then Michael's eyes became heavy, and he let himself relax more and doze, and he soon fell fast asleep, and had a dream. In his dream, the sky had become very dark and gloomy. Bolts of lightning flashed across the purple sky. Then a black cat appeared in the sky, with eyes as yellow as the sun, teeth flashing white as fear against the sparkling black of its fur. Great fangs bared, the huge predator yowled its challenge, then with fiendish ferocity it bolted out of the sky and raced toward Michael still lying in the lawn chair.

Michael tried to scream but he couldn't. He struggled to force himself to move or even just bite to defend himself but he couldn't do anything. The cat flew above Michael's head, flying through the air to pounce on him. In that instant, his arms flew up in front of his face to protect him from being scratched or hurt, and he croaked out a fearful cry for help. "Someone, please help me!"

As though he had heard someone scream, Michael snapped out of his terrible dream, and he leaped to his feet. The brightness of the sun was so intense it seemed to have a sound, and he raised his arms to protect himself, just as he had from the fiendish black cat. "Don't kill me again!" Michael screamed.

Then from the brilliant and blinding light Michael heard a voice. He heard the sweet voice of a woman speak to him, saying, "You're just dreaming, that's all." Surprised, he tried to see her through the glare, and he bolted up in his lawn chair, as though awakening from a restless nap. He shook his head and rubbed his eyes and squeezed the back of his neck, and looked around and discovered he could see just fine. He was sitting beside the great pool, on the lawn that stretched to the white castle a little way off.

Sitting in the other lawn chair across from him, was the most beautiful young woman he had ever seen in his whole life. In fact, she was the most beautiful woman he had seen all his life. Flowers began to bloom at her feet as he recognized her, and he gasped in delight that of all the people he could have met there, he had found Magellan Champs. The long dark red hair he had always loved fell on her bare shoulders and curled there along her graceful neck. The deep, melting and inviting honey and chocolate warmth of her eyes was more wonderful than anything Michael had ever seen or dreamed about. Her teeth flashed white as trust, white as the sands on the beach as she smiled at Michael. If any woman was a goddess, this tanned and satin-draped dark jewel was the one, sitting there by the pool with the castle and its towers looming in the distance behind her.

"You're Magellan Champs," he told her, as though he expected her to be surprised too.

She laughed, as though he should have known she knew everyone as well as everyone knew her.

"Where am I?" Michael asked her.

"San Carlos," she answered, and then waving toward the castle, said, "This is Castle Champs. It belongs to my father. He is the blind poet who wrote the book, *The Crack in the Wall.* You know I love my father very much, don't you? My mother died when I was a child. My father has taken care of me ever since I was seven. He has always told me wonderful stories about how much they were in love and about all the dreams that they dreamed together. All my life I have wished I had something like what they shared together. I have never fallen in love with anyone. I am every man's dream, but it is very lonely here in this dream world. I wish I had someone to share my life with, someone to hold in the cold, lonely nights. I wish more than anything else in the whole wide world that I could be in love. Is that too much to ask for?"

"Oh, no," Michael replied, and he sounded very

reassuring. "Not if you believe in love."

"Come on," she said as she stood up and reached out her hand to Michael. "I want you to meet my father, Mr. Champs."

They walked together to the Castle, then up a flight of stairs made of white marble with streaks of gold in it. At the top of the stairs were two huge glass doors with gold designs in them from the Plaza Hotel in New York City. Magellan waved the doors open for Michael, and they walked into the main hall of the castle. After a few steps, Michael stopped in the middle of the great hall, and stood there whirling round and round in awe and wonder. There were huge white Roman columns on all sides of the hall that rose up to the dome of the castle, where a covey of stained-glass angels let in the shimmering light of all colors.

"It's so beautiful," Magellan said, her voice husky with reverent awe.

"Yes, it is," Michael could only agree.

"Wait here," she told him. "I'm going to tell my father you are here." She turned and quickly began to walk down a long hall.

"You don't even know my name," Michael called after her.

"Spirit Man!" she yelled back to him. "I'll be right back!"

Michael stood ready to be there for a long time, smiling in surprise, and expecting something like a birthday party. Magellan came back in a few seconds or hours, and she told Michael her father was very eager to meet him. He had hardly time to react at all before she turned around and told him to follow her. "To my father's study," she said. Michael followed her across the huge hall of the castle and down a long hallway. They came to a door that bore an engraved brass plate reading: LIBRARY.

Magellan opened the door, and they walked into the room together. The room was very large and full of hundreds of books in highly polished oak shelves. There was one wall which was made entirely of huge windows overlooking the ocean below. As though each window was made of crystal, the rays of the sun darted and scampered through these windows in tiny sparks of rainbows, making Mr. Champs study very bright and cheerful.

Magellan stepped over to where her father sat in his deep plush executive chair by his wide polished desk. As she greeted him and kissed his cheek, Michael was surprised to recognize that the desk and the part of the room where he sat looked exactly like his own office at Spiritland Mansion. He paused to reflect for an instant that once again he felt the strange feeling that he was almost remembering something very important. Then Magellan waved for him to come on to meet her father, and he snapped out of the trance and walked to the desk.

Mr. Champs was a very tall man. When he stood to greet Michael, he rose almost a whole head above him, and Michael was a tall person himself. He was a classically distinguished handsome gentleman, well tanned and radiantly healthy. He moved with the grace of an athlete, and his handshake was firm and warm with generous energy. He ran his fingers through his long full-bodied silver-gray hair as he invited them to sit down with him. Only his distant gaze reminded Michael that he was blind.

"Magellan tells me you are Spirit Man," he said. "If that is true, then I've been waiting for this moment all my life."

Michael nodded his head and said simply, "I am."

Mr. Champs let out a big sigh, and leaned back in his chair just like Michael did in his own executive chair. "Hungry, Spirit Man?" he asked.

"Starving!" Michael confessed.

"I'll take care of it," Magellan said as she bounced to her feet. She swished away through an ornately carved door, and in what seemed like only seconds, came skipping back with a big silver tray of finger sandwiches, assorted deserts and drinks. She put the tray down on the table in front of them, and gave a little curtsey, just like a little schoolgirl at an afternoon tea party. Michael laughed in delight at her little pantomime, and Mr. Champs joined him as though he could see her himself.

"All right! Let's do this, shall we?" said Mr. Champs. His hands fluttered quickly over the tray, locating points on its edge, and observing the different shapes of the little plates. He picked up a slice of the most wickedly delicious looking Southern style pecan pie Michael had ever seen and chomped off almost half of it in one bite. "Mmm-MMM!"

Michael paused only long enough to decide whether to begin with the thick and inviting stuffed little sandwiches, or go directly to the confections, then he picked up a sandwich in each hand, and didn't say a single word as he thoroughly enjoyed each of the four bites it took to consume them. He chose a tall frosty silver tumbler of orange juice, drank half of it as though it were holy water gushing from a glacier, then indulged himself in a huge sigh of satisfaction.

"Eat up, my man. You'll need all of your strength for tomorrow's long journey," said Mr. Champs said as he took a bite out of his second sandwich.

"Journey?" Michael asked, trying a fat chocolate brownie smeared with marzipan.

"Just one more of those delicious little crab salad sandwiches, then I must stop," Mr. Champs protested. "No, what the hell, I was always a sucker for Bavarian cream, so I'm not stopping for anything. You should try those creampuffs."

"I will," Michael declared, and he picked up one of the crisp and warm little puffs and popped it into his mouth. It was the lightest and fluffiest pastry he had ever tasted, and when he bit into it, it gushed the most perfectly spiced cream filling.

"Are we ready for the coffee?" Mr. Champs asked. Magellan appeared at Michael's shoulder with two steaming mugs. "Magellan will take you to the wall tomorrow morning," Mr. Champs informed him.

"The wall?" Michael queried. He looked at Magellan, who turned away from him.

Mr. Champs sipped at his coffee quietly for a time,

then he leaned back in his chair and closed his eyes. After a moment, he said, "The wall is a thousand miles long and a mile high. It was built by slaves, hundreds of thousands of slaves driven to death in the work camps. When you get there, you will see so much human suffering, sorrow, and pain that you will wish that you could close your eyes and be blind like me, forever. That is the wall."

There was a long moment of silence in the room, then Magellan said, "My father is getting tired now. We should let him get some rest, and then you can talk more later." She walked to her father and gently kissed his forehead. For a moment Michael thought he had already fallen asleep, then he raised his hand and said, "Good to meet you, Spirit Man. There is so much we need to discuss."

"I'm looking forward to it," said Michael.

Then Magellan led Michael from her father's room, and they walked together across the great hallway. "Come on, I'll show you to your room," she told him.

It was the smallest room Michael had seen in the castle. It had only a narrow bed with an end table, and a thick red Persian rug. There was a small leaded-glass window across from the bed, and the afternoon sun shone brightly.

"Hope you like it," Magellan said. Then she gave him a hug, and kissed him on his neck, and said, "See you in the morning." She turned and walked out of the room.

Michael stepped to the doorway and watched her as she went down the long hallway and disappeared around a corner. "Am I falling in love with her?" he asked himself. He closed the door and turned to see the red and gold light of sunset flooding the room through the crystal panes of the window. "I ought to get some rest myself," he said. He lifted the white brocade coverlet from the narrow bed, lay down on his back, and spread it over himself, letting it settle smooth and straight like a draped shroud.

He awoke. There were candles burning in the dark room, their reflections winking in the window panes like the eyes of watchers in the dark beyond. Michael peered down toward his feet, and there was the black cat curled up on his legs and purring very loudly. It was the same black cat that he had seen in his terrible dream, and for a second he feared it would leap on him again. Then it leaped from the bed and ran out of the bedroom door which stood ajar.

At once wide awake, Michael jumped up and followed the cat down the hallway, around the corner to a spiral staircase, and then up the winding column, round and round as fast as he could climb. Twenty, forty, sixty, one hundred, two hundred, three hundred steps, and Michael still chased the cat! Though he had very long legs, and took very long strides, and had been a runner himself, the cat somehow always managed to stay ahead of him. When he finally reached the top of the spiral staircase, he realized where he was. He must be at the very top of one of the twin towers at the front of the great white castle.

And there only a few feet from him the black cat stood in the shadow of a dark archway, its bright yellow eyes piercing the darkness. It turned and stepped into the room, leaving just the tip of its tail still in the light where Michael could see it. Understanding, Michael followed it, crouching so he wouldn't hit his head on the top of the four and a half foot high archway.

It seemed quite dark in the tiny little room at the top of the tower, but after a few seconds, Michael could make things out. There were windows all the way around, and Michael could see a perfect view of the night sky. As he looked, he discovered he could see millions of stars and a thin crescent moon. In the middle of the room stood an altar of white marble, and as he leaned over it he could see a large, thick book. He could not make out the title in the dim moonlight, but he could see there was a stub of candle and a matchbook beside it. He lit the candle, and saw that the cover on the book read, "The Crack in the Wall, by Mr. Champs."

Michael carefully opened the book, and was surprised to find that the book was written in Braille, the language that blind people can read with their fingertips. It was a foot thick, and every page was covered with rows of raised dots. He started to ask himself what such a book would be doing there, then felt foolish when he remembered it would make perfect sense for a blind man to keep a copy in Braille. It was the candle that was out of place, since it could not make it easier for either a blind person or a sighted one to read the book.

Then as he watched, a cloud of white mist appeared on the pages of the book, words began to emerge from the cloud of white mist in printed form, and in a few moments, Michael could read them. This is what he read:

GOOD DREAMER
A poem by Mr. Champs

Every Good Dreamer notices
the shape of the moon,
dreams dreams and sees visions,
all day and all night.
All you got to do my friend,
is put up a good fight,
open your eyes and realize,
where the secret lies.
Mister Good Dreamer wears
many a brave disguise.
Don't you know that
you're living in a fantasy?
The world turned upside down
a long, long time ago.
Whisper my name,
put an end to my shame.
The earth will shake,
the wall will break,
that's all it will take to make
Mister Good Dreamer a myth.
Do you understand, Spirit Man?
Its me, Joey!

Alexander Champs

As mysteriously as they had come, the printed words began to fade away, and the book was in Braille once again. Like a playful kitten, a sudden single gust of wind swirled through the tiny tower room. It flipped the pages of the thick book and slammed the cover shut. For a moment the flickering of the candle flame made the title seem to dance on the cover, "The Crack In The Wall," and then the capering little gust blew it out and plunged the room into darkness again.

The thin sliver of moon lay almost on the horizon, and could be seen but gave no light to see by. Even the icy pinpricks of the stars offered no relief from the fearsome sudden blindness of the night. In the darkness, Michael somehow felt less protected, and not alone. He listened for the purring of the cat, but he heard only silence. He held his breath and listened again, and then he thought he heard something or someone breathing in the room.

"Who's there?" Michael whispered. A chill crept around the top of his spine, teased his heartbeat. He tried to scoff at his own foolishness, but still he found himself fearing the black cat he had dreamed of would come out of the dark shadows and attack him, for real this time, ripping him from limb to limb as he struggled and screamed and soiled himself in terror.

Then, Michael moved his head, and yes, yes, there was somebody breathing in the room with him. From the depth of the darkest shadow in the room, an unseen shape came toward him. Michael closed his eyes, and tried to listen and feel and smell. He wondered if the cat had transformed itself into a larger thing, a beast ready to pounce on him and kill him again and again. He wanted to scream, and to strike out and try to destroy the horror, and then he could feel the heat of the beast all around him. His terror and the mad fanatic intensity of controlling it was like the pressure of an unbearable sound, and his body shook and gasped as the beast wrapped its arms around his head.

Then a voice said, "Shhh. Its me, Magellan. Hold me."

Michael still had his eyes closed. He squeezed them

even tighter shut as he held onto Magellan, gasping and trembling. He could feel her warm body up against his, and he could feel the pulsing of her heartbeat as she flowed to him to soothe and calm his own rushing heart, and he never wanted to let her go, never in a million years.

## Chapter Twelve

Michael lay curled into a tiny ball, wrapped in warmth and security. For a moment he enjoyed the silence and the privacy of it, then he heard a sound softly reaching in to him, to stroke him gently. It was the gentle rolling of the surf, like the breathing of the sea itself. A soft breeze tickled around him, and he recognized the warmth was beaming down on him, not close upon him. With a trace of reluctance, he opened one eye just a peek.

He lay on a little blanket on the rolling white dunes of the beach, next to the great pool with its mysterious infinity shape, surrounded by the soft little crystals of pure white sand. The water in the pool was still as glass, and he could see reflected in it the twin towers of the mighty Castle Champs rising up to meet the dawn. The sun was just rising over the Franklin Mountains to the east, and it appeared between the towers as though it was hanging on a cable there.

"I wonder how they do that," he mused with a little smile. He closed his eye and lay enjoying the already-hot rays of the rising sun.

Then he heard a voice call out to him, a warm and inviting voice. "Michael, come on, it's time for breakfast, lunch, and tea." He opened his eyes and saw Magellan waving to him from a little balcony high up between the twin towers.

He laughed with pleasure and jumped to his feet. He ran to the pool, dived into the sparkling clear water and swam across it in a few smooth strokes, slaloming like a dolphin. He raised his arms to the sun and let its rays sear the water from his body, and let the sweetest morning breeze waft it away. He twirled round and round, marveling at the perfection of the sea stroking the beach like living jade, the white dunes stretching away to the horizon, the banded hills of the Franklin Mountains looking like carved onyx bookends against the polished turquoise of the sky.

It seemed a marvel to him, yet strangely not out of

place, that there was no one in this beautiful world but Magellan Champs herself, her father the blind poet, and a cat he mysteriously both sought and feared.

Magellan met him at the great main gate of the castle and greeted him with warm embrace. "I made a lot of food," she said, "and Daddy is waiting for you."

He was comfortably dressed in the soft jeans and work shirt he preferred when they arrived back at the heavy carved door with the brass plate engraved, LIBRARY. She led him into the room, where he noticed that all of the books on the shelves were very thick, and had the little telltale patches of dotted texture which identified them as written in Braille. "And some of them have magic written between the lines," he thought.

Mr. Champs sat with his back to them, staring sightlessly out to sea. "Daddy, we are here!" Magellan said.

"Hi honey," he said. Then he added, "Please sit down, Spirit Man."

Michael sat across from Mr. Champs, and as he stared into the vacant eyes of the blind poet, he thought he understood that blind people see where people who can see, see not, and can see within.

"I take it that you slept well?" asked Mr. Champs.

"Oh, yes," Michael replied, not quite certain it was true.

"Good. We'll eat a hearty breakfast, and then you will be on your way. I have been waiting for this day all my life."

Magellan departed, and in seconds came back with a huge silver tray piled high with food. Mr. Champs' strong and agile hands fluttered over the tray, and stroked each plate as she placed it on the desk before him. In an instant she had laid out a sumptuous buffet before them, and Mr. Champs jumped up and down in his chair like a child as he sampled the delights. She gave him a bowl of water and a large towel, so he could dispense with clumsy utensils, and eat with his long sensitive fingers.

When Michael watched him pick up a syrup-soaked pancake, smear it with a fingerful of whipped butter, roll it like a tortilla, and bite off half of it, he decided that was the right way to do it, and he joined his host. He wished he had another mouth and two more hands to enjoy the selection from fluffy scrambled eggs with fried potatoes to smoked fish in cream to gooseberry crepes to apricot empanadas.

"Come join us, won't you?" Magellan's father invited her.

"Why of course," she said, and sat beside Michael, where she sipped a cup of herb tea.

After a few silent minutes, Mr. Champs chuckled, and said, "Someone must really be hungry. Don't they feed you in the world you come from?"

"Not like this," Michael said, joining his mirth. "Your daughter can sure cook, sir! Back home, people are just so damn busy they don't have time to eat a good breakfast."

"What a shame," Mr. Champs said, with genuine sympathy.

"Daddy and I eat all our meals together all the time. Don't we, Daddy?" Magellan said.

"Yes, we do, Honey," he said, reaching out his hand for her to take. "I look forward to eating with my daughter every day, Spirit Man, just as much as writing my poems, taking my walks on the beach, and best of all, having Magellan read to me way, way into the night."

"Mmm," Michael agreed, unable to speak around the great bite of quince and rhubarb strudel he was so deeply appreciating.

"Today, is going to be the biggest day in your lives," Mr. Champs continued. "After this wonderful breakfast we are having together, you must begin on your journey to the wall." He paused dramatically a moment, and Magellan took a sip from her tea. "Magellan knows the way, and she can take you. It will take days to get there, but Magellan knows a place that will be safe for the night. Don't you, dearest?"

"Of course, Daddy," she said.

"Last night, I had a vision in a dream," said Mr. Champs. "I dreamed I saw you in the north tower, and you were reading my book, *The Crack in the Wall*, which as you know, only the blind can read and understand. But in my vision, I saw you reading words between the dots on the pages of my book. The title of the poem you were reading was Good Dreamer."

Michael was surprised, and could think of absolutely nothing to say.

"Go to the wall, Spirit Man," Mr. Champs said, earnest, and for a moment Michael was sure he could see right through him. "Whisper his name, put an end to his shame. If you are right, you will live. If you are wrong, God help us, we all shall perish forever."

Magellan got up and kissed her father upon his cheek in goodbye. "I love you, Daddy," she said.

Soon the castle lay far behind them as they walked down the endless beach for hours. The sun quickly rose high into the sky, and then stayed there, and with each passing hour grew hotter and hotter. Only the gentle breeze coming from the jade sea helped to cool them.

Magellan walked ahead of Michael, scampering barefoot along the very edge of the surf. Her satin drape exactly matched the honey gold of her perfect skin, and her dark and thick waves of hair perfectly matched the flowing curves of the surf. "This is the Goddess," Michael whispered to himself, again and again.

There was a break in the beach, a point that curved out a few hundred feet into the surf, and when Michael reached it, he was surprised to see that the beach beyond it was made of red dunes. As he watched, a flock of pelicans swept in from the dunes and began to dive into the surf off the point. In seconds, each bird came to the surface with a huge fish in its beak. He watched in fascination as each one flipped its fish into the air, caught it head first, and gulped it down with a smile and a wink.

Michael turned around and was alarmed that he could not see Magellan anywhere. He could see all the way down the white beach to where the castle was just the tiniest bit of rock at the farthest point away. The red beach he could see became rocky a couple of miles away, and the red dunes stretched away to sandstone bluffs in the distance. Then between the nearby dunes he could see patches of olive green and yellow, little gnarled trees and tall dried reeds. He started toward the nearest patch just as Magellan stepped from it and waved to him.

"Magellan, don't do that ever again!" he gasped. "I thought you were lost! Anything can happen out here, don't you know that?"

"We are here, you silly man," she said to him with a kiss on the cheek. "This is where we are safe. We will spend the night here, and then tomorrow we will head out again. Come on, now, and follow me."

She stepped into a clump of the tall reeds, and Michael followed behind her into a damp overgrown jungle. As the reeds and wide wet leaves stroked him as though they had reached out to touch him, he had to remind himself there was not a big tiger or a lion that would come charging out of the reeds to leap on him and devour him.

Then the reeds parted in front of him, and they stood together in a little jungle clearing, a little oasis with a red dune rising up behind it. Right in the middle stood a little hut of bamboo and boards and thatch.

"Do you like it?" she asked him.

"Yes, it looks like it could be made into a really neat place. Is it yours?"

"No, of course not, it's my father's place," she said with a gay little laugh. "Come on, let's get this place cozy, okay?"

"Do you want me to do something to help you?" Michael asked.

"No, just stay out of my way!" Magellan went to the little house and quickly got about a job she had obviously done before. She went to a trunk at the foot of the bed in the middle of the room, took out two blankets, and began to pound and beat the dust out of them, flapping them mightily. A swirling cloud of dust rose in the air, and Michael began to sneeze and cough. Then, a gust of the sea breeze swept over the trees and into the clearing and scampered through the house like a kitten chasing leaves in a pile, and the cloud of dust disappeared in seconds, leaving the hut sparkling clean.

"Works every time! Don't even need a broom!" she said and danced a little caper.

The sky turned dark red and brown like bloody mud as the sun was setting. Magellan took his hands in hers, and said, "This was the easy part. Tomorrow we enter into The Badlands of Chaos." Michael looked into Magellan's eyes, and saw the fiery orange and ruddy violet of the sunset reflected there, and he believed with all his heart that she was real.

Michael had a vision in his dreams again that night. He saw a huge black panther walking on the red beach in the middle of the night. It was so dark the beach was black, and the sea was black, and the sky was black. The great jungle cat opened up its mouth and roared into the night in a deep rough voice, saying, "Promise me that you will never leave me."

When Michael woke up the next morning, Magellan was gone. At first he thought she might be in the kitchen fixing one of her magnificent breakfasts, but she was not there. He found the things they had packed for the journey in a basket on the table, but nothing had been prepared. He called out for her, but there was no answer. He went outside, thinking there might be a spring, or a swimming pool where he might find her, but she was nowhere to be seen. He began to feel a sense of dread that he might once again find himself alone in a mysterious new world. The beginnings of fear began to bubble somewhere deep in his blood.

He looked up at the sun, and he was sure he could tell which direction the sea was, but he was not sure he could find his way back through the reeds to the hut if he left it. Instead of plunging into the jungle, he began to climb the red dune. In a few minutes he could see over the gnarled olive-green trees and the waving reeds and could see the surf rolling in on the rust-red beach.

"Magellan!" he cried out in anguish as he looked up and down the beach for her. His voice was lost in the vastness of the surf, and not even a pelican answered his cry. "How could I have lost her so soon," he moaned and fell to his knees and began to sob, then let himself fall back down the steep side of the red dune to lie beside the bamboo hut.

He knelt in the sand and beat upon it in frustration, and then noticed something very unusual. There was a set of paw prints leading from the house into the jungle toward the ocean. Frightened that she had not left him but instead had been taken from him, he jumped to his feet. "Oh Magellan, no, no!" he cried as he began to run through the reeds where the prints had led. In a moment he burst through the vegetation onto the beach, and he could easily see the single set of prints marching across the otherwise unmarked sand. Where the sand had been moist, the prints were perfect. They were clearly the prints of the paws of an enormous cat. The tracks led directly into the sea, and disappeared.

"No!" Michael cried to the sky, to the sea, and to the rolling surf. "Come back to me, my perfect Magellan! Don't leave me here in this strange world without your love!"

He remembered the good things in the basket on the table in the clearing, but somehow they just didn't seem worth going to look for. Instead he just began to walk up the beach, looking for paw prints he knew he would not find. The sun hung high in the sky, and there was no relief in sunset. His legs ached, and then became numb as he continued to walk. The beach became rockier, and harder to traverse, but still he kept on, knowing there was no point in stopping until he reached someplace. Perhaps if he kept walking, he would come to the wall, and she would be waiting there for him. Then his lungs could not drive one more step from his tortured legs, and he cursed the sun for refusing to set as he fell onto his face into the sand.

## Chapter Thirteen

The Strikers got to him first. Michael didn't even hear them coming. He struggled to regain consciousness, trying to force his tired and sunburned body to get up and defend itself. They came in a pack, howling and running alongside their caravan of junk-cobbled old jeeps and dune buggies. By the time Michael could get to his knees, they were all around him, tires skidding on the wet sand of the beach, and throwing up plumes of the dry sand as they slalomed to a stop.

In the jeep closest to Michael stood the man who appeared to be in command of the group. Like the others, he was dressed in old patched army camouflage fatigues, but his were less ragged than theirs, and he wore bright bands of gold braid around his sleeves at the wrist like a naval officer. "Well, well," said one of the others to him, "what do you suppose we have here, Baldy?"

The man in the jeep was indeed bald, as his head, face, and thick-jowled neck were baby butt smooth except for a long waxed black moustache. He was built like a lion—a sea lion, with a great blubber-laden torso supported by a pair of buttless short skinny legs. A sawed-off semi-automatic military shotgun was cradled comfortably on his right arm, and with his left hand he steadied himself on the jeep's rollover bar.

"I am not bald," he informed Michael, to the amusement of his troops. "One of my aides gives me a military shave every day. I am Colonel Baldonado Chavez, commanding officer of Conchita's First Buttkickulary Recon Division—the Big Green One. And you are what is passing for Spirit Man. Well, well, well."

Michael squinted to see Baldy Chavez' face in the glaring sun, and was repulsed to see that like the other Strikers, he wore white face paint with scarlet lipstick on his fat lips. "Who is Conchita?" Michael asked him.

Baldy and all of the others began to laugh and hoot.

"Conchita Champs rules around here, buddy," Baldy said. Then he waved to a group of his Striker troops. "All right, you vatos, round him up and let's get him back to Conchita. Get it on!"

With a whoop, six of the sinister clown like soldiers leaped forward and pounced on Michael before he even had time to twitch. They flipped him over, bound his hands and feet in seconds like a calf at a rodeo, then snatched him up and carried him like a trophy over their heads, passing him from one set of hands to others as they ran up the dune to the largest of the vehicles, an old army truck with enormous balloon tractor tires.

They tossed him into the back of the truck like a sack of rutabagas. Michael was glad they threw him onto his back instead of his face, since his hands were behind his back. Even so, he was surprised that the bed of the truck was so lumpy. Then he realized he had been thrown onto the feet of the men who were sitting on the benches on each side of the wooden side rails of the truck. He lay there staring up into twenty vicious-looking white mask faces. Slowly, each one of them pointed a rifle straight at Michael's face.

Michael tried very hard not to squeak, or to squirm, or to pee his pants. From behind the truck he heard Baldy Chavez say, "Cap'n Felix, I want you to prop him up somewhere on the way to Rubbleton, so he can see the wall. You got it? Roll it!"

"Ya betcha, Baldy," said the man sitting on the end of the bench. Then he yelled to his driver, "Yo-ooo, Arf!" and the truck lurched into motion. The big wide set tractor tires grabbed sand, and the truck accelerated up the side of a dune like a huge desert beetle.

In the back of the truck, Capitan Felix pointed to the big olive drab cooler can up front, and one of the troops dipped out a canteen cupful of green Kool-aid, which he passed down to Felix.

"Its time for the Spirit Man to wake up," Felix shouted in Michael's face as he poured the green water on him.

Michael spluttered and jerked himself to a sitting position. Then four pairs of hands grabbed him and pulled him up to sit on the bench so he could see where they were going.

"Where am I, Capitan?" Michael asked.

"Rubbleton," said the young officer with the red-smeared lips. "You are going to Rubbleton to see the wall and meet with the lady herself, if you can call her that." He and several of the other troops chuckled.

"Spirit Man, huh?" said another Striker. "Batman—Buttman, Superman—Pooperman, Spirit Man—Queeritman, har har har."

"Who do you think you really are, mister superstar?" Felix asked him. "I bet he doesn't even know the name of the man who plays many a cruel game, eh, vatos."

Michael looked from one of the leering bloodslobberlipped faces to the others, and he felt a very refreshing new resolve come over him. So these goon Strikers knew about the question too, did they? So they were amusing themselves making fun of him, were they? He knew these gibbering fools were no match for his highly developed martial skills, and he could easily defeat them and get away if given an opportunity.

Instead, he realized wanted to follow whatever destiny had brought him to that place, and to fulfill it. He began to feel very certain that meant he must go to the wall, and speak the name of the man who plays many a cruel game, and if he was right, and if he really did live on, and the Badlands of Chaos really did fall forever, then he might once again find his goddess love Magellan.

The caravan of trucks and jeeps rounded a bend, and there it was. A Striker snarled at Michael, saying, "On your feet, Spirit Man!" Two of them grabbed him and held him up as he first gazed upon the wall. His legs felt weak as the enormity of the wall struck him.

"We're still several miles away from it," said Capitan Felix with a wry grin. "Do you see those little rough places along the top, like cobwebs, sort of? Those are scaffolds, and there are thousands of slaves up there working right now."

The wall was an incredible spectacle, exactly as Mr. Champs had described it to him. The wall extended out into the ocean to the west, and disappeared onto the horizon. On the east it encountered a range of foothills, and was built over them to meet the highest crags of a range of snow covered peaks.

As they grew closer to the base of the wall, Michael had to look up, way up, to see the top, which disappeared into a thin layer of misty clouds. Everywhere he looked, he saw the tangled structures of scaffolding, ramps, pulleys, and cranes where masses of people worked near nude in the blazing red sunlight. Each worksite on the vast wall was like its own little community, with rows of tents and shacks made of refuse where the thousands of slaves slept, cooked their crude rations, and bred the next generation of laborers.

"It separates your world from ours," Felix told Michael. "Legend has it around here that the Spirit Man will come back one day and make the wall fall. Is that true, amigo?"

For a moment Michael stared into the eyes of Capitan Felix, and he was surprised to see a deep sadness, and something like fear there. "I am Spirit Man," he said. "That much is true."

"Do you know what his name is?" Felix asked Michael, and he turned his face away.

Michael gave a great sigh, and then he nodded his head "yes" but he didn't say anything. Felix did not turn around again, and did not see him nod, so Michael guessed he really did not want to know the name of the man who plays many a cruel game. So he just kept it to himself.

Rubbleton looked just like all the other workers camps they had passed, except that it was bigger, and apparently had some heavy industry. The village was nestled in what had once been a green valley among the hills that had been incorporated into the wall. Most of its area was covered with long rows of narrow barracks made of mud brick and construction rubble, with drainage ditches leading to sludge pools. A pall of greasy brown smoke rose up from huge dark buildings that looked like vast crude foundries.

"Where are you taking me?" Michael asked Felix.

"To the circle of death," the officer replied.

As they drove through the densely populated garbage dump that was Rubbleton, Michael noticed that he saw no children playing. What he saw was long lines of small children, naked or wearing only a rag diaper, bound in twos by carrying sticks. These were sticks crossed into a long X, with the legs on the shoulders of one child in front and one in back, and a bucket hung from the cross in the middle. The endless lines moved along like trails of ants, carrying buckets of water one way, and buckets of refuse the other.

"When do these kids spend time with their parents?" Michael asked.

The Strikers all began to snicker. "Parents? Who would have thought Spirit Man could be so stupid? Nobody has parents, you dope."

"It is much more practical than that," Felix told him. "When workers are off duty, they are assigned a sleep rack near their work site. For one hour every night they are encouraged to copulate. It is their reward for their hard work, and it keeps the sows pregnant all the time. The whelps are taken to nurseries, where they are raised and trained to work. Good little grubbers get water duty, like those you see."

"And the bad little grubbers?"

"Tunnel rats—hauling rocks and scum from the small, dark, and wet places that collapse on you." He smiled, sneering.

As they approached the base of the wall itself, the height of it seemed impossible. It was higher than some mountain ranges, and though not perfectly vertical, it was incredibly steep, and crisscrossed with narrow ledges and ramps leading ever upward. The truck lurched to a stop, and the white-faced Striker soldiers jumped from their benches, leaped to the ground, and began to line up side by side.

"All right, you yard-bird vatos," Michael heard a voice snarl out, "get the Spirit Man down out of the truck." Little short legs doing double steps to keep up with his ham-necked bulk, Baldy Chavez came marching up. Two of the Strikers leaped up into the truck bed again and threw Michael onto his face in the sand at the Colonel's feet. Then they jumped down after him, and snatched him back up onto his feet, then began to swat the dust from his clothes—the jeans and work shirt he wore at Castle Champs. They stuffed his shirt into his trousers and pulled his belt tight, and he stood there in a rough position of military attention. Felix gave him a thumb's up sign, and said, "Good luck, amigo."

Since they had come up a hill to the wall, Michael assumed they were at the bottom, but when they marched him a hundred yards along it, he was surprised to find himself on a ledge only a few yards wide, which dropped off several hundred feet into a narrow gulch cut along the edge of the wall. Michael was horrified to see the nature of the industry that took place there.

At the base of the drop-off there was an enormous pile of corpses, and another pile of skulls and bones. The gulch led to a building that looked like a cluster of teapots made of mud brick and stone, with a big pipe leading up to a cluster of buildings high on the wall above Rubbleton. Like the children in the street, Michael saw lines and gangs of workers, methodically processing the bodies of the dead, sluicing them into the rotting pools, where the gasses of their decomposition—which Michael could easily identify on the hot breeze—could be gathered and used for fuel.

"It's a retirement job for the weak and sick," Baldy told him. "Lots of the raw material that gas plant uses walks in there. Now, that is efficiency."

"Where does the pipe go?" Michael asked.

"East Rubbleton," said Baldy, pointing to the lodge like building high up on the hill. "That is Conchita's Palace, and the gas is used for the lights." He saw the look of dismay on Michael's face, and scoffed, "Hey, you don't want millions of people crossing over from the other side, do you? As long as Conchita rules, we stay ahead of the entropy on this wall. This is about responsibility, not power, don't you know that?"

The Colonel put his arm around Michael's shoulders and turned him around. "Have a look here, Spirit Man," he said. Michael saw he was facing an area on the wall that had been whitewashed heavily for about two hundred feet. Like the scarlet smears of the lips of the Strikers, there were large splotches of bloodstain down the entire length of the white.

"How many people have tried to guess the name of the man who plays many a cruel game?" Michael asked himself.

A roar and a skidding of tires caught his ear, and he turned around to see a black limousine come racing up the road to stop before him. Like the truck, it was mounted with tractor tires, so the body rode high off the ground. Two Strikers ran instantly to the black limousine, opened up the back door, and lifted out a set of stair steps. To the blaring of a retinue of assorted horns, a woman stepped from the car and coolly descended the stair step, gazing directly into Michael's eyes with the greatest of disdain.

"Magellan!" he gasped. There she stood, dressed in a black leather version of the satin gown Magellan had worn when he first met her, with her luscious living-liquid hair flowing upon her shoulders, and her dark bottomless eyes filled with.... but no, the eyes he beheld were not filled with love, but with sadistic contempt.

"Magellan, it's me. Tell them I am Spirit Man!" he cried.

"Don't call me that!" she snapped. She slapped him hard across the face, gave him a second to react, then slammed him backhanded across the other cheek. "Never." She began to laugh. "Of course you are Spirit Man, you simple hick," she said. "But so what? I am Conchita Champs, and that makes you nobody."

"I know the name of the man who plays the games," he said. "If I say the name, this whole place will go! I can make the wall fall down on all of it! Magellan, I can't do it until

I've saved you from whatever this is that has you."

"Shut up! Shut up, you miserable fool!" Conchita shouted as she slapped him again. "I am not Magellan, I am her infinitely superior twin sister Conchita, and I hate her, I hate her!"

"I love you, Magellan, whoever you are!" Michael cried out as he felt his whole world was crashing down on him.

"Teach this fool a lesson!" Conchita commanded. With a big grin, Baldy Chavez snapped his fingers at the two Strikers closest to Michael, and they leaped forward eagerly and knocked him to the ground and began to kick him in the belly and the back. Then Conchita brushed them aside and knelt to put her hand under his chin and hold his head up. "Do you know the name of the man who plays so many a cruel game to us who live in this dreamy place? Oh, Spirit of Man, can you tell us? We are waiting!"

"I can't," he groaned against his pain. "If I do, this whole world will come to an end, and I will lose you, Magellan."

"Aaaak! I am not Magellan, you stupid, stupid, stupid man!" she screamed as she kicked him again and again.

But still Michael did not answer her.

"So. You see, Baldy? What did I say? Spirit Man doesn't know! He is a fraud, a fake!" Conchita laughed as she walked around Michael as he lay in agony on the ground. "Prepare the firing squad! Lets get it over with! Spirit Man! Ha! Stupid, stupid, stupid man. Nobody knows the name! I will rule forever!"

As the firing squad was being prepared to execute Michael, Baldy dragged the hapless Spirit Man to the wall and leaned him against it. Seeing a moment, Capitan Felix sidled over to Conchita, bowing.

"Might I have a word with Your Majesty, Empress Conchita?" he begged. He huddled in very close to her, and whispered, "Suppose the Spirit Man really does know something."

"Like what?" Conchita asked.

"You know, the name of the man who plays many a

game. Shouldn't we clear out the place just in case the wall falls down on us?"

"Nobody knows the name, you puking idiot," she snarled. Then she looked at him with suspicion. "You let the Spirit Man talk you into this, didn't you? What did he tell you to ask for?"

"No, Empress, I was only concerned for your safety," Felix pleaded. With the toe of her sharp high-heeled shoe, Conchita kicked Felix in his groin, then she gave him a vicious chop on the back of his neck as he folded forward in pain. He flopped to the ground clutching his stomach and squealing.

"Put him up there too," she snapped at the other soldiers. Like children at a birthday party, they scooped up Felix and threw him against the wall beside Michael. With a saucy bounce in her walk, she sauntered up to stand before him. "So, Spirit Man, are you hungry now?" she asked.

Michael was so surprised to hear her ask him about food that he just stammered, "Now that you mention it, yes I am."

"Well, I am not Magellan, and whatever she fed you was your last meal," she sneered.

"And it was damn good," Michael said.

"That's what she does best, dearie. Now you are going to find out what I do best." She turned to her troops. "Colonel Chavez, when the circle of death arrives, you will execute the Spirit Man," she commanded.

"You got it, baby," Baldy replied.

"Give me his last cigarette," she said. Baldy took a pack of imported Turkish Dromedary Lights from his pocket and popped one out for her. A smiling Striker scurried forward with a huge flip-top lighter that issued an orange flame with a plume of greasy black smoke. Conchita took a great hissing drag, sucking up the plume and almost half of the cigarette. Then she leaned on the hood of the black limousine, and with a huge sigh let the smoke gush out from her mouth and nose in a swirling cloud that wrapped itself around her and then drifted away on the wind like a cruising shark.

"All we can do now is wait," said Baldy, relaxing in a military parade rest position facing the red-splattered white wall where Michael and Capitan Felix stood waiting to be executed. The six men of the firing squad stood at attention with their rifles at their sides, and sweat trickling from their white-painted faces.

One grossly fat Striker waddled up to Michael and stood shaking his head and clucking. "Didn't know anything after all, eh, Spirit Man? Well, you better try to guess the name anyway, before you get splattered all over that wall like the thousands before you."

"Yeah," said another with a silly giggle, "before you get tossed into Conchita's gas generator with all the other rotting stiffs."

For a time the sun seemed to stand still, and the heat grew more intense. Conchita kept looking impatiently up at the sky. Then everything seemed to pause for an instant, to hang in silence, and the sky began to darken. She looked at the terrified face of Capitan Felix, and his words kept nagging at her, "Suppose the Spirit Man knows something..."

A breath of wind came up, and then a swirl, and then a burst which picked up the dust and drove it against the wall. In seconds, a dark cloud began to pour over the top of the wall, and the first of dozens of blue white flashes of lightning cut down on top of them, accompanied by the loudest possible rumblings of thunder.

Baldy ran toward his firing squad shouting, "The circle of death has come! Take your firing position, but don't shoot until I tell you!"

Six wind-whipped Striker clowns in uniform raised their rifles and aimed them at the middle of Michael's chest. Then a cloud shaped like a perfect circle swiftly moved in front of the sun, blocking all of its light, casting a giant, round shadow on the earth below.

Baldy ran over to the Spirit Man as the storm rose to full force and the wind was whipping the Strikers' fatigues into tatters, and torrents of rain gushed down where

Michael was standing with his back against the wall. "The circle of death has come to take you away," Baldy shouted over the roar of water and thunder and wind. "This is the last chance you have. Tell me the name of the man who rules the world now, or have it your way and face death!"

Conchita stood screaming into the wind as she clutched the side of her limousine, "Shoot him! Shoot him now!"

"Magellan, I love you," Michael cried into the face of the terrible storm.

The earth began to shake and rumble as though the wall itself were shuddering before the fury of the storm brought by the terrible shadow of the circle of death. Michael lay his head back against the wall, and he began to recite *The Crack in the Wall*, as he had read it between the lines of Mr. Champs' book in Braille. "Every Good Dreamer notices the shape of the moon, dreams dreams, and sees visions, all day and all night." And his voice raised to a howl, and he felt the challenge rise in him as he continued, "All you got to do, my friend, is put up a good fight, open your eyes, and realize where the secret lies."

"Shoot him!" screamed Conchita, and Baldy repeated the order to the Strikers staggering in the wind. "Aim! Fire!"

The rifles barked, and as the bullets sped from their barrels, Michael shouted out, "Mister Good Dreamer wears many a brave disguise."

The earth shuddered, and a crack began to appear in the wall. A rain of huge blocks of rock suddenly began to slam the earth around them, crushing one after another of the scampering Strikers. A single monolith the size of a bus struck exactly on top of the black limousine, splattering mud in all directions and instantly squashing Conchita Champs to grotesque death.

Seventy miles of the wall came tumbling down in a single bone-shuddering lurch. Hailstones the size of coconuts created a deadly white downpour that splattered red brains from every Striker caught out in the open. The bald head of Colonel Baldonado Chavez was popped like a melon by the biggest hailstone of all. The earthquake and the storm swept Rubbleton off the wall like a cobweb, and blew every dwelling in the Badlands of Chaos into the great cracks that opened up in the ground.

Miles away, the sea rose up in a great wave, and crashed against the white towers of Castle Champs, sending them tumbling to the beach, where the thrashing water broke them up and scattered them for half a mile. Clutching his latest book of poems in Braille, the great Alexander Champs was swept out to sea.

The terrible earthquake in the Badlands of Chaos rippled across the land to faraway Fort Hauchuca and the land of Emmitt del Rio and the other drunken dwarves. "It is the end of the universe. Flee in terror!" squealed Emmitt as the earthquake ripped down the center of their fort, swallowing them all and flattening every sign they had ever existed.

Flatlands and great plains became bottomless pits and ragged gullies, and the tallest mountains were reduced to heaps of rubble and dust as the wall rained down an endless deluge of stone.

In the last instant before the bullets began to slam into his ribs and his brain and to splatter him all over the white wall like a bloody lipstick wound, he saw the face of Joey.

## Chapter Fourteen

A great silence fell upon the Badlands of Chaos, and as mysteriously as it had come, the circle of death slid away from the sun and slipped down the inverted bowl of the sky to disappear behind the horizon. With his eyes squeezed tight shut, Michael leaned against the wall. When it was apparent nothing more was going to happen, he opened them and took a look around.

There was only one place in the whole wall that had not fallen down, and that was the piece about ten feet tall where he stood. The rest looked like a range of utterly barren mountains—only half a mile high—that were made of piles of rubble. Near him were only the battered and dust covered remains of the Strikers, and the huge block that had crushed Conchita and her limo. At his feet lay the crumpled body of Capitan Felix, riddled by bullet holes. He saw that he was standing up to his knees in the crumpled body of Michael Seymour, who lay beside Felix.

"I will never get used to being killed all the time like this," he muttered to himself, and he stepped away from the wall. His body lay folded with his chin outstretched and his butt up against the wall. Michael shook his head to see the goggle-eyed stupid surprised look on his face, the tongue half-bitten off by the fall, and the hole in his forehead opening up the skull like a bowl of fruit salad. Several large and gory exit wounds had blasted big bloody ragged tears in the back of the shirt. "What a waste of a good shirt," he thought, and then noticed he was still wearing it, minus the bullet holes.

The new Spirit Man stood looking at Michael's splattered body, and it struck him as strange that he was still there in the same situation. So was he a ghost, wearing a ghost shirt? He walked over to one of the other bodies and kicked it, and it thunked and moved and stirred up dust quite naturally. When he made a tentative and queasy pass at kicking his own body, however, his foot passed right through it.

He thought about just beginning to walk, as he had so many times before, and letting whatever fate was driving his dreams take him to wherever it would. Then he thought perhaps the better thing would be to wait for something to come to him. He watched for a while as the fluids sank away from the dead Strikers' bodies, and as the green patches on the foothills began to spread up into the rubble, and new green foliage sucked the juices of the lost Strikers' lives from the rubble and created new life.

Then he stood awed as a new wave of Strikers swept through the valley, and began to rebuild at an astonishing rate. He stood slack-jawed as they created a gigantic bridge that arched all the way across the sky over the winding river which flowed from the Rubble Mountains. A half dozen huge ziggurats rose up to form an impressive skyline towering high in the sky.

Two hundred Strikers were standing in line to cross over the bridge, and Michael noticed that nobody was coming back. "What is the name of this place?" Michael asked a passerby. He received no reply, but in a short time, he overheard someone say they were thrilled to have arrived at New Chaos.

Up on a high place, a projection screen displayed Dean Martin and Jerry Lewis doing a straw-hat routine singing, "New Chaos, you're the best and worst of everything! You make us wanna sing! New Chaos, you slay us!"

Michael stepped into the back of the line of Strikers that were going to cross over to the city, and shuffled along with the others toward a toll booth. He could see each person give the booth guard a coin, and he wondered if the guard would see him. He reached into the pocket of his jeans automatically, and found a token stamped New Chaos Metro. He smiled, thinking if the guard would take the token, he could ask her—well, what would he ask her?

If he asked, "Where am I?" she would tell him he was in New Chaos. When he asked her, "What am I doing here?" she would say, "You tell me, Spirit Man."

He had decided the best thing to do would be to hand her the token and go on by, when he saw a teenaged Striker a few yards ahead of him draw a huge pistol from his belt and shoot the booth guard right between the tits. "The gun repeals all laws! The bridge is free!" he cried, and the crowd of Strikers began to cheer and to rush across the bridge. When the others saw what was happening, they broke out of line and tried to run to the front, and they began to scream and shout as they pushed each other into a raging mass. The ones closest to the gate were knocked down and crushed as those behind them climbed up over them and trampled them down in their mad rush to save a Metro token.

Michael rushed over to the stricken booth guard and lifted up her head. Her helmet and sunglasses fell off, and her long dark hair spilled down onto the ground. "Magellan!" Michael cried out.

"Welcome to New Chaos, Spirit Man," she said, and died.

A line of white-uniformed Strikers opened fire with machine guns on the crowd. A Striker in a fireman suit struggled to pull a ten-inch butcher knife out of his belly. A naked man carrying a pig with a Striker face ran by screaming, "Not me! Not me!" The pig ripped its long curved tusks into his belly, spilling hot-links and little things wrapped in paper.

The white coat soldiers marched up the bridge, shooting rockets and tear gas at the savage Striker mob crushing itself to death on the bridge.

"Clear the area. Come on, move it out now," barked a soldier through his megaphone. "Show's all over folks, go on home now."

Tear gas exploded on the bridge, and a cloud of acrid smoke swirled and gushed out to pounce on the masses, to render them retching wretches, kicking and clawing at each other trying to find a breath of air. Like muttering locust, a flight of helicopters swirled around the mob, and sent a hail of tracer fire into them from their snarling machineguns. Whistling bombs came down one after another, exploding with the crash of cymbals, flinging bodies up into the air like rag doll clown acrobats. Michael was surprised to see that the pilots of the helicopters were Emmitt del Rio and his troop of Cavalry dwarves, waving their black hats and singing The Ballad of Garry Owen.

In a few seconds, the crowd dispersed like a pile of cockroaches when the light comes on, and Michael could only hear the whimpering of the wounded, and the yowling of sirens coming. He began to walk across the deserted bridge, pausing only long enough to kick once at the boot of a dead man, with a satisfying thunk.

He turned up Baldwin Street, as he had done so many times, and there like an old friend was the little white house with the green trim. The only thing that seemed to have changed was the door was painted black, and on it were stenciled the words MISTER GOOD DREAMER.

He put his hand on the doorknob and gently turned it to the right. It clicked once, and then swung open to reveal a completely dark house. Feeling he had no choice but to do so, Michael stepped into the dark, and let the door close behind him.

## Chapter Fifteen

He stood for a moment waiting for something to happen, and when nothing did, he started to take a step. At that instant, the lights came on, and a group of people began to sing out, "Surprise! Surprise! Happy birthday to you! Happy birthday to you! Happy birthday, dear Spirit Man, happy birthday to you!"

He was standing in Cindy's Cafe in Benson. The place was trashed. The windows were all shot out, and bullet holes marred the walls and counters. There was broken glass everywhere, and every surface and object was splattered with blood. The people who stood singing and applauding him were all mangled by bullet holes and the slashes of flying glass, wearing torn clothing soaked in blood, with bits of tattered flesh hanging from their ragged wounds.

Some of them were wearing pointed party hats, and Allansworth and Kailey produced a tambourine and ukulele to accompany the happy song. There were the two old tourists, grinning like proud grandparents, and the high school kids who had cut class to make out in a van before stopping at Cindy's for a burger and shake. The kid was chomping on his burger as he cheered Michael, oblivious to the fact that half his stomach had been blown away by a shotgun blast. Right in front stood Betty Lou, foxy tight-assed Betty Lou, looking as good as ever, except for the fist-sized hole in her forehead, which she covered with a wave at her bangs. "Hiya, ramb'lin man," she said. "Where's that Lohman guy? Does he still want his double dicker? I'm keeping it hot and juicy, and he can have it any time he wants."

Though the scene was jarring to him at first, Michael could see everyone else seemed to be having a good time, so he tried to relax and get into the spirit of the event. Then to his surprise, the man sitting at the table closest to him began to speak as though he were a narrator telling the story. "Though the scene was jarring to him at first," the man said, "Michael could see everyone else seemed to be having a good time, so he tried to relax and get into the spirit of the event."

Everyone agreed, nodding and humming, and they stood smiling and looking expectantly at Michael, waiting for his reaction. "Are...are we all dead?" Michael asked.

"Nope," said the old tourist with his arm blown off. "I'm not dead. I'm not the late Grandpa George, I'm the early bird."

"We all know about your dirty old bird, Georgie," said the grinning old crone at his side.

"So how come John Lohman's not here?" Michael asked, looking around.

"Maybe he wasn't killed," said Allansworth.

"Sure he was killed," said Kailey.

"Maybe he caught a bus," said Allansworth.

"Maybe caught a bullet," said Kailey.

"He could have had me," said Betty Lou.

"He could have had lunch," said Grandpa George, as he took a chair and moved it to sit close to Michael. "Come on, sit down, Spirit Man, and tell us about yourself. How come your dreams are so violent and angry?"

Like bad actors in a community play, the others in the room made a great show of crossing their arms, putting their fists on their hips, their feet up on chairs, leaning on their elbows, and listening with great attentiveness.

Michael slouched into the chair, and looked from one of them to the other. He frowned, tried to reach deep within himself for a sincere answer, and said, "Well, maybe it's because I am in a hospital somewhere, dying of an incurable disease."

"Aren't we all?" clucked the scrawny and grizzled old George. "You should read the obituaries. Every day you will find someone who has died before you. Of course, for someone who has died as many times as you have..."

"Oh, yeah, but I mean for real," said Michael.

"What? Getting shot to pieces wasn't real enough for you?" old George asked. "Or do you expect the real death to take you somewhere else?" The dead chuckled wryly.

"Are you trying to tell me there isn't a real world?" Michael asked.

Betty Lou brought Michael a frosty milk shake and a hot sizzling juicy burger. "Is that real enough for you?" she asked, with a saucy jiggle of her pretty bloodstained titties.

"If what happened to you here wasn't a real death, then where are you now?" Grandpa George asked. Michael looked around the room uneasily, and felt the sweat grow cool on his forehead as the desert wind blew in through the shattered windows of the Cafe.

"You know there is no Cindy's Cafe in Benson, don't you?" Betty Lou taunted him.

"I had lunch here with John Lohman," Michael affirmed. "A real lunch, on a real trip."

"From the Spiritman Mansion to go fishing in Mexico?" Kailey asked. "There is no Mansion. Your family lost all their money trying to pay the doctors to save you from your fate. You live in an old house on Baldwin street."

"Oh yeah? What about John Lohman? I didn't dream him up, did I?"

"That wasn't John Lohman, Michael, it was Don Johnson doing a cameo," said Grandpa George. He pointed to one of the men standing in the group at the back of the room, wearing the same jeans and denim jacket Lohman had worn. "That guy is Nick Panszczyk. He did the body double and took the fall."

"And got killed?" Michael asked.

"Damn right," said Kailey. Then he chuckled and said, "Go on, eat your burger while it's hot. Those bloodstains on the bun won't hurt you a bit."

"How could a little of that sweet Betty Lou's blood upset me?" Michael grumbled, and took a bite of the sandwich. After a couple of bites, he said, "It doesn't matter what you say. Like I said, I came in here with Lohman for lunch, and some pissed-off dickhead ex-employee came in with a bunch of guns and blew everybody away."

"OK, so how do you feel about that?" Allensworth asked, as he picked up Michael's milk shake and slurped the froth off the top.

"How do I feel? How the hell do you think I feel? The son of a bitch came in here and blew us all away!"

"Damn right. You bet," the dead agreed, nodding and displaying their wounds as Kailey and Allensworth rattled a chord on their instruments.

There was a crashing as someone kicked open the kitchen door and leaped into the room. "Who you calling dickhead, you pinche pendejo?" he yelled as he began to spray the room with the urban-guerrilla 9mm assault weapon he was carrying. The party members all began to scream and scatter, as the bullets ripped into the ceiling, the walls, and splattered new wounds from their flesh. Then he slipped on an order of biscuits and gravy and fell on his ass with both heels over his head. The gun spun from his fingers to land exactly at Michael's feet.

Michael snatched it up, fired it once at the ceiling, then pointed it right between the eyes of the mad mass murderer.

"Do it, do it," the dead all cheered.

Michael stared down the barrel of the gun at the crouching man before him. He frowned. "Don't I know you?" he asked.

"Michael, meet Joey Pachuco," said Grandpa George. Michael glanced up to see that he had not moved an inch during the shooting. "Are you going to shoot him?" old George asked.

"Well, I guess....only if he moves."

"Only if he moves. Well, good for you, Spirit Man.

For an instant there was a pause, as though all of the living and the dead in the room were about to applaud and cheer. Then Joey Pachuco let out a scream of feral rage, and launched himself at Michael, howling, "I'll get you yet!"

"No!" cried Michael, trying to back off from the savage attack. Then the gun bucked in his hands, and he saw the bullets strike Joey again and again.

"See you at the hospital, Spirit Man," said Grandpa George, and for an instant Michael could see he had the face of John Lohman, and then he struck Michael on the jaw with a perfect John-Wayne right cross. The lights went out for Michael Seymour.

## Chapter Sixteen

Michael Seymour, reknown as the world famous Spirit Man, lay alone in his bed. His eyes popped wide open and he leaped from his bed as though shocked. He stood looking in all directions, to his far left and to his far right. He looked at the empty bed next to him, glanced at the clock on the wall, then sighed and relaxed. It was nearly midnight, Halloween eve – time for the Spirit Man to leave this world and especially this dismal place. The doctors had tried to treat Michael and find a cure for his so-called illness but Michael knew the only thing that would help right then was for him to leave. His soul was ready to go "wandering off to another place and time" (as he explained it to his doctor). "I'll be free, Doc," Michael had told him in a happy voice.

Michael took off his white hospital robe and stood naked in the middle of his room in the glaring bright light. He walked over to his bathroom, looked at his reflection, and grinned. He swept back his hair with his fingers and nodded. He took out his long-sleeved white shirt and black Guess jeans, and quickly got dressed, starting with under shorts pulled from a pocket of the jeans. He looked at himself in the mirror and smiled again.

Michael took a black hefty bag from a concealed place beneath the sink, and from it removed a brown uniform he recognized as belonging to the janitors who worked at the hospital. He put the big comfortable brown jumpsuit uniform over his street clothes. There was a nametag on the left front pocket that read "Johnny Lohman." With a "Hmmph," and a tug, Michael tore off the name tag and stuffed it into the black hefty bag. Then he reached into his pants pocket, and pasted a new tag over his shirt pocket, which read, "SPIRIT MAN."

Michael hoped that by dressing as a janitor he would fit in with the rest of the hospital staff and not be detected. "Nobody who thinks himself important ever pays attention to people who push a mop for a living," his friend Lohman had told him. Of all the people Michael had met in his long stay in the hospital, it had been the old janitor who had been his best friend.  The doctors had been very professional, but it had been Lohman who had been there for him always as he struggled to confront the horror of his terrible disease.

Michael picked up the blue plastic wastebasket and dumped its contents into the black bag to give it some volume – then just dropped the whole wastebasket into it. He turned off the lights with a swipe of his hand and walked out into the hallway, holding the black hefty bag in his hands, and whistling softly.  The "janitor" dumped the black hefty bag into a cleaning cart in front of room 345, and kept on walking down the hallway.  As he passed the staff lounge, he encountered a rowdy group who had just come from the hospital's Halloween party, all dressed up in costumes. He kept to himself gliding along the wall, and with a smile of friendly greeting to the revelers, passed undetected just as he had predicted. The group seemed to be nurses and doctors dressed as clowns, witches, and vampires, with faces painted white, and great smears of bright red lipstick. They were so grotesque, fat bodies stuffed into their uniforms, scrawny bodies sticking out of collars and sleeves, that he could not be sure they were not witches and vampires dressed in the costumes of doctors and nurses.

At a door marked STAIRS, he stopped and looked all around him to make sure nobody could see him, then ducked inside.  He walked down several flights of stairs, down a short hallway, and then left the hospital through a side door.

Michael stepped out onto the small cement stoop beside the unmarked staff entrance, and was surprised to see someone else there, leaning against the wall holding a cigarette.  He was startled at first, then pleased to see it was John Lohman, wearing janitor's overalls like himself. The parking lot was still, as no other people appeared to be around, so Michael stood beside him and leaned against the wall also.  He didn't say anything right away, but took several long slow deep breaths of the cool night air.  The full moon was almost straight overhead, creating a strange, flat, shadowless light. He looked up at it, and the dark image of the Man in the Moon gazed down on him with blank staring eyes. He took another deep grateful breath of open air, noting that even the powerful air conditioning system of the hospital left the place feeling close, stuffy, and fetid.

"Didn't know you smoked, John," he said.

"I don't," the janitor replied, "but if I came out here and stood for ten minutes without holding a butt, they'd say I was loafing."

"Yep, I reckon you're right," Michael agreed. "Guess I'd better be moseying along."

"Guess you had. Good luck, Spirit Man."

"Thanks, John. You should have been a minister."

"Nah. It would get in the way of my ministry." Lohman grinned, tapped the ash from his unsmoked butt, and waved.

Michael walked across the parking lot, pausing only once beside a white Mercedes Benz in its designated parking spot. He turned to look up at the hospital, noting that the back wall of the building was entirely without windows.

Michael crossed Telshor Boulevard without seeing a single car on the street. He went up University Avenue a block or two, then made a turn onto a dirt road which led into the desert. He walked quickly and steadily, noticing that as he proceeded, his dark shadow began to move out from beneath him to extend farther and farther in front of him. Soon, the desert road became a narrow path which went straight up a steep hill known as Mount Solitaire. As the Spirit Man reached the top of the steep hill, he turned around to look back at the hospital in the distance far behind.

"The farther from that place the better," he said to himself. "The farther from the real world with its petty problems and pathetic lives the better. I'm pretty damn tired of doctors trying to find a cure for what isn't wrong with me." He knew exactly what was wrong with him. It was time for the Spirit Man to leave this world and go onto another one full of adventure and new challenges for him to face and overcome. "If I ever come back here, it will have to be for a terribly good reason," he said aloud.

There on the top of Mount Solitaire, he began to feel free again. The real world with its real problems seemed far away. He sighed, turned his back on the distant town, and began to follow a path that led around the top of the mountain toward a dark forest of tall pines. He smiled and danced a couple of steps in anticipation, as he knew there were no forests between Mount Solitaire and the high crags of the Organ Mountains east of Las Cruces.

When he reached the dense forest of gigantic pine trees, they were swaying in a cold harsh wind. The wind rushed through the tall pines and moaned and whined in his ears as he walked along the narrow path through the enchanted forest. The tops of the trees soared so high above him that a billion dew-dropped pine needles glistened and sparkled as the full moon settled behind them in the sky.

Around another bend he came to a small clearing, where stood a huge yellowish rock, an ochre monolith over two hundred feet tall, rising up through the towering pines. In red blood dripping down the jagged surface of the huge yellow rock appeared the words STRIKE THIS. Michael stood by the edge of the clearing in the woods and stared at these words in blood for a long, long time.

Then something else caught his attention. The sound of drunkenness and music fading in and out were mingled with the blowing winds in the far distance, a warbling, swirling of sounds, like fragments snatched from songs or the cheering of crowds, tumbled together like leaves in the wind. Michael strained to make out the sounds, and then with a little gasp like the whole world had just sucked in its breath, the forest fell absolutely silent.

Michael's whole body tensed to fight or run as a man of massive size and strength stepped out of the dark shadows. The stranger wore a long royal blue robe that seemed to float just off the ground behind him as he slowly strode around the yellow rock. He wore a white mask over his eyes, with red lipstick heavily smeared upon his thin lips.

From the sides of his white mask flashed lightning bolts a few inches long, sparkling and crackling. His hair was long and even in the moonlight it shone like gold in the New Mexico sun as it cascaded upon his broad muscular shoulders. Through the eye holes in the mask, his eyes blazed like fireballs and flashed with ominous promise like the leering come-on of the shills of Las Vegas.

Michael did not move an inch or blink an eye. With a deep and smooth voice, he said, "Don't be afraid, Spirit Man. Your adventure is about to begin!"

"All right. Who are you?" Michael asked.

"I am Lord Striker! I come from the Dream World called Shook," he said. He paused a moment as though sizing up Michael, then told him, "Before you cross over to the Other Side, I must strike you!"

"And what...?" Michael began to ask. With no further warning, Lord Striker leaped through the air and pounced, throwing him down to the ground. The wind came rushing up again as though from all sides at once, and a cloud of smoke and dust and mist swirled up into the sky around them as Lord Striker pinned Michael down on his back. Lord Striker drove his knees into Michael's chest, and spread apart his helpless arms. Michael tried to free himself but the blue warrior was too strong and heavy for him. Then Striker opened his mouth and growled like a mountain lion, exposing a mouthful of six-inch long, razor-sharp white fangs. Sabre teeth flashing in the bright moonlight, Striker swung his monstrous head from side to side, roaring, "I must strike you! Strike you! Strike you dead!"

Lord Striker's hands transformed into the massive paws of a Grizzly bear, covered with dark golden tangled hair, and bearing seven-inch claws. With one mighty blow, he struck Michael across his face, tearing a gobbet-sized piece of flesh from his cheek. Blood gushed down the side of Michael's pretty face and ran into his mouth. He choked on his own blood, and when he tried to spit it out of his mouth, the hole in his cheek kept him from spitting. Then the golden-haired bear monster tore the borrowed janitor garb into shreds and bits and pieces, exposing Michael's naked chest. With a savage thrust, Striker stuck his bear-claw fingers into the middle of Michael's chest and tore his rib cage apart like a Cajun opening a crab. He reached deep into the chest cavity, wrapped both hands around the bloody pounding heart, and ripped it out.

Throwing back his blue cape, Striker rose and held the heart in his huge bear-like hands with those sharp and deadly claws. He lifted the heart up to his face so he could see it better in the moonlight. He rotated it around and around in his bloody hands, being very careful not to drop it on the ground, smiling approval as it pumped up and down in his hands.

Like a chameleon with a rattlesnake tongue, Striker licked Michael's heart. The forked tongue, pink in color and prehensile as a tentacle, shot out of his mouth to hold and caress the heart for just an instant before it recoiled back between the huge lips smeared red with lipstick and blood.

Striker raised Michael's beating heart up to the full moon, and for a brief moment the moon became red, dripping down from the sky above, dripping down to settle behind the trees, flowing down behind the horizon.

To the east the sky began to lighten. Michael's blood dripped upon Lord Striker's white masked face as he howled into the last dark hour of the cold windy night, "Where are you now, Spirit Man? Where are you? Aren't you going to come to save your friend Michael? I have his heart. It is mine, mine, do you hear me? So come and get me, Spirit Man! Come and get me if you can!"

# SPIRIT MAN

## Chapter Seventeen

Dressed in his long flowing royal blue robe, the dark shadowy figure of Lord Striker stood all alone on top of Mount Solitaire in the last glow of moonlight, the first glow of dawn, still holding Michael's heart in his bloody hands. Michael's blood ran between Striker's long fingers and onto the ground by his feet, not yet red with the daylight, but still black with the night, pooling in tiny hollows, splattering the black-polished boots of the golden-haired giant from Shook.

Striker tossed back his head and howled at the setting full moon, and the moonlight reflected upon his blood-streaked white-masked face as he cried out again, "Come on, Spirit Man! I just cut your heart out! Don't you want it back? Come and get it, Spirit Man, world-renowned corpse on a nowhere mountaintop." A cold wind blew over the land as Lord Striker howled and screamed, "You belong to me now!"

Lord Striker looked down at Michael lying on the ground still and lifeless. He took a long, slow breath, and then with a rumbling that began deep in his gut and rose to a gurgling thunder in his throat, he hawked up and then spat a huge gelatinous glob directly into the gaping shattered cavity in Michael's chest. "That's for your heart, boy."

Striding back and forth with steps so long and smooth he seemed to be gliding, Striker faced the setting moon. He stood like a giant on the mountaintop, shaking his long hair from side to side as he looked north and south. "Where are you now, Spirit Man?" he crowed. "Where is the champion who will rescue the heart of this worthless bag of guts?"

As though the trees and the stones themselves could hear him, he taunted, "I expected the mighty Spirit Man would come to destroy me utterly for taking this heart. But no, he is not here. Well, well, well. Then this is what he will have to do. He will have to track me down, hunt me like an animal in the wild, chase me to the ends of the world if he would like to claim his friend's heart back."

Lord Striker turned to face the huge yellow rock with the words "STRIKE THIS" dripping in streams of red blood down its jagged face. Holding Michael's grisly heart between his palms, he pressed his hands together like a monk at prayer. Then with a hiss of breath between his teeth, he thrust his hands forward and speared both of them directly into the stone. With a thunderous crack, the stone split, and pieces flew out to the sides. Like a spring-steel whip, Striker's grasping hands plunged into the stone, grasped something, and snatched it back close to his chest. Once again the stone rang like thunder as the pieces snapped back into place.

Lord Striker held a crystal decanter, a beautiful glass jar about a foot in height, intricately engraved. On each side was a sweeping curved silver handle, a single piece of gleaming metal which also firmly held on the crystal stopper in the top of the jar. Inside the vessel was Michael's heart.

Striker laughed with childish amusement as he shook the decanter and the heart made a sloppy thumping sound. "Now Spirit Man," he said, "wherever you are, whoever you are, whatever you think you are, come looking for me." He shook the decanter again. "And when you find me, I will kill you again," he said to the heart. Then just in the last seconds before the sun rose up over the horizon, he swirled his cape around himself, stepped into the last bit of moon shadow behind the yellow rock, and disappeared.

For a long moment, the tree-crested top of Mount Solitaire was silent. The baleful dawn was an instant from breaking. Then as though the sky itself refused to become light, a haze began to gather about the clearing and the great yellow stone. The haze began to swirl slowly, and to thicken and spread, and to rise up as a gray cloud bank which grew to cover the eastern horizon. The sky grew darker instead of lighter, as the swirl became a wind, and the clouds began to surge and churn. The trees began to sigh and sway, and then to shriek and roar, as tiny branches were ripped from them to swirl and fly in a frenetic dance around the stone.

# SPIRIT MAN

Michael lay like the gutted sacrifice of an oracle, blood draining into dark glistening globs of grisly mud. The swirling winds rose up from him, and the clouds above arched high over the mountaintop, great nimbus masses joined at their crowns to form a huge cathedral, with walls as dark as raging smoke. The body began to shudder, as though every muscle fiber in the flaccid flesh had begun to twitch, as the earth beneath it shook in seismic awe of the gathering storm. The rumble of the earthquake rose like tympani, then was split by a shuddering crack that began in the top of the great dome of clouds, crackled and echoed from its swirling sides, sharp-edged, chattering, ragged and violent. So loud it seemed the mountain itself had cracked wide open, the first thundering bolt drove itself down upon the land. Brighter by a thousand times than the storm-shuttered sun, the bolt flashed, danced, and flashed again. With a sound that could only be made by a crowd of applauding archangels, it was joined by a dozen, a score, and then a hundred more, each striking the top of Solitaire, and dancing before the great yellow altar stone.

The ground around Michael's body began to smoke, and the smoke rose and swirled around the body to form a cord, and then a column. In the column a form began to grow, a human form, as though cocooned. A face came forth, and then hands crossed over the chest. As the legs appeared, the arms of the spectral form swept open the column of smoke like a robe and the apparition stepped forward to stand on the mountaintop beside the shattered corpse.

The thunder fell off to a distant rumble, the final sigh of a giant retiring. In the hush of that instant, a gentle pattering of rain began to fall. It swept to a peaceful shower, darkening the scorched earth of the mountaintop, flushing away the last wisps of smoke, and washing the bloody words from the great ochre monolith. It washed the blood from the face of the desecrated body, and it washed the smoke-like cocoon from the face of the one who had stepped forth. The face was Michael's. As the water flowed down his chest and arms, soaking the white shirt he wore and the black jeans, the walls of clouds broke open, and the warm glow of the morning burst through, filling the great celestial hall with light. He faced the dawn, and its rays drove the water from his clothes in a swirl of steam. He took a long slow breath, sighed with a great smile, and the Spirit Man opened his eyes.

He looked down at Michael lying on the blood- stained earth, then knelt and gazed at the body drying in the morning sun. He reached down and gently touched the gaping wound from which Michael's heart had been so savagely ripped. "That really sucks," he said. The Spirit Man closed his eyes a moment, raised up his hand and took a white stone out of his mouth. He held it up to the sun, and it glowed as though it held a shining bead of pure moonlight deep within its milky crystal. Then the Spirit Man placed the smooth white stone deep inside Michael's empty chest cavity where his heart had once beat so freely and mightily. Then waved his hands over Michael and he chanted a prayer in his native tongue, called English.

"This is my vow, my good friend and soul mate Michael, that I will not rest nor return to this world until I find the perpetrator of this sacrilege, and revenge myself upon him. I bullshit you not, fact, truth, and deed."

His head came up and his eyes snapped open, as though he had heard the step of an approaching attacker. Quickly he looked from side to side, tensing himself as though to fight or flee. He gasped as he looked at the great yellow rock. Though the rain had washed off almost all of the bloody message Michael had seen, a few letters were still visible after the sun had baked the great stone dry. "Lord Striker," said the Spirit Man, with both contempt and awe in his voice. "I might have known," he said, standing, "and I know what I have to do. I must search to the ends of the earth, hunt the infamous and notorious Lord Striker down like an animal, and face him in a battle of spirit and will."

He closed his eyes, and then when he opened them again, the body had disappeared, and Michael stood alone before the stone. He clucked his tongue and looked around carefully. "I think I know what to expect here," he said, and he stepped around to the back of the great stone. He was hardly surprised to find a magical door on the other side of the huge yellow rock. The magical door was blue as the New Mexico sky, and it had a blazing yellow sun in its upper left corner. Though he might have expected it to be in the stone itself, it stood about ten yards away from where he was standing with his back to the stone. As he walked over to the blue door and stood in front of it, he saw that it was not really a door at all, but instead a patch of crystal clear blue sky with a fiery sun in it and a thin layer of white clouds swirling around and around the sun. The blue door was a rectangle about ten feet high and about five feet in width. It did not touch the ground at all, but seemed suspended in mid air several feet above the dark earth. Above the blue door was a sign lit up in neon pink. Flashing manically on and off, it read, "IN SHOOK, IT'S THE DEAD ONES YOU DON'T HAVE TO WORRY ABOUT. NO SIREE, IT'S THE LIVE ONES THAT GIVE YOU ALL THE SHIT!"

The Spirit Man watched the clouds within the blue door slowly drift across the deep blue sky, and then drift behind the yellow sun. He reached up his hand and discovered that the glowing sun was really a golden door knob. He grasped it, turned it, and the door opened before him.

It was as though he had opened a clear glass door. He could still see the same blue sky, and appeared to be looking down from a great height through an opening high in the sky. The clouds before him swirled open, and he saw before him a beautiful young woman, almost naked, dancing on the sunbeams. She had long golden hair and her eyes were blue as the sky, and she wore several heavy gold necklaces around her long slender neck, and clusters of silver bracelets on her strong and graceful arms. She danced like an angel swaying in the wind with grace and beauty, and then with a smile she beckoned Michael to come to her. "Come, pretty boy, come to me," she said. "I am Shaker, Goddess of Shook. I'm a dancer, entrancer, I'm a sweet romancer, and I'm here to show you the way. Come to me now."

She put her hand out toward Michael. Dazzled by her beauty so close up, he put his own hand out to touch hers. Just the instant when he leaned out to take her hand, she jerked it back with her thumb over her shoulder. He tried to grab the side of the door, but there was nothing to grab, and he fell through into empty space. With a scream, he struggled an instant, then spread his arms to stabilize his fall as the wind began to whip past him. He was falling toward a deck of clouds far below. Then from behind he heard the deep voice of Lord Striker rumble in derisive laughter, "Shaker, your ass, Chumpo."

Michael fell into the clouds and when the white mists surrounded him, he lost his sense of which way he was falling. The winds in the cloud seemed to tumble him and come from all directions. Every second he expected to break out and see the ground below, but the clouds just got darker and darker. Then just when he thought the sky would black out completely, he broke out above a broad green sea sparkling in the sun. With a cry of surprise, he looked around to see there was not a cloud in the sky. He could not tell if the sea below was a few hundred feet beneath him, or thousands. The sound of the wind rushing past him began to rise in pitch, as though he were falling faster and faster. It rose to a whistle, and then a scream. He pulled his hands in to cover his ears, but that made him tumble, and he stuck them back out into the stream, screaming against the pain of the shrieking wind.

Then below him something caught his attention. At first it looked like a bit of flotsam floating in the jade-green sea, and then like a great jagged rock sticking up out of the water. Then he could tell it was really a rocky island far below. As he fell toward it faster and faster his path began to swing toward it until he was flying not downward, but forward, flat above the surface of the sea, rushing toward the island at what seemed hundreds of miles per hour. Instead of hurtling toward the sea, he was flying straight toward the rocky cliffs.

He struggled to scream into the rushing wind, but couldn't make a sound against its pressure. He tried to turn to the right or to the left, but could not make any change in his path. He felt a rush of cold, and was astonished to see he was not flying, but riding the front of a huge wave, a rolling ridge of living jade a hundred feet high. Sticking out of the gleaming wall of water were the dorsal fins of a dozen dolphins which were cavorting and slaloming along beside him as he rushed directly toward the high black cliff. As the rock filled his view, and the crashing of the wave upon it filled his nostrils with the smell of salt, he struggled to hold back his scream. Then he braced himself as the wave drove him at full speed directly against the gleaming obsidian cliff.

He felt he was still falling, but there was no rush of wind past him. It was completely dark, and completely silent. He tried to yell, but the sound did not seem to go anywhere at all, and did not echo or fade. He could hear himself, but the sound seemed to be just sucked up by the darkness.

Then he sensed something that made him gasp with new fear much greater than that of falling. In the total darkness, Michael smelled something rotting, the overpowering sweet stench of Death itself. He was reminded of the time when he was a little boy and found a dead deer in the desert, and he imagined he could see again the rotting body lying before the great yellow stone. The stench grew greater and greater; he felt gusts of warm moist air blowing past him, and he tried to keep from peeing his pants as he envisioned the monster mouth that exhaled such breath. As if to confirm his fears, before him appeared two huge glowing white eyes. In the light from the eyes he saw huge jaws, scales flecked with gobbets of rotting flesh, a long sinuous neck ringed with bony plates. Recoiling, Michael turned and fell away past the monster into the darkness.

"It's just me, Smeller, the Sultan of Shook," the great reptile said in a whining voice. "I thought you wanted some help."

And again Michael heard the rumbling voice and derisive laughter of Lord Striker. "I guess he just doesn't like dragons, Smeller."

And the whining voice called out after him, saying, "No way out of this nightmare, Spirit Man, no way out at all!"

Not knowing if he had passed an obstacle or failed a test, Michael floated into the darkness. Before he could give another thought to his situation, his eye was caught by a tiny speck of light which seemed to be far away. Moving so fast he did not even have time to react, the speck grew to a spot, a circle, and then a flashing disc as it rushed toward him. He threw up his arms to shield himself, but the disc flashed right past him, leaving him hanging in space in light so bright he couldn't see a thing at first. He dropped down and forward for what felt like about ten feet, and landed on solid ground. He struck, twisted, tumbled backward in a clumsy somersault, and came to rest lying on his face.

He lay there for a few moments waiting to see if something else was going to happen, then he lifted up his head. Though he was in some pain from the landing, he checked himself over, and was glad to see that nothing appeared to be broken or missing. He used his elbows to brace himself as he slowly got to a sitting position and dusted himself off. For a moment he sat with his head bowed, catching his breath. Then he looked up, and gave a cry of dismay.

Before him rose the great yellow stone, looking almost exactly like it had the last time he saw it. Across its rugged face were splashed new words, in thickening blood: "SHOOK: TO HELL AND BACK AGAIN."

"Damn it, I'm back on Solitaire," he said. Then he took a second look, and a very strange sensation swept over him. "No, I don't think so," he muttered to himself. "This is Striker's Shook, and Striker's doing, and I don't like it one bit."

## Chapter Eighteen

Michael sat in the brown and yellow dust of the mountaintop and stared up at the new blood-dripping letters on the stone above him. SHOOK: TO HELL AND BACK AGAIN.

"No, I'm not yet back from hell," he muttered to himself. Even so believing, he looked in the direction of the path he had first taken to get to the great yellow stone, hoping it might be possible to just walk back down the path and return to the world where he had left Johnny Lohman standing at the back door of the hospital. He shook his head. "No, it's not going to be that easy."

He heard a strange sound begin to rise around him, and he looked to see what was causing it. It seemed to be coming from behind the great stone. As he watched, a cloud of the yellow dust began to rise up behind the stone, swirling slowly at first, then faster and faster around and around. Then looking like an enormous swirling balloon, a tall, fat dust-devil rose up into view. The sound coming from it was like the humming of an old-fashioned singing top, but louder than the roaring of a huge dynamo. It rose up over him, and he saw the tip of the tornado searching back and forth, as though looking for something.

To hide from it, he began to crawl toward the great stone. He noticed that his body seemed to feel as though it had been bruised over every square inch from head to toe. The whirling fat cloud of yellow dust hovered high over him, its obscene twitching tip probing and searching, its great bulk blocking out the sun, and casting a sinister shadow over Michael's cowering body. He crawled to the stone, gasping in pain, then fell against it heavily, striking his head with a loud and very painful "thunk." He leaned back against the cold stone and looked up into the darkening sky. Like an exploring finger, the tip of the dust-devil stroked across the tops of the tall trees crowning the mountain, while the trees whipped back and forth like blades of grass beneath the whirling blades of a lawnmower.

He took a deep breath, steeled himself against the aches in his body, and struggled to stand up. He staggered a couple of steps, then found his balance. At first he started to make his way around the stone to conceal himself, then he remembered how he had found the blue door behind the stone. "It's a dead end," he said. "That sleaze ball slime ball Striker is just laughing at me. There has to be another way."

As he watched, the dust-devil touched one tree after another, plucking each one up from the ground like a stalk of celery, and sucking it up into the fat body of the storm. One by one, the trees were stripped from the mountaintop, to the macabre howling of the spinning yellow mass. Michael stood gritting his teeth, looking from side to side as the forest was ripped from the mountaintop, leaving the earth torn and tumbled like an ochre desert after an earthquake. When the last tree was gone, the swirling cloud hung in the sky before the great yellow stone.

Then instead of extending its fatal finger down to touch the earth again, the entire storm began to settle until it just rested on the torn soil of the mountain. The side of the swirling mass began to flex up, as though the winds were flowing over an inverted glass dome. Then it parted open, and Michael saw a tall imposing figure standing in the midst of the storm. It was the blue-robed golden-haired white-masked figure of the sinister Lord Striker. Like the Colossus, he stood with feet apart and hands on hips, and the ringing of his laughter echoed from the face of the bloody yellow stone, louder even than the howling of the spinning tornado. "So, Spirit Man, you wimpy weenie boy, I thought you were going to hunt me down and make a big hero of yourself. Har har har! So what's the matter? Could it be you just don't have the heart for it?" He held up the crystal decanter with the silver binding on its stopper, and Michael could clearly see the bloody heart inside. Striker shook the bottle over his head, his mocking laughter swirling away with the dirty yellow-brown torrent of dust.

Michael cringed against the face of the rock, clinging

SPIRIT MAN

to a crack to shield himself from the whipping wisps of the edges of the storm. Mesmerized, he watched Striker rapidly moving his fingers up and down along the metal handles of the glass jar. He lifted up the jar to his ear as if listening to hear if Michael's heart was still beating. Michael was dismayed to find himself wondering if his heart was still beating, and dismayed again when Striker laughed as though he could see his uncertainty and fear. The blue-robed demigod from Shook began to shake the jar back and forth, the heart slapping against one side and the other, thu-thunk, thu-thunk, thu-thunk, louder and louder. The pounding of the heart against the sides of the jar felt like great drumbeats against Michael's chest, and then it seemed to come from within him, the pounding of his own heart.

He struggled to get to his feet, gritting his teeth against the wind. "You can't have it, Striker," he yelled into the howling rush. "You're not getting away with this."

The mass of dust swirled around Lord Striker again, obscuring him from view. The storm rose straight up into the air like an enormous spaceship, blotting out the sun at first, then disappearing right into it. "No!" Michael yelled, raising his fist to the sky. "What are you, chicken? Come back here, you big ugly blue chicken!"

He leaned back against the stone, then banged his head against it several times in frustration. He closed his eyes and took a few deep breaths, then something made him snap his eyes open. Above him a spot grew right out of the sun, quickly growing large enough to blot it out and plunge Michael into shadow. He saw it was a huge bird, in plumage as bright blue as Striker's robe, diving straight down onto him. With a screech louder than a fighter plane, and a wingspan wider than a bomber, the enormous white-faced bird swooped down on him, slashing at him with a red-smeared crow-black beak as big as a racing boat, and grasping at him with claws that could snatch up a car like an eagle snatches a rat. With a cry, Michael pressed himself against the rock.

The huge bird swept gracefully up into the air in a

steep turn like a crop-duster, and for a moment, seemed to just hang in the air. "You'll have to do much better than that," screeched the bird in Striker's voice. Then it dropped a wing, dived for the ground, and sped away toward the western horizon, skimming the ground so fast that plumes of dust rose up after it.

Feeling very unsatisfied with his own performance, Michael shook his shoulders, hitched up his jeans, and began to walk toward the direction in which the great Striker-chicken had flown. It took him a few minutes to walk through the shattered area where all the trees were uprooted, then he found himself stepping out onto a broad ridge overlooking a valley. It was certainly not the Mesilla Valley of New Mexico from which he had come.

Michael's breath caught in the back of his throat at the awesome beauty of the place. From where he stood, a path began to wind through softly-rolling hills and gentle hollows, where the ground was a magic carpet full of wild flowers and tall grasses bending and waving in the playful breeze. A little way off, where the flowered carpet met a grove of shimmering aspens, he could see the taunting figure of Striker, his golden hair waving and flashing.

Shaking off the pain he had been suffering, Michael got a grip on himself and began to walk rapidly down the trail. Then he began to run, jogging at first, and then striding. He felt the adrenaline rise in his body, and with it a sense of deep physical determination, and he began to relish in its driving power. "Whoo! Whoo!" his breath rushed from his cheeks as he pushed his body harder and harder. Not like a deer he ran, but like the streaking cheetah that chases the deer, shuddering in anticipation of the taste of blood. Ahead of him Striker turned and walked into the shadow of the trees, following the path on which Michael was leaping and striding.

When he ran into the shadow of the grove of trees, Michael was barely skimming the ground, as though just flying above it and reaching down with his feet to claw the ground to drive himself hurtling forward. In shadow,

Michael squinted, and checked his speed, but it was too late. An arm-thick branch struck him squarely across the forehead, flipping him all the way over backwards as he flew forward, so he landed flat on his face in the middle of the trail.

He had no idea how long he lay there. It might have been seconds or hours. As he began to regain his consciousness, he felt his breathing grow calm and slow, and the ringing pain in his head gradually subside. He raised his head, and was surprised to find a sculpture had been erected exactly in the middle of the trail. It was a tall and gaunt man in tattered black clothes and the top hat of an undertaker, and he held a wide signboard in his hands. It said, "KNOCK YOURSELF OUT, AND FIND YOURSELF IN A NEW WORLD."

Lord Striker was nowhere to be seen. As his eyes became adjusted to the shadowed grove, Michael saw that the trail led him beside a tiny shallow lake, a pretty pool surrounded by lush greenery and dark-colored blossoms that seemed carved from translucent wax. In the manner of a Japanese garden, a lovely bridge stretched over the pool. When he stepped onto the bridge, he gasped in delight as a cloud of white snow geese rose up together from the lake into the sky. Thousands of wings all beating together created a thrilling sound as the geese flew up over the tops of the trees. He stood, clutching the railing of the bridge, which he noticed was made of ivory or polished bone, rubbed smooth and stained coffee-brown as though with centuries of human contact.

High above, the cloud of geese shaped itself into a long "V" which turned round and round above the lake, and then finally departed into the distance.

Michael leaned over the railing and looked down into the clear water. He smiled at the tall slender green reeds and light brown cattails which grew at the base of the bridge pylons. There was a school of large gold fish and white carp swimming at the bottom of the shallow lake. It was very pleasant there and for a moment he found himself lulled into a nostalgic reverie. This beautiful place, surrounded by snow dusted mountains in the far distance, reminded the Spirit Man very much of the Bosque Del Apache, the bird sanctuary south of Socorro, New Mexico. Homesick, sad and lonely, Michael wanted to go home right then, to give up whatever mission had brought him to this place.

Then from behind him he heard a voice, a strangely familiar squeaky voice. "To err is human; to andy, divine," said the voice. Michael spun around on his heels, ready to face his enemy, and was surprised at what he saw. Before him at the end of the bridge stood a man as strange looking as anyone he had ever met. He was not four feet tall, and his waist could not have been farther than a third of that height from the ground. His hips and his butt were wide and round, as though a clay model of a normal man had been squashed down to spread out into short fat bulby legs which ended in peculiarly tiny feet. His shoulders were narrow, and his arms short and gnarled with muscles. Most astonishing was his head, which was tall and round like a melon, with a high forehead and a face all squnched down close to a broad but very short chin. "Hey, Spirit Man! Glad to see you made it here to these tricks of the sticks!"

"Do I know you?" Michael asked, his jaw gaping open in awe in spite of himself. From the very top of the little man's head sprouted a wooly bristle of curly black hair, and from the very bottom of his wide jaw sprouted a scraggle of long red beard which extended all the way to his fat little pot belly. He was wearing a pair of dark purple tights, a pair of dirty white tennis shoes, and a bright yellow sweatshirt stained with spaghetti sauce and chocolate pudding. He shuffled—or more accurately, bounced—on his stubby bowlegs over to Michael and put out his stubby-fingered hand to shake. "Sure you do," he said in his wheezy voice. "I am Lazaro Hitchcock, and I am the wizard in this crack of the track here in mother-shaking Shook! Pleased to meet you, Spirit Man! Heard so much about you! All good of course!"

Michael put his own hand, and the two of them shook hands vigorously for a long time. When they had shaken hands so long it began to seem ridiculous to Michael, he broke out in a big grin. Lazaro let out a whoop of laughter and popped right up into the air, doing a back flip and landing right on his fat butt to bounce up to his feet. Michael laughed in genuine delight. "Lazaro Hitchcock, Wizard of Shook, I am pleased to meet you. I hope you don't turn out to be Striker, like all the others. You seem like an OK guy."

The diminutive wizard Lazaro jumped up and down, then spun around in mid air and popped right over in a back flip again. He crash landed on his fat butt, bounded to his feet, and squeezed his fat belly with his fat kewpie-doll fingers. "You're a big fella, ain't ya? Yes, you are! Wow! They make them real big where you come from. Come on now, Spirit Man, follow me! We got to get the scoop on all the poop around here! That's an expression around here meaning we got a lot to talk about! So let's go, Spirit Man! What say we go chew a shoe?"

"What? Where are we going?"

"To go eat! What else? Isn't your tummy tum hungry? Plenty of grub at my humble abode!" Lazaro scampered down the bridge and began to bound along the trail. Though Michael was a tall man with long legs, and a champion runner as well, and Lazaro was a short fat man with stumpy hams for legs, Michael found it difficult to keep up with him. The red-bearded bubble-butt apparition bounded along like a bouncing ball, his fat little legs pumping madly back and forth. As the narrow dirt path led through the thick woods, the little cheerful guy was always a step or two in front of the Spirit Man. Tall Popular trees grew in this part of the woods and their golden leaves clapped against one another in the gentle wind, filling their ears with sweet sounds. They ran for hours through the woods with the warm sunlight filtering through the trees and dancing upon their faces and shoulders. Soon, they came to a small clearing in the woods and they stopped at the edge of it. And in the middle of the small clearing stood Lazaro's magnificent brown stone castle.

"Wow! That is some humble abode!" Michael shouted out loud. There was something so secure about it, so warm and welcoming, that for the first time since his arrival in Shook, the Spirit Man felt completely safe and far from danger. "Nobody could find us here," Michael thought.

"I call this place The Little Dakota," Lazaro told him and then added, "Hope you like it, Spirit Man! Hope, hope, hope you like it! I do!"

"It is beautiful," Michael told him and then asked, "Who lives here?"

"Just little old me. Nobody else can bother me that way if you know what I mean! Like it like that. Keep to my little old self, the little old elf! Come on, let's go. We don't got all day and I could eat a whole shuffle of buffalo if they had them out here on the range!"

They walked on a wide pathway made of blood-red pipestone carved with thousands of fishes, lizards, and tiny men with big lemur eyes and long twitching tails. Michael looked up and saw twin towers on top of the castle's roof, which was made of thick tar and old worn gray shingles. Though the castle was five stories tall, and its walls were made of huge square stones, he could see it was constructed in proportion to Lazaro's body. There was a wide and short archway in the front of the castle, which served as the main entrance. As they got closer, Michael could see a small courtyard inside. Michael had to duck his head as they walked underneath the archway and soon they stood together in the middle of the small courtyard.

Delighted, Michael thought he must have been transported in time to a little town in Europe. A white marble water fountain in the middle of the small courtyard was flowing with crystal clear bubbling water. The water splashed down the white marble fountain and the sound of the bubbling water echoed from the dark walls, making a playful sound very soothing indeed. It washed away all Michael's worries away. Across the courtyard stood a wide old weathered wooden door, just five feet tall. Above it on the wall was a beautiful sign, carved in white marble to match the fountain. It read, THE WAY TO A MAN'S HEART IS THROUGH HIS STOMACH!

"I once had a girlfriend who told me that," Michael said. "She was a great cook, but I confess she sometimes touched my heart while dinner was still cooking, and we managed to burn more than one soufflé."

"Without appetite, there is no fulfillment," said Lazaro. "Let's see what you have an appetite for."

Lazaro then opened up the old wooden door and they went inside it. They walked down a long hallway and then they came to the kitchen and dining room area. It was a very large room with a half dozen or more round tables in the middle of it. There was a long row of big picture windows that went all the way around three sides of the spacious dining room. The big picture windows overlooked Lazaro's splendid flower and herb gardens.

"Sit down where ever ya like, Spirit Man! I'll be right back with the soup of the day!" Lazaro told him and then he left the dining room scurrying into the main kitchen.

Michael sat down at the nearest table by him. Every table in the dining room was neatly decorated with a white table cloth. There were neatly folded green napkins on every table and pure crystal glasses and highly polished silverware as well. Michael held a spoon up to his face and he could see his own reflection in it. For a moment Michael thought that he might see Striker's image in the silver spoon but he did not. He put the spoon back down on the table next to his dinner plate, white with blue trim.

Soon Lazaro came skipping out into the dining room, carrying a silver tray with two hot bowls of steaming soup. The scent of the hot soup filled up the entire room and swirled round and round in Michael's nostrils. It reminded Michael of his grandmother's home made chicken soup which she cooked with fresh vegetables from her garden, along with a handful of spices and herbs. "Smells Great!" Michael said.

"Ever heard of Murff Ball Soup?" Lazaro asked.

"No, what is it?" Michael asked, not really sure if he

wanted to know.

"It's your basic chicken soup—little of this, and a little of that!" Lazaro then sat down, smiled at him and then he leaned over his bowl of Murff Ball soup and took a huge slurping sip. Using a big silver spoon, Michael took a sip from his own bowl—but not as loud or as rude as the wizard's. Lazaro took another, louder than the one before, fully enjoying himself. When he saw Michael's face light up at the delicious taste of his famous Murff Ball soup, he bounced up and down in his chair.

The Spirit Man chuckled to himself, thinking, "I don't know whose balls go in Murff Ball soup, but it probably makes wizards out of ordinary men." He began to eagerly dip into the bowl, and brought out big chunks of tender chicken, mushrooms, and tiny golden squashes. No matter how much he ate, the bowl seemed to be bottomless.

"Oh, forgot," said Lazaro as he reached into the pocket of his baggy pants and brought out a crusty loaf of fresh-baked bread. He tore it in half, gave half to Michael, and dipped his own piece into the soup. Michael did the same, and by the time the bread was gone, the bowl was empty, and Michael couldn't eat another bite.

The wizard let out a big burp, and wiped his mouth off with the sleeve of his bright yellow sweatshirt. He leaned back in his chair and gave a deep sigh. "OK, Spirit Man, here's the real deal, the deal of steel. You want to know about Striker, Lord of Shook, who tests the hearts of men."

"I do," said Michael.

"You do, do you? Well, you're a lucky ducky, Buck, 'cause I'm going to tell you. There is so much you need to know and so little precious time for me to tell you the whole story, because it is a very long one filled with history dating back to the beginning of time itself. Lord Striker belongs to the Clan of the Dangerous Gods, which is the cruelest and most violent of all the Orders of the Pantheon here in Shook. Lord Striker is The God of Hearts who tests men's spirits to see if they have courage or not. Lord Striker's sole mission in the universe is to steal people's hearts.

Murder is his business and has been ever since the beginning of creation itself. He brings death and destruction upon the land and he shows no remorse for what he has done. Spirit Man, here in Shook we are born to die, not to live. That's how it is under Lord Striker's rule and reign of terror here in this sad place. Innocent men, women and children, have been killed by his mighty hand, one by one, limb by limb, heart by heart, and all we have has been taken away from us throughout the ages. Everything Lord Striker touches dies, and becomes death itself. No man, woman, or child, no elf or fairy, no demigod or demon can ever escape The Ultimate Law, which is death by His Hand of Punishment."

"Is he some kind of avatar?" Michael asked.

"No. He only acts like he thinks he is the One True God of all the Universes Himself. I don't know if he is a god or a demon, if he is good or evil, or maybe a little good and a lot of evil, but around these parts of the carts, he carries a very big stick, and it's a very tricky stick, Dick, let me clue you."

"Does he live around here, or just come through kicking butt once in a while?" Michael asked.

"That's a good question. You're no dummy, Chummy. Striker lives in a place called Terminal Island and that is where you will find The Tower of Views and The Garden of Two Deaths."

"Can you tell me how to get there, Lazaro?"

"Nope, 'fraid not. Nobody has ever seen his secret places and lived to tell about them. Terminal Island, The Tower of Views, and the Garden of Two Deaths, are all myth to everyone dying here in Shook. We don't believe in Heaven or Hell, because we know Shook is a magical world, but we do know there is more to everything you see than what you see. That's the catch of the latch here, y'see what I mean. Spirit Man, until you can see it with your own eyes and feel the ground below your own stinking feet, well, piss on it, it will always remain an illusion."

Michael stared at him, trying to make some sense of what Lazaro was trying to tell him.

"I am very sorry, Spirit Man," said the little man with the wheezing voice and jiggling jowls. "I can't tell you much more about the towers and secret gardens. You might be able to get there, but here among us they are only legends. Truth is, they don't do us much good, no they don't. They don't do for us at all. But I will tell you this much. My gut feeling, which is about the only thing I trust, tells me that the hearts Lord Striker steals—taking our breath and life away, sending us into a bottomless pit of darkness—are not lost. My dear friend, can you guess what he does with all of those beating hearts? I have spent many long years guessing what he does. You know what I guess? Striker takes those hearts to his Garden of Two Deaths. I am only a wizard and a little one at that, but, I have a hunch about what he does with all the hearts of the people of the world. Once he gets to his garden, he plants them there!"

"Plants them? To grow into what?"

"I don't know. Subjects, maybe. He's a ruler, and rulers all like to have lots of subjects. I guess he must have over six billion of them by now! Anyway, Spirit Man, if my gut is telling me the truth, you'll find Michael's heart still alive in The Garden of Two Deaths at the Tower of Views."

"Will I have to die to get there, Laz?" Michael asked, as if it was just another casual question.

Lazaro grinned and winked. "Well, after a while you get used to that, don't you? Now, let me tell you something about what dying twice means. The first death is the killing of the body  like when someone murders you, or you get killed in a war. The second death is much more difficult to reach, which makes the Garden a particularly fearful place to think about. The Second Death is the death of the spirit. Only an act of God can destroy your spirit. Man cannot kill a man's spirit no matter what he does to his body, because spirit is much stronger than earth. That's the basic fact of the act around this place, Buck Ace. Myself, I don't think it is possible to destroy a man's spirit, but that is my own belief. You must decide for yourself what you believe, and what you are willing to risk. If the Blue Lord really has the

Second Death in his garden, that means he has some really powerful connections, you hear what I'm saying? Be very careful in your pursuit of your heart and dreams. Even if they can't really destroy you, Spirit Man, they can make your life a cesspool, a puking pit of living shit."

"Where do I find Terminal Island, Lazaro?" Michael asked him, and it wasn't a question so much as a demand.

"Haven't you been listening to me? I don't even know if these places exist at all. You may never find them for the rest of your lives."

There was a long moment of silence between them, then Lazaro got up and waved to Michael to follow him. Michael got up too and went outside behind the Little Dakota. There was a small patio with a hammock made of rope tied between two branches of an old cottonwood tree. Next to the hammock was a wooden picnic table. Lazaro sat on top of it and pointed to Michael to climb into the hammock and take a nap there.

"OK, a nap. What are you going to do?" Michael asked the wizard as he climbed into the hammock.

"Don't worry about me. I'll sleep right here on top of the table. You ain't able, Mabel, but I do it all the time. I can sleep anywhere, anytime, start with a fart and stop on a dime." Lazaro lay down on the table, shuddered, sighed, and relaxed, his fat round butt and melon head seeming to settle and squash out like sagging clay. In seconds, he fell fast asleep, and began to snore with a sound like a pig gargling pancake batter.

Michael lay in the hammock amazed at how fast Lazaro fell asleep. Though he had not even considered going to sleep, he decided he might as well take advantage of the opportunity, and soon his eyes grew heavy as he swayed gently back and forth.

Not a single dream or vision disturbed the Spirit Man while he slept in the hammock tied to the huge branches of the old cottonwood tree. When he awakened, he stretched and yawned, and then looked around. In an instant, he jumped up, lost his balance, and fell out of the hammock.

There was no one around. There was no five-story brown stone castle, no pipestone walks, and no Lazaro Hitchcock. The sun was setting behind the distant rolling hills and the Wizard of Shook was gone.

The cottonwood tree stood alone in the middle of a clearing in the woods. Michael could easily look around and see there was nothing else in the clearing except one thing. A few yards away from him stood a tall gold door, over eight feet tall and five feet wide, with scrolls and cherubs carved all around it. No sixteenth-century palace ever had a grander one.

"I've had about enough of this," Michael muttered as he picked himself up and walked to the door. Beautifully engraved in its gold face were the words, DON'T BELIEVE IN WHAT YOU SEE. With clenched jaw, he took a deep breath and grasped the gold doorknob.

The door swung away from him, revealing a cloud of mist which parted exposing none other than the blue-robed figure of Lord Striker, still holding the crystal jar with Michael's heart in the bottom of it. Before Michael could catch his breath and move or speak, Striker spoke to him, saying, "All are created in my likeness and image!"

"No," Michael snarled at Striker. "No, we are not created in your likeness. We are not all like you. Give me my heart back!"

"Didn't you learn anything from Lazaro, Do-do Man? If you want to beard the lion, you must do it in his den." With a move like a diver doing a back layout, Lord Striker raised his arms and dived backwards into the darkness behind him.

"Damn," spat Michael, stamping his foot. "Damn, damn!" With the mad resolve of a man leaping out of an airplane without a parachute, he dived headfirst into the darkness behind the golden door.

# SPIRIT MAN

## Chapter Nineteen

It felt like Michael was falling, and he struggled for balance like a skydiver frogging out, but there was no rush of wind to press against. He could breathe—though he was gasping for air through his teeth like a runner before the hounds. He struggled a moment, then tried to get hold of himself and relax. At first he thought it was absolutely dark, but then he found it even more strange to think it was absolutely lighted and utterly empty. He could see his own body clearly, well lighted but without shadow cast in any direction. Beyond that, a flat dimensionless void, not black, but void like the sensation of trying to see with your foot. He tried to turn and look in all directions, but he was unable to tell if he was rotating, tumbling, falling, or just hanging in space.

He didn't see it coming. There was a blinding flash of blue light that exploded upon his retinas, showering him with stars. It was so bright that it seemed more like a single spike of piercing sound than a burst of light. It left behind a numb tingling sensation and a metallic taste in his mouth, as though he had been falling through space and had struck a perfectly flat and utterly hard surface.

He didn't know if it knocked him unconscious or awake, if he had been falling through the void for seconds or hours, or if he had been comatose for weeks. He felt a world rush upon him, sounds, and a warm redness he realized he was seeing. He opened his eyes and immediately snapped them shut again, wincing against the brightness of the sunlit sky. His hands clawed at hot sand, and he sat upright, lifting them up to cover his eyes. Carefully, he opened his eyes to slits and took a peek around.

Michael was sitting exactly in the middle of a crossroad in two perfectly straight two-lane dirt roads, which extended to the horizon in all four directions. There were street lights – broken and completely rusted out— hanging on dark cables, swinging back and forth just slightly. There were no power lines. The sand on which he sat was the rust-red of his home in New Mexico, and as far as he could see it was heaped in mounds by the clumps of mesquite which grew in it. "Jeez, I'm back on the Jornada," he said to himself, refusing to acknowledge it was obvious there were no mountains, neither the Organs on one side nor the Robledos on the other.

When he held out his hand, it cast a shadow straight down. He passed the shadow over his leg, and he could feel the difference in the temperature as it gave its scant relief from the blazing high-noon sun. Again he looked around, refusing to acknowledge the obvious fact there were no trees, nor anything else tall enough to cast a sheltering shadow. He squeezed his eyes shut, trying to hope he was still in the void, and not in the middle of...well, somewhere.

But he was in the middle of somewhere, and he could not ignore the heat, nor the tickling bead of sweat trickling down the side of his neck. He opened his eyes again. The broken street lights were making a tiny, just-perceptible squeaking sound as they swung back and forth in the thick flow of hot breeze. "Like I've been here forever," he thought to himself.

He stood up and drew a deep breath, and took a serious look around. "Where's the sign?" he asked some unseen listener, with a twist of sarcasm in his voice. He even looked up to see if a blimp would sail by towing a banner. Then as though in answer to his question, he saw them – tiny signs low to the ground, just sticking up out of the sand along all four roads.

He could just read the first one: "YOU CAN GO FORWARD." It was the same on all four roads. He took a deep breath, snorted the dust from his nostrils, and picked one. In just a few steps, he could see that the next sign read, "IN ANY DIRECTION." New curiosity giving him a reason to get to the next sign, Michael picked up his pace, almost to a jog. Soon he could read, "BUT YOU CAN'T GO BACK." His pace broke, almost to a halt, then to a resigned walk toward the place where he could read the inevitable, "AT ALL. Burma-Shook."

Feeling very sad and lonely, he kept walking a few feet, then stopped to take a second look at his situation. "I can walk, or I can wait," he said to himself. "If I'm going to wait, the best place would be the crossroad, so I should go back." Then he looked at the sign again, and did not even turn around to see if the street lights he had left behind were still standing there. He started walking across the desert.

The hot wind blew across the mesquite-studded red sands. It was almost unfair to call it wind – it was more like a hot, thick mass that flowed by in unsteady swirls. It seemed to suck the water from his skin almost on contact, so although he was sweating heavily, his skin was never even moist at all. There was a certain comfort in the familiarity of the scene, as though he actually was back in New Mexico, and could feel "at home" in spite of the fact he was quite lost. The comfort was quickly offset by his recollection that the rolling sea of sand there was called the Jornada del Muerte – the Journey of Death – because people had often died trying to cross it.

Michael tried not to dwell upon the fact that he had no water. He trudged along with his head down, protecting his eyes from the glare, then he looked up at the blazing sun once again and saw swirling heat waves pouring out from the hot ball of fire. The sky turned white with the intensity of the shimmering heat, and he began to feel nauseous and weak. For a moment he thought he was going to pass out and fall onto his face in the sand, but the glassy rush passed and he took a deep breath and went on. Squinting, he looked along the road, and right at the point where it met the horizon, he saw a little plume of dust.

He watched it a few seconds, then clucked and nodded. "Well, here comes fate," he muttered. He paused in his step, as though to wait for whatever it was to arrive. Then he kept walking, and watching the burble of dust draw closer to him on the sandy desert road. It was moving at very high speed, and in only a few minutes, he could see it was a truck of some kind, painted bright yellow. Soon he could hear its engine's roaring hum and the yellow Hummer sped right past him.

Michael waved his arms and began to run after the big power-jeep. Having seen him in the rearview mirror, the driver hit the brakes, and the truck slid to a stop a quarter of a mile down the road. In time he knew would have broken every record, he ran the distance to catch up. The thick, sultry wind carried the plume of dust across the road and began to drop it between the mesquite hummocks, so when he arrived, he could see who was driving.

"I thought you were going the other way, Hon," said the beautiful young woman behind the wheel of the Hummer.

"Only because I didn't know any better," Michael gasped. "I'd just like to get out of this desert."

"Well, you better jump your skinny ass right on in here, then. There won't be anybody else along this road for days - nobody you'd want to meet, anyway. There ain't nobody but me and them."

"Them? Who are they?" Michael asked.

"You better hope you don't find out," she replied. "Shut that door, now, we got better things to do than wait around here for them to show up."

"OK," he agreed. He settled into the seat as she picked up speed again, and took a moment to actually look at her. She was a knockout, a showgirl top-model Amazon knockout. She wore her long red hair loose upon her shoulders, bare except for the straps of a sleeveless white muscle shirt. Her eyes were large and dark, her lips very full, and her skin a soft warm olive. Michael's usual reaction to seeing a beautiful woman well-displayed had always been (to his eternal gratitude) to enjoy appreciating her voluptuous pulchritude. But he recognized there was something about the way she wore her jeans, workboots, and hat that set her apart from all that sexy stuff. She was certainly sexy, but it just wasn't an issue.

"My name is Solitaire Bianca," she said, "but you can call me Ace."

"Thanks, Ace, I'll do that," he said. "I am..."

"Save it, pretty boy! I know who you are. You're Spirit Man, aren't you?"

"Yes, I'm afraid I am," he said, with a helpless chuckle. "So where was I headed?"

"Middle of nowhere."

"I thought that's where I was."

"Things are like that here in Shook," she agreed. "I'm going to take you to my place and then we're going to look for The Tower of Views and your secret garden."

"The Garden of Two Deaths," he affirmed. "Yes." He sat watching her drive the powerful big vehicle, relaxed, but serious and watchful. He almost asked her how she knew about those things, but it seemed somehow pointless to question the obvious. He hadn't drawn Ace by chance – there was more going on than he could know.

For a long time they didn't say anything, then she said, "Check this out, OK."

"What?" he asked.

"Pain is to pleasure as darkness is to light," she said, as though quoting from a book. "What do you think?"

"Meaning you can't have one without the other?" he ventured.

"Yeah, maybe," she agreed. "So does it mean pain is like darkness, or like light? Is pleasure an absence of pain, or an absence of light?"

Michael pondered a moment, almost asking, "Is this a game?" Then he started to say, "Well, light is something, and darkness is nothing, so since pain is certainly something, does that mean pleasure is nothing?"

But before he could say a word, Ace looked into her mirror and snarled, "Shit, piss, and corruption! We've got ourselves some unwanted company!"

Michael turned around to look out the back window and saw a band of ragged bikers tailing them. "Who the hell are they?" he asked.

"Strikers," she said, with both contempt and a certain fear in her voice. Riding motorcycles, tires slashing back and forth across the desert road, they were gaining speed on them.  The Strikers were dressed in black leather jackets with gold and silver chains, and bright red pants. White masks covered up half of their faces, and their lips were smeared with gobs of bright red lipstick.

Ace dropped a gear and made a sharp left turn off the road, and began twisting and bounding between the mesquite hummocks. She zigzagged across a flat stretch of red sand, kicking up a cloud of red dust to blind the Strikers, and cutting deep skid-ruts to throw their bikes off balance.

"How many of them we got, Spirit Man?" Ace asked as she stomped the pedal to the floor.

"Forty, fifty maybe, I don't know!  I can't see through the dust."  He looked up and saw that the thick winds of Shook had formed a swirl that was gathering up the dust of their zooms and turns and holding it in a twirling cloud around them.  As the wind whirled round them, Michael was astonished to see some of the ugly white masked Strikers riding through the flying sand like the Wicked Witch of the West on her bicycle.  "I sure hope you know a way out of here, Ace," he said with tension straining his voice.  "These ugly bastards are right on our ass!"

Ace nodded, then raised her hand toward them with her middle finger extended in the universal symbol of ill will. The big jeep broke out of the swirling dust, struck a hummock, and went airborne, flying over a clump of mesquite.  "All right!" she crowed as the vehicle bounded over the hummock and landed on a stretch of paved road. "Now we're getting somewhere. That's the Cisceron Gorge Bridge about a quarter of a mile up there ahead."  She looked up at her rear view mirror and saw the Strikers were also turning onto the road. "Have I got a big surprise for you white-faced blubber heads!"

Michael couldn't imagine what use a bridge could be in the middle of this flat desert, but in seconds, they passed a road sign that read:  "CISCERON GORGE BRIDGE. DREAM ON, YOU FOOLS, DREAM ON."

As they drove onto the bridge, Michael looked down

to see the mighty Cisceron river fiercely flowing through a narrow canyon far below him. Ace reached down beside her seat and pulled up a short lever. "Look out the back," she said. From two pipes at the back of the truck came two black sprays of thick oil, which spread in a sheet to cover the entire road.

A dozen Strikers rode their big motorcycles onto the bridge, six abreast. The leader raised his front wheel up off the road in a wheelie and zoomed forward, and then hit the slick oil patch. The bike lurched back and forth, and then crashed into the bike beside him, and then into another. As the first row crashed, the second row crashed into them, and bikes and Strikers tumbled madly, breaking up into pieces. Michael saw four, then five Strikers go flying up into the sky and over the steel guardrails along the sides of the bridge. They plunged to their deaths into the white water rapids of the Cisceron river far below, going all the way down to the bottom of the steep canyon.

"No mercy for you rotten suckers!" Ace yelled out of her window at the band of Strikers. She stuck her hand groping for something underneath her seat, and pulled out a long red flare. She bit off the trigger cap, lit the fuse with her cigarette lighter, and threw the blazing torch out of her window. In very slow motion, they watched the red flare soar up into the sky and then fall down through the air until it landed on top of the bridge. The red flare rolled, spun around several times, then stopped in the middle of the oil-covered road. For a moment, nothing—then a huge explosion of fire and black smoke engulfed the old bridge. Strikers flew through the air, killed on the spot, or screaming with a limb blown off. A fat Striker who probably weighed at least three hundred pounds was screaming at the top of his lungs because his pants were on fire! Then, the entire bridge began to crumble and break up, splitting right down the middle. They drove off just in the nick of time before the entire bridge collapsed and fell the mile or two down to the bottom of the Cisceron Gorge.

Ace cheered wildly and jumped up and down in her

seat. "Gotcha!" she shouted out loud in delight. "Them chicken-lickin' Strikers can't beat me. They'll learn not to mess with a real live woman! Whoopie!"

"I wouldn't pick a fight with you! You're one tough lady!" Michael affirmed.

"You got that right, partner!" she agreed. "Had enough adventure for one day, Spirit Man?"

"Yeah, no more surprises, please," Michael said, and they both laughed.

"Hey, listen, I know of a quiet place up ahead from here. It's called The City of Rocks, a nice place to camp and spend the night. The moon is full tonight so there will be plenty of light. How does that sound to you, Spirit Man?"

"Great!"

"Good, get some rest then, okay?

"Sure, you got it, Ace!"

Michael leaned his head back in the jeep, feeling very sleepy and worn out and tired. The instant he closed his eyes he fell fast asleep while Ace drove across the empty Wastelands of Shook. A couple of hours passed before she turned off the highway and down another road full of pot-holes and bumps, leading to the main entrance to the park. She stopped there sat looking at the sun setting in fiery colors over the sea of rolling sand called The Wastelands of Shook. She nudged the Spirit Man to wake him up. "Wake up, sleeping beauty! "We're here, at The City of Rocks! Look at the beautiful sunset!"

Michael sat up and rubbed his sleepy eyes, still feeling groggy with cobwebs in his head as he looked across the wide valley that stretched in front of him. There were all kinds of weird rock formations all around him for miles and miles in every direction. He sat there in total silence as he absorbed the boundless beauty of this strange land.

"A long, long time ago, there was a huge volcano," she said. "It blew up and all the rocks flew up into the sky and then they all landed here on top of each other like a giant kid's building blocks." She paused for a moment and then added, "Or maybe it was a big dragon that breathed fire and smoke across the land and used this place for nesting."

There were round rocks, oval ones, rectangles, squares, and rocks in the shape of a triangle that looked like the Egyptian pyramids. Michael saw a tall, slender rock standing steeply up into the sky, like a duck with its neck stretched straight. Then, he saw another pile of rocks that looked like a camel's back with two humps on it. "Wow!" Michael cheered as he pointed to the rocks. "Look at that – a big duck and camel's back!"

"Yeah, yeah, yeah," Ace replied, pointing to the tall, slender rock standing stiffly up into the dusky sunset sky. "That rock looks like a dick to me, a big hard dick, not a duck. And those two humps over there look like a camel to you? Come on, boy, anyone can see that's a fat girl with her heels in her ears."

At first he was astonished to hear her speak like that, then he saw the little smirk tickling the corners of her mouth, and he knew she was just teasing him to put him at ease, and they both cracked up laughing. Ace slowly drove past an old main entrance gate under a sign which identified the place as "The City Of Rocks, an Ephederal Snate Park of the Ninth Diosnese of Shook." A rusted broken padlock dangled from the gaping gate, and it seemed they had the place all to themselves. There were no campers here, no people drinking beer, partying their asses off, playing loud music which would disturb their neighbors and shatter the deafening sounds of silence in this very strange natural world. Michael felt that the road, and the concrete picnic tables, were just other weird natural features, and no one had ever been there before he and Solitaire Bianca arrived.

Ace drove the Hummer around a bend of the dirt road and pulled into a campground area with a picnic table and a small shelter made of tin sheets on a metal frame. As though she had known exactly where she intended to park all along, she pulled in and turned off the engine. "You've heard of a four-star hotel?" she asked. "Well, you're not going to believe the number of stars this place has."

He walked to the shelter and in the waning twilight he could read a park sign that had been nailed to the side of the shed. Painted on a sheet of metal, it had once been white, but the sun had yellowed the paint, and the rain-run rust had browned it. The words had once been black, but time had reduced them to faded brown on the lighter brown of the sign. At the top, it said simply, "PARK RULES," and beneath in block letters, "If you let the dream die, the world will never meet the spirit, man. Keep the dream alive, and please put all your trash in the receptacles provided." He smiled, and felt very reassured that he was where he was supposed to be, wherever that was. Someone had known he was going to come there, and a long time ago, by the look of the sign.

She knelt by an old fallen tree limb and gathered some dry pieces of firewood to make a campfire. Bemused by the message on the sign, he stood watching her and he found himself smiling and feeling unusually affectionate. As though she had read his mind, she turned around and gave him a pointed glance. "I hope you are enjoying yourself. I could use some help around here, Mr. Big Strong Spirit Man."

"Right!" he said, and jumped to help her. He picked up more firewood and helped her pile it in the right order, starting with a big handful of dry desert grass, and then bigger and bigger pieces. By the time they were finished, it was growing quite dark. Ace lit the grass, which lit the small twigs, which caught the dry firewood, and in seconds, they had a growing fire. They fed it more wood, and soon the flickering flames of the dancing fire reflected upon their faces.

Ace went to her Jeep and brought two sleeping bags out from a panel built into the back. Before he could make even a joking comment on the fact that she had two sleeping bags in her truck, she said, "Before you say a word about why I have two sleeping bags, let me tell you that I actually carry four of them, a tent, ten gallons of water, and emergency rations for a week." She handed him one bag, and spread out the other on the clean desert sand beside the camp fire. He spread out the other nearby, and soon sat Indian style, smiling and feeling quite happy, and impressed with how capable, and competent, and completely together was his new friend Ace.

It got dark, and the firelight spread out and glowed from the truck, and the tree, and the shelter, and even from some of the closer rocks. Then Michael noticed that instead of getting darker, it seemed to have grown brighter. He looked up into the sky, and gasped. He had never seen so many stars anywhere in the many worlds through which he had traveled. There were so many stars that their total light actually cast a soft shadow. He held up his arm and noticed that it cast not a shaped shadow, but just a darker fuzzy place on the ground. He laughed, seeing that was because no star was bright enough to cast a separate shadow by itself. Then, as if in counterpoint to his thoughts, a small but very bright moon rose to cast a soft sepia shadow from the horizon. With the moon, the stars, and the fire, there were eerie shadows cast by all the weird rocks and overhanging branches.

Michael waved his hand in front of the fire and feeling quite silly, he made a shadow rabbit from his hands, and then a rooster, and a kangaroo. Ace watched him with great curiosity as his long fingers twisted and entwined. He made a horse, an elephant, and a dog. She laughed and clapped, simply impressed and delighted to see the Spirit Man so resourceful in repartee and overflowing with talent.

"That's great, Michael," she said, "but did you know there are monsters roaming these parts out here?"

"Really?" Michael asked, for a moment jarred to think she was serious.

"Yep! Let me show you how it's done by us pros!" Ace stood up and made her own shadow figures, using her whole body, and the light of the moon and the fire to cast them on the side of the nearest big rock. Her first one was a tall dragon, with a spiked tail. With a hoot of laughter, Michael applauded. Then she bent down and made a cat with its back arched. But when she stood back up, the shadow was clearly and horribly none other than The Wicked Witch of the West.

Michael broke out in a sudden sweat and gasped as he envisioned that Ace had transformed herself into The Lord Striker himself, and would pounce on him, tear him up into tiny shreds and kill him on the spot. But, it was Ace that was standing there in front of him, doing her shadow figure of the wicked witch, and not The Striker at all.

"Scared ya, didn't I?" she teased. She laughed as she sat down on her sleeping bag once again, no longer a witch in the dark. "Shook is a world filled with much pain and great beauty, Michael," she said. "Plenty of Strikers too, everywhere. They call themselves Strikers after their leader, Lord Striker, who breaks people's hearts in two, but the fact is most of them can't even wipe their own butts."

"Are they not likely to come here?" he asked her.

"Nah, not tonight anyway. They'll be held up fooling around with that bridge instead of coming the other way."

"There's another way?"

"Sure. There's another way to get anywhere. Hall's balls, Spirit Man, you ought to know that." Ace looked directly into his eyes, then put her warm soft hands over them and told him, in a sweet soft voice, "Listen to me, please. There is so much you need to know and so little precious time for me to tell you my story..."

She paused for a moment, and he closed his eyes and sighed. She began to speak again, and as he listened he began to feel he was listening to the Wizard of Shook, the bell-bottomed bouncing Lazaro Hitchcock, all over again. Had the Wizard magically transformed himself into The Striker? Was Striker really the Wizard of Shook all along—and the Sultan, the Secretariat, the Supreme Saladin, and everybody else?

Who was who in this dream world anyway? And now, he was facing another fateful dilemma. It didn't feel like a dilemma, but more like a night in peaceful paradise. Was Striker disguising himself as a beautiful young woman? If so, what was Ace going to do with him? He sighed and stared into the fire, hoping that she was not the man in royal blue – while knowing that he wanted to be with her even if she was—and hoping that he would make it through the night and be alive in the morning.

After a while, she stopped, and they just sat there quietly together.

"What's wrong?" Michael asked her. Ace's voice seemed to be very far away as she held back her tears and whispered to him, "Your heart, my sweet Michael. What are you going to do if you can't get it back from The Striker? Suppose we can't find Terminal Island and The Tower of Views and The Garden of Two Deaths?"

In that moment, he could see the Michael Seymour he had left lying on top of Mount Solitaire in a pool of red blood in front of the huge yellow rock with the words STRIKE THIS! in red blood. The Spirit Man also saw the lights of the small town hospital in the far distance, He closed his eyes and looked away. And when he opened them again, he was staring into the emptiness of the lonely desert, at the endless metropolis of gnome stones.

"I didn't mean to upset you," she said. "You came here for a reason. It's your mission and destiny for you to find your heart and go back home with it. Follow your dreams, Michael! Never give up, you will get your heart back!"

Michael did not say a word to her. He just looked into her misty eyes, and then past her beautiful face and at the moon hanging in the Shook sky. The bright little Shook moon had grown fat, and looked exactly like the full moon above Mount Solitaire back home in New Mexico on that terrible Halloween night when Michael the one and only Spirit Man mysteriously disappeared from the hospital.

"Hold me, Spirit Man, please," Ace whispered. He wrapped his arms around her to hold her for the rest of the night. Soon, they fell asleep together on her sleeping bag underneath a sky full of stars and one bright white-faced moon.

That night, the Spirit Man had a very strange dream. He dreamed he got up from the sleeping bag, and was walking among the weird-shaped rocks beneath a huge full moon. A rolling fog crept across the land as Michael walked between the huge boulders. When the fog touched him, his entire body became white as snow and he looked exactly like a Striker himself. His heart was beating and pounding wildly in his chest and it became visible inside his rib cage. His heart glowed with a bright orange light and boiled with red hot blood. Michael then ran up to the top of a ridge as his heartbeat grew louder and louder like a steady drum beat pounding over and over again. Michael raised his hands up to the Shook sky and he screamed out loud. And then, the doors to the heavens above opened up, and Spirit Man saw a vision there. He saw Lord Striker appear in the night sky, holding the glass jar which had Michael's heart in it. At that moment, the Spirit Man's own heart stopped beating. The world became very silent all around him. Striker spoke to him, as though to a child, saying, "The One is One! There is nothing more profound than that, my friend! Nothing!"

Then, in Michael's dream, the little Wizard of Shook magically appeared, wearing the white mask of a Striker, and dancing madly around the feet of the blue-robed giant. He leaped into the air, flipped over in a back flip, and yelled, "Picasso!" just as Lord Striker dropped the glass vessel containing Michael's heart. The glass jar slowly fell down through the star-filled sky and it landed right on the top of the big-dick rock and it shattered into millions of tiny bits and pieces. For a brief moment, the Spirit Man thought he had suffered the final death itself, and he was horrified beyond sensation, and he cried out in his agony.

But Ace did not hear him. She was still sound asleep.

## Chapter Twenty

It wasn't the silence that woke Michael, though that was the first thing of which he was conscious. He became aware he was not asleep, and he reached out his consciousness to listen long before he opened his eyes. It was not a perfect silence. He could hear a distant chirping, and a sigh of wind unfelt which told him he was not in a room, but somewhere outside. He rolled to his back on the sleeping bag, rubbed his eyes, and opened them.

The sky was perfectly black, but there were so many stars that the space between them seemed to have a texture of its own, like polished obsidian. To the east, he could see a hint of color, too dark to tell if it was just beyond the reddest crimson or just beyond the most purple violet. Without moving, he watched it spread like a gaseous amoeba across the sky, without an edge, but ever advancing.

In what seemed like only seconds, the sky began to flame in swirls of red and gold, with flashing tones of colors Michael found unlikely, but surprisingly right - colors like chartreuse, heliotrope, turquoise, and coral. As the disc of the sun broke the horizon with a blaze of light like flaming blood on polished gold, Michael marveled that it did not seem to him like a normal sunrise, so much as a recording of a sunset played backwards.

Beside him, Solitaire Bianca sighed, stretched, and then sat up. "Dawn," she said.

"Mm-hm," he agreed, not yet wanting to break the silence of the morning. He watched as she rose, slipped on her boots, and then went to poke the coals in the fire pit. She added a few pieces of wood, blew on them until they began to smoke, then touched the smoke with the flame of a large wooden match she took from a pocket in her jeans. A lively fire immediately flared up, and in seconds, the water began to boil in her blue enameled coffee pot. A cloud of steam rose up around her, swirling and twisting like a tiny dust devil, and with it came the delicious aroma of fresh coffee.

Michael sat up in his sleeping bag, and he smiled with the pleasure of seeing her. Though she still had her back turned toward him, and he could not see her beautiful face on this fine morning, his heart told him she was truly Ace and not The Striker at all. His smile became a wry grin as he observed himself relieved to find her still there with him and not vanished into thin air or turned into a monster. After all, this was the dream world and not the real world, he tried to remind himself, and he expected many strange things to happen.

Ace turned and smiled at him. "Seems to be ready, Spirit Man," she said. "Would you like a cup?"

"I sure would!" Michael said. He stretched his back and shoulders, and took the big silver cup of hot coffee she brought him.

"Sorry, I don't have any cream or sugar," she said. "Just coffee, tea, or little old me!"

They both laughed out loud at this and then she sat down right behind him and gave him the most wonderful massage that anyone could ever dream of. She massaged his shoulders and neck for a long time, digging her strong fingers into his hard muscles. Her touch was very soothing and relaxing to him. "Wow! That sure feels good," he said, with a long sigh of pure pleasure.

"Shhh. Be still, Spirit Man!" She gave him a karate chop or two along the ridge of his broad shoulders. "Chop! Chop! Chop!" She went along his upper back with her cupped hands as Michael sat Indian style, bouncing up and down slightly. Half an hour later, they gathered all their belongings and packed up the Jeep for their long trip across the wastelands, the sinister deadly Outshook.

"The place is about four hundred miles from here," she told him. "It'll take most of the day to get there." They jumped into her bright yellow Hummer and she started up the engine, put the powerful vehicle in gear, and drove off, going all the way around The City of Rocks on a dirt road. A huge cloud of smoke and dust swirled behind them as she zoomed past the main gate and then headed south on

Highway 280.

During the first couple of hours into their long trip across The Wastelands of Shook, Michael kept busy looking out his window and taking in all of the magnificent sights along the way. There were extinct volcano ranges in the far distances, tall palm trees that surrounded deep blue lakes and wide open spaces that stretched for miles across the vast deserts and plains of Shook as far as the eye could see.

Then ahead of them he could see tall plumes of smoke, and by mid afternoon, they came to a tiny village in the middle of the desert. A smoking sign announced the place as "Shakey Town." There were long rows of rundown shacks on both sides of the road that went through the deserted town. Almost every one was in flames, or was a pile of smoking and smoldering ashes. A thick blanket of black smoke covered the sky above them.

As Ace drove through the abandoned town, there was no sign of life anywhere to be found. Soon they drove into the center of town, and they parked at the main plaza there. To Michael's dismay, there were dozens of signs nailed up on the sides of the ruined buildings, most of them made from sheets of plywood. One read, "It's a wall, that's all!"

"Tell me, Ace, what do you make of all these signs?" He pointed to one that read, "If you have never been there, what are you waiting for? Get going!"

"I don't know," she said with a shrug. "I've never paid much attention to them. I kind of like that one." She pointed to a sign that said simply, "Hire Consciousness."

One after another caught his attention.

"Dreams are so stupid, only a fool is smart enough to follow them"

"Believe in me, The Lord Striker,
even if I don't believe in you, Spirit Putz.
See you at The Tower of Views
and in the Garden of Two Deaths!"

He saw one sign lying on its face in the dust, and he bent over to pick it up. It read, "What color is the wind, you idiot?"

He turned to Ace and asked her, "What do you make of it? Why all these ridiculous signs here in Shook?"

"Don't call them that," she said. "Shook is full of signs, wonders, and miracles!" She paused a moment and then added, "Misfits, mistakes, and plenty of misfortunes, too, of course."

Ace pulled out of the plaza and drove down a side road. Half a block later, they were astonished to find a group of dead people lying on the ground and slumped over in the dark doorways of their homes. They stopped and stepped out of the big jeep to see if anyone could be helped. In a few minutes, it was clear to them that everyone in Shakey Town was dead and all of them had their hearts ripped out of their chests just like Michael's own heart had been stolen from him on top of Mount Solitaire back in New Mexico.

Ace struggled for breath, her whole body trembling. Though he had seen many terrible things in his travels, Michael too was stunned. He started to gasp, "What happened here, Ace?" Then when he looked into her eyes, his words caught in the back of his throat.

In her stunned silence, Michael saw a terrible vision unfold in his mind's eye. A band of Strikers came roaring down from the tall mountain behind town, and they rode through Shakey Town on their huge chromed motorcycles, burning every block and building to rubble and ashes. They howled and cursed as they killed everyone in their sight, turning their path into an avenue of death and destruction. In his vision, the band of Strikers killed all of the innocent men, women and children in Shakey Town, every one, with sharp knives, axes, long fangs and bear-like claws, until they were all dead, dead, dead.

After the defenseless people of Shakey Town were all butchered alive, the band of Strikers took great care to preserve their bloody hearts. They carefully placed them into hundreds of glass jars which they had brought in the saddlebags of their magnificent throbbing and gleaming bikes. Then they put the glass jars with the hearts of the people back into their saddlebags and roared away with them, leaving Shakey Town to return to the lair of their sinister leader, The Striker, who dwells in the Tower of Views and in the Garden of Two Deaths on Terminal Island.

Without a word, Michael took Solitaire Bianca in his arms and held her for a long moment. She took a few deep breaths, then stood straight and nodded that she was all right. The vision of the band of Strikers faded. "Come on, Ace, we got to get out of here right now!" He said.

"Do you mind driving?" she asked. "I don't feel like doing that right now."

"Sure, I understand," Michael said. He held her door open for her, then went to the driver's side and got in, started the engine, and drove off.

They did not speak a word to each other as they left town. He fumbled with the radio but found nothing. Half an hour later, Ace sagged deep into her big comfortable bucket seat and fell asleep, while Michael drove across the Wastelands of Shook. In the silence, Michael was thinking about his own life and his journey to Shook. Why, he wondered, was there so much death and destruction in this dream world? Why, when there was so much death and destruction in his own real world back in New Mexico? "What is all the hating and suffering and dying for?" he asked himself.

As if in answer, another thought popped into his cloudy head. "Can Spirit Man be killed? Is that even possible? Could even one as powerful as Lord Striker actually destroy him?"

What could possibly be the divine purpose or rational reason to kill any living thing at all, he wondered. For any god of any world, to be The Mass Murderer of his own people could only be purely evil and unforgivable—which is not a pleasant thing to think about one's god. People on God's Earth die and are killed every day, but for Michael, it was a very strange notion to think that perhaps gods and unworldly powers should be blamed and held accountable for this mess we are all in! Weren't gods the reason for death itself, in all the different worlds since the Beginning of Time? What were they thinking when they created suffering and pain and sadness and tears? Could the existentialists and nihilists be right, in complaining that God gives us life only to snatch it away from us in the blink of an eye? One breath, and then we are gone like the dust in the wind? That too, was a very unpleasant thing to think about one's God.

In spite of all of his many strange travels as the Spirit Man, Michael thought as though he still really believed he had absolutely no assurance whatsoever that when we die we are going to another place and another time better than the one we leave.

Then he remembered he had left his shattered dead body at the foot of the Great Yellow Stone – or was it in a café in some small desert town, or lying dead in a hospital? He had seen a lot of people die in that hospital in their clean beds. He frowned, and tried to grasp the reality of that place, but it was far from the hot jolting ride of the Hummer across the bleak Outshook.

This made the Spirit Man very sad indeed and he wept as he drove along the road. "So much for being some kind of hotshot avatar, Spirit Boy," he said to himself. "Yeah?" he replied in angry self-defense. "Well, all those other avatars have failed just as miserably. So what?"

Without even answering himself, he knew what. There was only one thing left for him to do and that was to get Michael's heart back from Lord Striker. There were no answers here in Shook. He had to confront The Striker Himself if he would ask his burning questions.

"All right, I'll do it," he declared. "Whatever I've let myself in for."

As though in reply, Michael heard the voice of the helpful Lazaro Hitchcock say to him, "The Garden of Two Deaths. The first death is the killing of one's perishable body, but, oh Spirit Man, the second death is much more difficult to attain. You can kill a man off easily enough but you can never destroy his spirit." It was a most comforting thought.

Two and a half hours later, Michael came to a wide intersection in the middle of the road. He slowed down and then brought the powerful truck to a stop. He looked down the roads and could see nothing that would tell him which way to go. He looked at Ace, and saw she was still asleep. She looked so peaceful resting there and so beautiful to him that he wanted to kiss her on her lips at that moment but he dared not to because he did not want to wake her.

Michael might have been surprised when a white door with a shiny brass doorknob magically appeared in front of him in the middle of the wide intersection. There was an old wooden sign hanging on the white door, bearing antique letters reading, SEBASTIAN the Eternal SPIRIT. But he had seen such doors before, and he found himself almost expecting it to be there.

Michael put on the parking brake and stepped out of the jeep, then walked over to stand before the mysterious door. He started to reach out to touch the doorknob, then hesitated. It occurred to him that in all the times he had found such doors beckoning him, he had always opened the door and stepped through into some strange world. He turned and looked back at Ace as she lay still sleeping. He frowned, and he wondered if the right move might not be to just get back into the Hummer with her and drive away in any direction. He took a step to go and wake her, to ask her where she thought they should be going, and then he hesitated again.

"I'll just take a peek," he said to himself. He reached out his hand to the brass doorknob. The instant his fingers touched it, the entire door disappeared in a blink, and Michael was sucked into the hole like a mosquito caught by a vacuum cleaner. He tried to scream, but his voice was literally frozen in his throat. His body jerked to a tense bow as swirling winds drove subzero blasts of ice crystals into his skin. He tumbled through blinding white frozen space, whipped and twirled by the fierce blizzard winds. At first he was terrified he was up in the air somewhere tossed by the winds, then he was even more terrified when the wind luffed a second, and he felt himself being dropped. In spite of the burning pain of the cold, he tried to stretch himself out to strike the ground flat. In spite of his effort, his body jerked itself into a fetal cannonball, and he hugged his knees to his chest and waited for the end.

Before he knew he had hit something, he plowed into a snow bank and came to a stop buried in frosty powder. It was over before he realized it had begun, and his first awareness of the event was that it was over, and he had survived. The answer to his next question – how deep he was buried – came when he tried to sit up, tossed the snow from his arms, and discovered himself sitting in the bottom of a crater blasted six feet into the snow.

He crawled to the rim of the crater and took a look around. Everything he could see was white and swirling. Apart from being able to see where he was putting his feet, he might as well have been blind. By crouching down in the crater, he could give himself a bit of protection from the freezing winds, but since he was still dressed in the jeans and shirt he wore on the deserts of Shook, he knew he would freeze to death in minutes there. "Can the Spirit Man freeze to death?" he wondered.

Blinking off the icicles forming on his eyelashes, he struggled to climb out of the crater, and began walking in the direction he was blown by the wind. All of his body parts were either numb or in pain. He couldn't feel his feet, and kept falling when he couldn't control them. Every few steps he raised his head and yelled into the screaming wind, "Son of a bitch! I will survive, do you hear me, you cheesewood bastard?"

He stumbled and tripped over something that was protruding from the snow. "Yeow," he cried as his knees banged against a stony edge. For a split second, the wind cleared all the snow away, and Michael could see before him a flight of black stone steps leading steeply up into the depthless white mass of the arctic storm. Michael struggled to get to his feet, but it took a few tries before he finally was able to get a foothold on the steps and to begin to climb them.

"One hundred, two hundred, three hundred," steps he counted as he struggled up the steep, slick tower of stone. Ignoring the fact that his skin was all covered with half an inch of frost and the snow piled up inches on his head and shoulders, he labored on. After a while he noticed that the winds were less, and the sky above a lighter shade of white the higher he went. Then to his surprise, the clouds broke over him, and he saw a brilliant ice-blue sky above. A few steps higher he was able to look out over the top of the great cloud bank he had climbed out of, and also up the stairway to his destination.

He had no idea how far he had climbed, but his breath caught in his throat when he looked up the long narrowing ridge of black stone he was ascending. Like a huge blade it rose up out of the clouds, growing narrower and steeper with every step. At the very top, he could see it was only a few inches wide, and the steps so tall it was almost like a ladder, its polished black sides falling off a sheer thousand feet. Though he had felt some fear of falling on the slick stone steps while in the clouds, he had not endured the sense of height. "They are just stairs," he tried to remind himself. "I'm not going to fall down just going upstairs."

The top of the blade of stone steps just reached the very top of a great crag of gray basalt, a flat-topped mountain which thrust up from the swirling fog beneath, so steep-sided as to be approachable only by the staircase, or with pitons and ropes. Gritting his teeth against his fear, and the vertigo of the great height, he took one more step, breathed deeply, then took another, and another. The last steps were only one foot wide, two feet high, and four inches deep, so he had to use both his feet and hands to climb them. When at last he reached the top step, he was shaking and sweating, so afraid he would pee his pants and make ice that he would slip on and fall, and fall, and fall, that he lay flat on his stomach and crawled away from the edge onto the flat cold stone mountaintop.

He closed his eyes and lay gasping for many minutes until his heart stopped racing, and he was able to sit up and look around. Though the air was still terribly cold, the warmth of the sun on his skin was welcome, and he was pleased to see the frost melting away. He heard something squeaking softly, and turned to see a metal sign hanging in a stand-rack, swinging just a little in the gentle breeze. Painted and lettered exactly like the signs at City of Rocks, it read, "Welcome to Pony Hill Recreational Revelation Park." To his great dismay, behind the sign stood a tall white door with a brass doorknob, exactly like the one he had seen in the intersection of desert roads in the Great Outshook. "Aw, crap," he muttered.

Michael sat before the second white door on top of the black mountain for a very long time. He did not open or touch it, nor did he look around to see if there was somewhere else to go, nor did he consider trying to climb back down the long stone staircase. He just sat on the cold stone in the icy clear air and waited.

He had just decided that the door was the only choice he had, and he might as well just get up and go through it, when the white door opened. From the darkness beyond it, a tall Striker emerged and stepped out into the light, dressed in a long black robe and a baggy black hood. His face was painted white, and great gobs of bright red lipstick covered his slobbering lips. Michael jumped to his feet, ready to fight or leap off the cliff. The Striker laughed and waved a hand. "Hey, take it easy. My name is Sebastian. I'm the spirit of the mountain here."

"What do you want with me?" Michael asked him, still peddling backwards and holding up his guard.

"Don't be afraid of me, Spirit Man. I have come all the way up here to the top of the world overlooking all the kingdoms of Shook, just so I can teach you about the ways of the world and the secrets of the human heart. Come on, follow me." The spirit of the mountain walked past the Spirit Man to the far edge of the mountain, and sat down inside a small circle of white stones. Michael followed and sat down across from him, trying not to notice the abyss only a few feet away. With a deep sigh, the Striker reached up and took off his face. He set it aside like a mask, revealing beneath it the face of a compassionate monk. "Now, let me teach you about the ways of the world and the secrets of the human heart," Sebastian said.

He began to speak to Michael about the things that were troubling him, and the problems he was facing in his many travels in the worlds of the spirit. Michael quickly found himself very touched by the depth of the Striker monk's understanding, and he began to ask him questions eagerly. Soon Michael began to laugh, and tears began to stream down his face. All that he had ever wanted to hear, he heard. All that he had ever wanted to ask, was answered. It was the ultimate meeting of two great visionary sages.

Then Sebastian held up his hand to let Michael know it was over. "OK, Spirit Man, that's all of it," he said. "You go ahead and take the door back."

Michael stood to leave, shook Sebastian's hand, and then walked directly to the door, opened it, and stepped right through. He immediately stepped out onto the red sand of the Outshook, and the door winked away behind him. Michael took a big breath, so relieved was he to find himself back with Ace. He started toward the Hummer, ready to swear to her that it had been the most productive time of his truth-seeking life. He could remember exactly how he felt listening to the black-robed monk, but to his surprise, he could not remember a single word of what had been said.

Ace was still sound asleep as if he hadn't been gone for more than a few seconds. With a sigh, he climbed into the Jeep and drove off, passing right over the place where the first white door once stood. Ace gasped at the motion, then sat up, smiled at him and asked, "How long have I been sleeping?"

"A while," Michael replied.

From the top of the great stone mountain, The Striker Sebastian the Eternal Spirit looked down upon the Hummer driving across the barren red desert. He shook his head, then reached up and took off his monk's face. Beneath it was one bright white, with great slobbering red lips. His jet black robe slowly turned into a bright royal blue. "I will never give your heart back, unless you show some fire in your belly," he said. "Half an eternity to sit on a mountaintop in Personal Audience with me, and he wants to talk about philosophy and religion? What a bozo."

"Are you all right?" Ace asked him.

He smiled, shrugged his shoulders, and told her that he was. But he knew that he wasn't. "Close your eyes and visualize winning the prize," he thought to himself as he drove down the road with Ace's hand upon his shoulder.

## Chapter Twenty-one

It began innocently enough. The sky began to darken on the far horizon ahead of the cruising Hummer. Michael was taking advantage of the long drive to try to relax, to let the heat of the Wasteland of Shook soak him through and through, to enjoy listening to the hum of the engine, and the thrum of the knobby tires on the endless dirt road. He leaned back against the firm padded seat of the vehicle and enjoyed the feeling that even if something was going to happen when they got to where they were going, for the moment he could just drive down the road in the company of the incomparable Bianca Solitaire, the Ace of Aces.

His reverie was rudely interrupted by a sudden knife-edged wall of sound as a bolt of lightning struck the ground only a few feet from the side of the truck. The flash of blazing light was so much brighter than the burning glare of the desert sun that he was instantly blinded, and he leaped up in the seat, jerking the wheel sharply away from the staccato explosion. Ace let out a shriek and grabbed hold of his neck as he struggled to regain control of the careening jeep. "Oh, Michael, hold on," she cried.

He looked out the window and was astonished to see that he had not noticed how quickly the storm on the horizon had risen over them. The entire sky was filled with roiling clouds of every shade of black, and among them flashed bolts of blue lightning. Another blinding blue bolt blasted down to the earth beside them, and then another, and in seconds, they were surrounded by sheets of rain whipped to swirls and torrents by howling winds. He groped around the dashboard for the windshield wiper switch, and Ace reached across to do it for him. The windshield wipers went back and forth at a furious pace but it did not help. The water completely covered the glass, like a waterfall, and not like drops at all, and the wipers just swished the flow back and forth, and never opened a space behind themselves. "Dammit, dammit!" Michael yelled as he fought the wheel to keep the vehicle on the road while he tried to see where it was.

"Don't worry, Michael," she yelled over the roar of the storm. "Storms here only last for a while, and then they go away just as fast as they came along in the first place."

"I sure hope so," Michael spat, "'cause this is becoming a real pain, real fast."

"Stop worrying! You're going to come up to Exit 115 soon. Make a right hand turn there. My house is right up the road from there."

"Exit 115?" he marveled. "We haven't seen one exit all day."

"You'll get used to it," she said.

The thundering sky beat down lightning bolts all around them, from horizon to horizon. Then there was a change. They began to flash closer and closer, like huge beasts two miles high moving across the desert flashing step by flashing step, marching closer and closer to them. Dozens of the crackling blue bolts, and then hundreds of them crashed down, ripping the sky with their constant booming and roaring.

Then Michael saw something even more astonishing than the army of marching lightning bolts. Every time a bolt touched down on the earth around him, there stood an ugly white-faced, slobbering red-lipped Striker. Each stepped out of the burst of blue light as though it were some kind of magic elevator that had transported it from another even more horrible world.

Each Striker was dressed out in a bright royal blue uniform, like a broadly-double-breasted tux, with big bright brass buttons, and each wore a bright royal blue cape with hood thrown back, and face to the wind and rain. The horde of Strikers began to march like an army of leering corpses, closing, closing, ever closer to the road, and to the jeep, and to Michael and Ace. Holding his head out into the rain through the opened side window so he could see around the flooded windshield, Michael could see the wild flaring eyes and slobbering lips of the manic Strikers. Row upon row on them flanked the road, and then they reached around behind themselves and all as one brought out their strange weapons. Each held a big fat clown rifle, a blunderbuss with brass trim and bright-painted stock. With the wind whipping their hair and their capes, they all fired their guns at once. From the barrel of each gun popped a large flag on a stick, and each flag had a letter. All seen in a row, they read, "T H I S I S H E L L A N D A L L O U R F R I E N D S A R E H E R E."

"All right, you rotters are asking for it," Ace shouted into the wind. She reached over her head and pulled open a panel in the roof, letting in the whipping rain. She reached down beside her seat and pulled out a big leather purse, from which she drew a tiny bright red pistol. Then she stood up through the opening and began to blast away at the Strikers with deadly fire. The explosions from the little pistol were as loud as the lightning bolts, booming like an artillery cannon firing. The little red gat spat and spat. Each bullet she fired blasted the head right off one of the leering Strikers. In a few short seconds, she killed ten, twenty, thirty of the mug-ugly buggers. "Who the hell you think you are?" she shouted, so loud he could hear it over the roar of the storm and over the incredible jarring blasts of her pistol. "Who the hell you think you're dealing with, eh?"

Michael tried to watch her and still drive the careening vehicle through the swirling winds. The road became rutted with gullies and arroyos, and with puddles that hid chuckholes. Even the powerful and rugged Hummer slammed and lurched when it hit them. "Drive!" she yelled at him. "Drive like your life depended on it."

He did. He discovered the window in front of him would swing open, and he pushed it and took the rain full in the face so he could see where he was going. He dropped down a gear and ran at higher engine rpm to give him better quick response to the increasingly-rutted and ragged road. He grabbed hold of the steering wheel, both his hands surging with determined strength, and he began to aggressively press the big machine forward. She let out a whoop and a howl like a wild mountain wolf with the smell of blood in her nose, and began to fire faster and faster, deafening the storm with a sound like the hammering of a huge heart, relentless and driving.

With each hammering heartbeat, the little red gun spat a bolt of fire that blew the head off a Striker, and the ranks of blue demons burst and fell in a bloody row like dancing swimmers plunging into a pool.

"How many of those exploding artillery cannon shells can she have in that little pocket pistol?" Michael wondered. "Isn't it ever going to run out?" But it didn't run out. She kept on firing away, shooting every Striker right between the eyes, popping every head like a melon with a grenade in it, and leaving piles of bleeding bodies, dead, dead, dead.

"Yippee!" she hooted once again. "Don't you mess with me, you worthless cow-pie blue-bellies." She stopped firing and pulled her head down into the inside of the truck. "Get ready to turn off to the right," she said. In seconds, he came to a road sign, a huge green road sign big enough for an eight-lane highway. "The One And Only Exit 115," it read.

Michael took the exit, and followed the road as it turned around a little hill. As soon as they were behind it, the rain stopped. In what seemed only seconds, the sun came out between some scattered clouds, and the inside of the truck quickly dried out.

"What did I tell you, mister?" Ace grinned and pointed out the window as the sky turned into a perfect blue all around them, just as she had predicted it would.

"Yeah, right, lucky guess, Spirit Woman!" Michael laughed with her as he headed down the road.

"Spirit Woman," she repeated, with a hint of laughter in her voice. "I see you're beginning to catch on." She pointed toward a mountain peak ahead of them. "That's Torpedo Peak!" she said. "That's where we're going."

Michael put the Hummer into a lower gear and drove up a steep hill with cliffs of red clay on both sides, and then he drove down the other side. He crossed over a dry creek bed identified with a small sign. He was interested to see what it would say, and was almost disappointed when it read only "Stony Brook." Around a corner onto a dusty road he found himself in a pleasant little valley with clusters of fat round trees. A closer look told him they were apple trees. He drove down the dirt road a hundred yards or so, the Ace signaled to him to make a right hand turn onto her clean-swept paved driveway. With a sigh of completion, turned off the engine and sat looking over her place.

It was a very small house made of tiny rose-colored bricks. The two windows in the front were trimmed in light blue, and her front door was a bright royal blue. That made Michael a bit uncomfortable, but he put it quickly out of his mind as Ace jumped from the vehicle and began to collect her things.

"The dream girl from the dream world could all be mine," Michael thought to himself. He wondered if it was really possible for Spirit Man to fall in love with her. He wondered if that might not be dangerous. If she were just another mask worn by Lord Striker, he would surely fall victim, for he was quite taken by her. But if she were not a Striker, might not his falling in love with her be dangerous to her too?

Ace turned around then and called back to him, "Come on, Spirit Man! Are you going to sit there all day looking at my cushy buns or what?"

He jumped up like he had been poked, grabbed an armful of her things, and followed her to the door. She opened it right up and walked in. Michael was surprised that Ace had not locked her door, and as if she could read his mind, she explained, "I never lock my door around here. It's real safe in this part of the country, Michael. No Strikers ever come out here this far! So are you coming in or what?"

Michael stepped through the front door, noticing as he did that the tiny bricks of her house were actually rose-colored dominos. He put her stuff down on the floor against the wall, and when he looked up again, he found himself staring right into her hypnotizing eyes. A sudden rush of fear swept over him and almost expected to see the fiery gaze of The Dangerous God named Striker Himself in her innocent eyes.

"Spirit Man, what is it?" she asked.

"Ah, its nothing really," Michael mumbled, and then added, "I just thought you were..."

"Who? The Boogie Man?"

He almost blubbered some kind of stupid confession of his fears, but then he could see the humor in her eyes, and the warmth and compassion and understanding, and he relaxed and joined her in laughter.

"Okay, then, good looking," she said, "How would you like the grand tour of my living room right now?"

"Sure," he agreed.

Ace took him by the hand and together they turned round in a circle. It was a very small living room with a short little couch on one side, and two straight wooden chairs beside a card table on the other. An opening without a door led to a little kitchen on one side, and a tiny hallway led to a pair of doors on the other. Though very plain, it was a homey and comfortable room. She led him to the card table, and his attention was caught by a framed photograph hanging on the wall above it. It was a picture of Ace, in sepia monochrome. She was holding a tennis racket, and wearing the polo shirt, baggy shorts, and saddle shoes of a 1940's tennis outfit. Behind her extended a railing, and several rows of bench seats, like pews, overlooking a bay, and a cluster of smokestacks. "That's the Catalina Island ferry," he said, surprised he recognized it, "about 1941."

"Don't be silly," she said. "That's just down the street." She pointed to the chessboard set up on the table. "Maybe you can give me some help with this problem."

"Sure, if I can," he said. He addressed the board, and observed there was a game in progress.

"You can pick either side to play," she said.

Since the Spirit Man had spent many long nights playing with such fine strategists as the janitor John Lohman, and such fine tacticians Lazaro Hitchcock, he thought himself well-versed in the ways of chessmen. He saw that the sides were fairly evenly deployed, but something very strange caught his attention. There was only one Queen on the board, and she was neither black nor white, but royal blue.

"All right, how about a clue here," he said, pointing to the blue Queen. "Who does she think she is?"

"You know exactly who she is," Ace replied. "Here's how it works. Either player can use the Queen. The only rule is that if I move the Queen, we both must make one move with another piece before you can move the Queen—and then vice versa."

"What about capturing her?" he asked.

"Don't be silly, willy," she laughed. "Why would you want to take your own Queen?"

"She makes the game almost meaningless, don't you think," he said. "She is going to slaughter half the pieces on both sides, and no matter which side loses, she wins."

"She is truly the most powerful piece in her universe," Ace agreed, "but she is not more powerful than the player."

"That's poor consolation when she takes out my Knight," he argued.

"When you move a Knight, are you a Knight?" she asked. "When a Knight falls, do you? Come, we'll play this game out later. I think it's time for something else."

She led him to the little hallway, and to the two doors. One was slightly open, and he could see the end of an old-fashioned lion-footed iron bathtub within. The other, closed, was the brightest shade of royal blue, and marked in the gold letters of a star's dressing room, "ACE'S DREAMING PLACE." She turned the brass doorknob.

The door creaked as it swung wide open. Michael had to lean to one side to peek into the darkened space. There was just enough light to see the room was completely empty except for an ornate 19th-century psychiatrist's couch, upholstered in royal blue with blood-red brocade. If there were any windows behind any of the floor-to-ceiling drapes, they were not admitting a photon.

Michael started to turn to look at Ace, when she

startled him so that he jumped back and gasped. He stared at her. She had her head back and her arms were raised up into the air, like a melodramatic high priestess. With a voice that boomed and echoed in the tiny space like the inside of a tympani, she chanted, "Oh, Spirit Man, go you right now into the room of dreams. Oh, yes! Go you in to dream of visions. Go you in to envision images. Go you in to imagine all that you can dream. Oh, yes! Go you in to dream of all the lessons in your life..." Then she dropped her arms and drew close to him, and almost whispered to him. "...the lessons that will show you the way back to Michael Seymour's heart."

Michael's eyes widened when Ace spoke his full name. Without more hesitation than it took to give her a sign of grateful acknowledgment, and without a word, he quickly walked past her and into her room of dreams and visions.

"Here is another question for you to think about," she called after him. "When you rise from a dream, do all those you met in the dream awaken?"

The old door creaked once again as she shut it, leaving the Spirit Man all by himself in total darkness. He groped around the tiny room bent-kneed like a man newly blind. Then he stopped, took control of himself, and reminded himself that he had seen the room, and knew exactly where the couch was located. He chided himself for fearing that obstacles had been placed in his path as soon as the light was gone, and he took two steps, turned around, and sat down – exactly on the middle of the little lounge bed.

He lay down on the bed on his back, folded his hands over his chest, and tried to stare up at the ceiling. All he could see was the usual purple and green display of his retina fatigue. He rubbed his eyes to make the colors flash and move, but he knew he was seeing nothing. He took a deep breath, sighed, then closed his eyes and fell asleep. He slipped into a very dark deep dream.

In Michael's dream, he saw The Striker wearing a black hood tightly wrapped around his head, his white-painted face barely visible in the darkness within. A gust of wind blew across the universe and Michael heard Striker cry out, "I am sorry for what I have done! Will you ever forgive me?"

Still dreaming in Ace's bed, Michael felt his spirit leave his body to soar through dark skies and millions of stars, until the Spirit Man stood before The Striker Himself. Michael's spirit then asked the Dangerous God from Shook, "Why is there so much suffering in the world and why must we all die?"

Lord Striker turned his dark visage upon the Spirit Man and said, "That has got to be the stupidest question anybody has ever asked. You might as well ask why there is sunset and night."

"You mean, like there can't be light without darkness, that sort of thing?" Michael asked him.

"No, dummy, it is not that complicated," said Striker, shaking his head. "Here is the answer to both questions: The sun is always shining."

Michael's feet then gave out from underneath him and his body fell spinning out of control. He fell backwards through space and time in his dream, through a landscape of darkness and shadows, down, down, down, and back to Ace's room.

Next morning, Michael woke up in her small bedroom. He got up, put on his blue jeans, and walked down the short hallway and into the kitchen. He found his dream girl making breakfast for both of them, and by the looks of it, she had been up since the crack of dawn. A white apron was tied around her shapely waist and she was holding a black iron skillet full of scrambled eggs and ham in her hands. There was a huge spread of food on a small old oak table—a slab of bacon, roast beef, links of sausage, home made bread with peach jam, a fresh pot of hot coffee, and a pitcher of freshly squeezed orange juice.

"Good morning, Spirit Man! Sit down and dig in," she greeted him.

"Wow! What a feast," Michael said as he sat down. She handed him a huge plate of food, and he didn't even look up as he dug in like he hadn't eaten in weeks.

She took a cup of coffee and sat down across from him. "I don't have it all figured out yet, but here is my plan, Stan! We will leave today after you eat your breakfast. I will take you as far as the wall that separates the two worlds, and then you will be on your own. Understand?"

Michael sighed and nodded his head. "Yeah, I do," he said with resignation in his voice. "So tell me, Ace, will I find what I am looking for at this place you call the wall that separates the worlds?"

"That's all going to be up to you, Spirit Man," she said. "Now finish up those waffles and be ready to go in five minutes, or I'm leaving without you."

"Without me? Why, where are you going?"

"I'm out of teabags," she said. "If I can't go shopping, I don't know what I'll do."

"Oh, I see, it's like a woman thing, something like that, right?"

She shook her head. "Yeah, something like that. Now come on, cowboy, let's get cracking." She walked out of the kitchen, leaving him to himself. He quickly scooped up another huge mouthful of his delicious breakfast, gulped down another glass of orange juice, then jumped up and followed her. Minutes later, they climbed into her truck, and Ace pulled out of her driveway and headed north on Highway 25.

## Chapter Twenty-two

Night fell upon the dream world like a manhole cover slamming shut as Ace drove across the barren Wastelands of Shook. It seemed like many hours before she finally took a right turn off Highway 25 onto a new road, proclaimed by signs to be Noway Highway. She took the exit, then turned back to the left into the same direction they had been moving. It seemed curious but strangely not out of place to Michael that they were driving along parallel to the other highway, about five hundred feet apart. Noway Highway was flat as ice, and much narrower than the road on which they had been for most of the day and night. Ace was driving very fast down the abandoned highway, and the Hummer's big engine hummed its deep-throated roaring hum.

It seemed curious to Michael also that in all the time they had been driving, he had not seen another car or person. Again, he made note of the strange fact, but it did not seem to be unreal or improbable. Then he saw something that did seem astonishing. As they drove through the dark night, the ruins of an old fort appeared alongside the road ahead of them. Ace glanced at it, and gave no reaction at all, as though it were just another long-abandoned lifeless crumbling shack. The old fort appeared to have been in a terrible war and fire a long time ago. Most of the walls were falling, and there were huge holes gaping. The lookout tower was badly charred and tumbling down as well and it looked quite unstable, as though it were somehow impossibly swaying back and forth in the windless night sky.

The place was lighted by a row of pale yellow streetlamps, the only lights he had seen all night. Michael for a moment thought he would stop and pull in to see the place, but there was no exit, no place to park. There were no signs of anybody around, nor of any business offering services to passers by. To his surprise, Michael recognized the fort.

"That's Fort Huachuca," Michael almost said aloud. "But it looks like it has been abandoned for a hundred years." A flood of memories overflowed his brain as he remembered all the good times that he had getting drunk and partying the night away with Emmitt del Rio and the rest of his diminutive Cavalry at the very same fort in the Badlands of Chaos.

He started to ask Ace if she knew how they could get from the Wastelands of Shook to the Badlands of Chaos in the same world by simply turning off one road and going onto another in the same direction. Then he changed his mind and decided to keep to himself the strange feeling that he was in two places at once. "Maybe it isn't the same fort anyway," he muttered to himself.

Then Michael felt a bump, and then another. Very quickly, the smooth road became rough and bumpy, and then turned to chunks of broken pavement, then a field of ruts and potholes, and patches of gravel and sand. Ace had to wrestle with the wheel to control the truck, as the terrain challenged even the strong and agile Hummer.

"What happened? We've run out of road," Michael asked.

"That's because we're almost there," she replied, pointing ahead. He turned and looked, and out of the darkness loomed a huge gray steel tower. She pulled up right next to it and stopped. With its base imbedded in cement and huge square stones, the steel tower soared straight up into the dark sky, disappearing into the night above them.

"What is it?" Michael asked her as he looked out of his window.

"We're at DW #15 Main Station," she told him as she turned off the engine. She put her hands inside her coat pockets of her blue jean jacket and settled down into the seat.

"What do we do now, Ace?" he asked her.

"Wait," she said. "Get some rest, Spirit Man."

Ace took two long slow deep breaths, and fell fast asleep. Michael sat next to her, watching her, and listening to her breathing slowly, gently, in the quiet of the night. "Well, if she says so," he muttered to himself. He tucked himself into the corner of the seat, then wrapped himself in his own visions and drifted away in his own thoughts to another place and another time. He was in his bedroom at the Spiritman Mansion listening to his extensive CD collection. Bob Dylan was whining and creaking a song about the darkest hour always being right before the dawn.

What seemed like only minutes later, Ace's eyes popped wide open and she bolted straight up in her seat. "What time is it?" she asked out loud. Getting no immediate answer from Michael, she punched his shoulder and shook him. "Get up, quick!" she demanded.

Though quickly jarred awake, Michael was amused by her urgency, and put up his arms to defend himself. "Damn, woman! You don't have to beat me up!"

"Quit barking, you mutt," she snapped. "I overslept, and we're late as hell! You better hop to it if you don't want to miss the next train, pretty boy! Now let's go!"

Ace jumped out of the truck and began to run across the dirt field toward the steel tower. Michael shook his head then began to run after her. When they arrived at the base of the tower, he saw a flight of steep stairs leading up into the night. Without even slowing down, she sprinted up the stairs, five flights, then ten, and more. When they finally reached the top level, they found a small platform lighted by a single pale yellow bulb, which illuminated a sign that read, DW #15 Main Station. Ace walked along a yellow painted railing and toward a long line of monorail cars which sat in dark silence on a single track. When they got within a few feet of the first monorail car, bright lights inside automatically turned on, flooding the entire area with light. Two doors then opened up, sliding from its left and right sides.

"Come on, slowpoke," she said. She grabbed his sleeve and dragged him into the monorail car with her. "There," she said with satisfaction. The doors hissed shut behind them and the lights dimmed to a comfortable level. "Wow! That sure was close," she told him as she wiped the sweat from her forehead with her sleeve.

"Was it?" Michael asked. "Looked to me like the thing has been here waiting for us for years."

"Well, of course it has," she replied, "but if we hadn't got here, it wouldn't be leaving at all."

As he pondered the logic of that, an electronic bell sound announced a message, followed by a deep voice which spoke with the intimate confidence of a senior-citizens' tour guide. "Welcome to the DW Main Train, where we maintain the mainframe, retain the main game, and you gain the fast lane. Enjoy your trip! It may be the last one you ever take." The voice then rumbled in deep-throated laughter and faded away in a series of distant echoes.

With a series of quick bumps and jolts, the monorail train lurched into motion. As they left the station, Michael saw a single tall pole rising up from the darkness below, supporting a sign. Just legible in the light of a pale yellow bulb was its message, "Dreams come and go. It is up to you to catch them."

The monorail car began to glide faster and faster along its lone trackway. Shooting stars flared across the dark skies as Michael asked, "Where are we going, Ace?" But she did not answer him as they zoomed along in the darkness and deep silence.

They arrived at the next stop, DW #17 Station, about seventeen minutes later. The monorail car pulled into the tiny station at the end of its line. With a bump and a jolt, the car hit a thick rubber stopper at the end of the tracks.

Michael and Ace sat up on their hard plastic seats, listening to the humming sound of the engine. They waited in the darkness for the two sliding doors to open up, then stepped out onto the crumbling concrete platform. There was only one pale yellow streetlight at the tiny station, which barely lit up the area right in front of them. Michael could see the station was badly run down and appeared to be completely empty. "Sure is quiet out here tonight," Michael said in the eerie flickering light of the streetlight. Ace took his hand and squeezed it hard, and he was surprised to recognize that she was very frightened to be there.

As if someone else were expecting to be captured, there was the sound of footsteps running toward them. The sound of heavy footsteps landing one after another on the hard cement platform of the tiny station grew louder and louder as they waited beside the monorail car. Then Michael saw something he hoped he would never see again, a large group of Strikers rushing toward them at full speed. They were all dressed in their royal blue uniforms and they were heavily armed with rifles and swords. They ran through the dark doorway of the tiny station and onto the cement platform where Michael and Ace were standing. The Striker soldiers quickly surrounded them and pointed their guns between their eyes, and their swords at their chests and hearts.

The ugliest Striker stepped up and pushed his red-slobbered white face right in Michael's face, and shouted, "Let's go, Spirit Man! Make one funny move and you're both dead!"

They turned to go with them, when a bigger and uglier Striker strode up the stairs and appeared as a dark figure in the poorly lit doorway of the tiny run down station. The first Striker stepped back and waved a gloved hand at the dark silhouette of the newcomer. "May I introduce Captain Tyja Shapolsky, our fearless leader and Commander in Chief of this local division, which happens to be Number #73."

Captain Shapolsky was a very tall man, well over six feet, five inches tall. He had long black curly hair and he wore a black eye patch over his left eye, making him seem more like a pirate on a ship lost at sea than a Striker in an army. He had a wooden peg for his right leg, which gave him a very noticeable limp, a kind of bold swaggering limp. The most curious thing about Captain Shapolsky was the parrot which perched upon his right shoulder. The epaulet and sleeve of his dark blue long coat were crusted with crumbly globs of greasy gray guano. The most curious thing about the parrot was that it had almost no feathers left at all. Its back and neck were roughly scabbed, and its scrawny body shook almost constantly.

"So," rumbled the deep voice of Captain Shapolsky, "look who shows up on my beat."

The parrot extended his long scrawny featherless neck and squawked, "Drop dead, One-eye! Drop dead, One-eye!"

A group of soldiers stood behind their captain as he drew his long silver sword from his thick black belt wrapped around his waist. He then raised his long shiny sword up in the air, and shouted out to his men, "Take them away to the compound!"

"Drop dead, One-eye!" squawked the parrot.

Several soldiers grabbed Michael and his dream girl from the dream world by their arms and legs and marched them across the cement platform of the tiny station at gunpoint. All of them had their swords drawn out, and they took turns pointing the tips right up against the small of their captives' backs, cackling with enthusiasm.

As they approached a small building, the Striker soldiers marched them through a small plaza, which was deserted, except for a few drunken Strikers and a skinny black dog. The beast was panting as though it had been running all day, and it looked like it was starving to death. Immediately two Strikers ran over and began kicking it.

The soldiers marched Michael and Ace past Captain Shapolsky, who glared at them with his one good eye as they went by. He muttered to the Spirit Man as he passed, "The darkest hour may be right before the dawn, but you ain't ever gonna see the next sunrise, baby face, You can trust me on that one, you freak!"

After the soldiers dragged them past Captain Shapolsky, they took them out the front door and onto a street of cobblestones. There was a line of beat-up green army trucks and jeeps parked side-by-side. The soldiers took both of them over to a big truck which had a long flat bed in the back of it. Wooden railings went around three sides of the flat bed truck, but it did not have a gate in the back of it at all.

A group of soldiers then picked up Michael and Ace by

their arms and legs and tossed them into the back of the flat bed truck like two sacks of fresh green chile to be roasted. Then they jumped up into the truck with Michael and Ace so they could guard them in case they tried to escape. Once the soldiers climbed into the back of the truck, they sat down on some wooden crates along the sides of the truck. They aimed their guns and swords at the Spirit Man and Spirit Woman as Captain Shapolsky hobbled over to the back of the truck.

"Drop dead, One-eye! Drop dead, One-eye!" the annoying parrot screeched out over and over again.

Over the parrot's cries, Captain Shapolsky belted out his orders to his men, saying, "Head out, mates!"

Captain Shapolsky then limped back to his green army jeep, climbed into the passenger side, and drove off with his cousin Sonny, a short, fat Striker with a huge butt and a huge bushy black beard almost as big and round.

The night was very hot and humid and it felt like it had just rained as the caravan of army trucks and Jeeps slowly pulled away from the tiny station. One of the soldiers in the back of the truck took a cigarette out of his shirt pocket and lit it up. The young man took a heavy drag from it and Michael watched the smoke curl up into a long and slender white snake. He followed the trail of white smoke drifting out of the back of the truck and disappearing into the misty dark night.

They rode in the back of the truck well into the night along the bumpy cobblestone streets of Old Shook City. Michael was wide awake and alert as they made their way through the ancient city in the dream world. Most of the buildings in the city were boarded up and there wasn't a living soul around.

"Murdered by Lord Striker, each one of them, no doubt, so he could add to his fine collection of beating hearts," he thought to himself as they bounced up and down in the back of the truck.

Soon the caravan of army trucks and jeeps made a looping right-hand turn off the cobblestone streets of Old

Shook City and onto the soft white sands of South Gehenna Beach. Michael was very glad to get off the cobblestone streets of the ancient city because his butt was getting sore sitting and bouncing on the hard bed of the old truck.

Looking between the splintered wooden railings which went around the three sides of the flatbed, he could see ocean waves pounding a long sandy shoreline. A strange sense of peacefulness and pure happiness swept over the Spirit Man, and although Michael knew that they were in harm's way, he did not want to think about that or about his mission in Shook. At the feet of his captors, riding bruised and scraped in the back of a trashed-out old truck, he was surprised to discover that he was very happy, and he wanted to cherish this rare and very special moment in this strange world. "Happiness for me in this world, any world for that matter, dream or real like back home, is a lot like the puff of smoke coming from the young man's cigarette— here one day and gone the next," he thought.

They rode along the beach for another hour or so before they turned once again, then slowed down to a snail's pace going five to ten miles per hour. Captain Shapolsky and his cousin drove into a clump of red sand dunes on top of a small hill which overlooked the southern shore of the Bay of Gehenna. Among the red sand dunes was a row of old buildings and tiny shacks made out of pieces of rotten wood and gray cinder blocks, and lighted with a row of the baleful pale yellow streetlights. The army trucks and jeeps that followed behind Captain Shapolsky and his cousin pulled up next to them, and they parked in front of the row of old buildings and shacks.

Sonny turned off the engine as Captain Shapolsky got out of his jeep and stepped onto the graveled parking lot. Taking a wide-spread stance like Mussolini, he shouted, "Got dog it, don't just stand there, you slobbering goons. Put them in the jail house, lock them up, and throw away the keys! If they get away, some Strikers' heads are going to end up in the taco machine, you hear me. Now move it!"

The soldiers ran to the back of the truck and yanked Michael and Ace out.  They gang tackled them to the ground, picked them up by their hair on top of their heads, and dragged them across the parking lot.  They pulled them to their feet, and then marched  them once again at gun point, waving their swords above their heads, and chanting over and over, "Dreams are for fools!  Dreams are for fools!"

Perched upon the heap of crusty guano on Captain Shapolsky's shoulder, the parrot screeched, "Drop dead, One-eye!  Drop dead, One-eye!"

One of the soldiers opened the door to the dank and crumbling jailhouse, and the other militant Strikers threw Michael and Ace into their cell, and slammed shut the door behind them. Michael went flying across the room, and came to rest in a tangled pile against the back wall. He turned at once to see if Ace was all right, but she was already at his side, asking if he was all right. He assured her that he was.

It was very dark inside their new home except for one small square window which gave them a glimpse into the outside world that lay beyond.  The night sky was full of distant galaxies and twinkling stars, and their faint light barely lit up their prison cell.  It could hardly dispel the aura of gloom and doom but it did give them some comfort and hope. Michael looked up at the thick steel bars that went up and down and back and forth across the small square window of their prison cell. "It is going to be impossible to get out of here," Michael whispered into the darkness.

Michael felt the most completely lost and confused and depressed that he had ever been, and on that night he began to cry.  His sobbing was punctuated by the sound of guns popping off in the distance, and the sound of drunken laughter coming from Captain Shapolsky's men, who were partying on the beach.  Every so often the booming voice of the Captain could be heard issuing some order, or some insult, to which everyone else either yelled, "Yes Sir!" or laughed mightily.

Each time the peg-legged cyclopean Captain spoke, the screeching parrot had a few words to say as well. "Drop dead, One-eye! Drop dead, One-eye!"

Ace came close to him, and leaned her head against his shoulder, and said, "Shhh... Be still, my dear Spirit Man! Have I ever told you my story about the two prisoners?"

"No," he sobbed.

"There were two prisoners who shared the same cell, as small as this one just like us tonight," she began. "They had been there for many long and hard years, both serving life sentence with no chance of ever getting out of prison at all. It was night time, dark as hell, just it is here right now in this little hell hole of ours. The two prisoners woke up exactly at the same time in the middle of the night, and they stood up together and they looked through the small window in their prison cell. They both had the same view looking through the steel bars of their only window." She paused for a long time, and in the total silence she looked out through the steel bars in the window of their own cell. She then said, "Do you know what the two prisoners saw on that night through the steel bars of their tiny window?"

Michael shook his head, but he did not utter a word.

"One saw mud," she said. "But the other one...the other one saw stars."

"Who told you that beautiful story?" Michael asked.

"A friend of mine," she said, "a friend with a very bad reputation." As she stood looking up at the night sky through the steel bars in the small square window, Ace seemed to be in some kind of trance. Michael too looked up at the night sky, and together they saw a galaxy of stars swirling around and around in circles, and it filled up their hearts with hope.

"Everything is gonna be okay, Michael, you wait and see. You are going to get your heart back, I know you will," she told him, wiping away the tears from his eyes. "I love you, Spirit Man," Ace whispered into his ear.

"I love you too, Spirit Woman," Michael told her, staring deep into her eyes, and still wondering who she really was. And then they fell fast asleep on the hard floor, holding each other in their arms.

# Chapter Twenty-three

The morning sun rose above the Sea of Gehenna. The bright sunlight glistened upon the waves of the sparkling sea there in that strange land. Michael woke up, opened his eyes, and saw that his dream girl from the dream world was gone.

The rays of the sun filtered through the steel bars of the tiny prison cell where Michael and Ace had spent the night before imprisoned together. When Michael first opened up his sleepy eyes, the bright morning sun blinded him for a brief moment. After his eyes adjusted to the brightness of the sun, he looked all around for Ace—but she was not there. Michael got up off the floor and he ran to the tiny window in their jail and he yelled out the window, "Ace? Where are you, my love? Come back to me!"

But there was no response at all from the dream girl of the dream world. Only the wind blew and nothing else was heard.

Michael jumped up and ran over to the old wooden door in their prison cell. He was very surprised to find it was slightly ajar when he pushed on it. Then he kicked the door open with one mighty blow of his boot heel, sending it flying off its hinges and soaring through the sky a hundred feet.

He darted out of the cell and ran along the sandy beach looking for Ace. She was nowhere in sight. Nor was there any sign of Captain Shapolsky and his soldiers. There were only the tire tracks in the sand left behind by the caravan of army trucks and jeeps. Everyone had disappeared in the night, including his dream girl from the dream world. At that lonely moment, the Spirit Man fell down to his knees and cried out for his lost love, saying, "I love you, Ace! My dream girl from this terrible dream world! Come back to me! I miss you! Where are you? Why don't you answer me? I want you! I need you! I love you!"

But once again there was no response from her to his bitter cries. The only sound that he heard was the wind whistling around his head and the waves pounding upon the shore and a seagull screeching and circling the blazing sun above him.

After Michael cried for a long time, he got up to one knee and then he stood by the edge of the sea where the waves were gently rolling in and out in long sheets of white foam. He then looked up at the hot boiling sun in the hazy Shook sky.

"Is this really me, Lord?" he cried out. "Is this more real than reality?" Full of doubt and fear, he began to walk away along the empty beach looking for Ace and endlessly following the tire tracks in the sand.

Hours had passed and the hot sun was too much for him to endure. Feeling quite dizzy and sick to his stomach, he watched in slow motion as the world started spinning around and around him in full circles. He then collapsed on the white sands of the beach.

His head hit the ground first and he lay there for a very long time, motionless as if dead. When he awakened hours later, he was lying in front of a huge dark structure rising up out of the white sandy beach. At first glance, Michael thought that the large and dark structure was the famed Tower of Views which he had been searching for all these long drawn out days and months. A second look quite astonished him. It was not the great tower of the land that he had discovered, but a gigantic black wall. "The wall that separates the two worlds," Michael said to himself.

The black wall seemed to stretch for miles out into the sea, and to disappear up into the clouds on the dawn horizon. On the other side, it occluded the entire north sky all the way to the mountainous horizon on the west. The Black Wall was so long that it started from the Sea of Gehenna and it crossed over the land as far as the eye could see, disappearing into the distant blue horizon where the lowland deserts of the far west lay beyond the mountains. The black wall was as high as it was long. It went straight up into the clear blue sky and vanished into a thin layer of clouds high in the sky above him.

Michael rolled to his left side, groaning to discover how stiff and bruised and sore he was. He was relieved to see the tire tracks still in the sand. They headed straight toward the wall, then turned and followed it into the desert to the west. He stood in front of the huge black wall, full of awe and wonder as he admired it towering way up into the deep blue sky. His neck got twisted and snapped back as he tried to follow and look at the wall way up in the sky and beyond. "Whew!" he gasped.

He began to walk along it, thinking sooner or later there would be a gate through it. When he saw the light reflect from something on the wall ahead of him, he smiled in anticipation. "I think I'm beginning to get the hang of this place," he said to himself. To his surprise, the flash was from some words, huge words, carved into the face of the black stone like an enormous tombstone. The words struck him like a slap.

> "Get it through
> Your big thick head.
> Spirit Man
> Is already dead."

Hands on his hips, Michael stood and shook his head. "Oh, is that right?" he said aloud. "Is that a mother-striking fact?" He picked up a clod of dirt from beneath his feet and threw it against the wall as high as he could throw. Then he turned and kept walking along the wall away from the Sea of Gehenna, still following the tire tracks in the sandy soil, still hoping to find his dream girl from the dream world. He resigned himself to the idea that Captain Shapolsky and his soldiers had taken her away with them—or she had gone with them willingly—but he tried not to acknowledge the premonition that he would never see her again.

Hours later, Michael stood in the middle of a green meadow full of blooming yellow and gold and deep purple flowers. Before him were seven tall and majestic mountains, which rose above a carpet of deep green forest like seven angels robed in granite gowns, each trimmed with snow-white plumes of ermine. Long flowing waterfalls splashed down their faces, and clouds wreathed their highest peaks like crowns. He looked around for some kind of sign that might tell him the name of the place, and to his surprise, he saw one. Made of two upright logs and a stone base like the park signs in New Mexico, the sign said,

"Historical Marker.
These mountains do not have a name
because no one has ever been here before."

"I think I'm going to stop reading signs," he muttered to himself, and ran on. Soon he stopped in the middle of the meadow to catch his breath. A bee buzzed by him and landed on a nearby flower sucking nectar to make honey. Michael watched the bumblebee with great interest, when he heard a familiar voice behind him. Michael turned around fully expecting to see either Lord Striker or Captain Shapolsky ready to pounce upon him and kill him once and for all, but it was neither one of them. Instead it was the one and only kind-hearted, thunder-farted Wizard of Shook, Lazaro Hitchcock himself. The fine little wizard was standing right in front of him. Lazaro's fat and round face beamed with a huge smile from ear to ear and his eyes sparkled, filled with great joy at seeing the Spirit Man once again. "Hello, my good friend from the real world," he said. "Good to see you again. How have you been?"

"I'm all right," Michael told him, "but I really miss Ace a lot. I guess she has turned out to be just another Striker too."

Lazaro clucked his tongue and shook his head. "I understand the pain that you must feel, Spirit Man, but I am afraid there's nothing I can tell you about that. Now listen, we don't have very much time here together, so pay attention. We live in very dangerous times right now, so I'll tell you what I know. You must go to The Garden of the Dangerous Gods and wait for a sign there."

"I've had about enough of signs," Michael said.

"Believe me, it will come to you in a beautiful vision, so don't get your liver in a quiver," Lazaro continued. "But before you go on to your next destination I must give you your lesson for today. Ready? A journey of a thousand miles begins with the first step. If you want your heart back, start hoofing it!"

They both laughed together, and as though their laughter had conjured it up, a strong gust of wind whipped up and blew across the green meadow. It raced up and down the rolling hills, parting the tall grasses and wild flowers, revealing a narrow path all the way through the green meadow toward the seven majestic mountains in the far distance. Michael followed the narrow path with his eyes until it disappeared into the far horizon. He asked him, "Are you coming with me to get my heart back?"

Lazaro shook his head and said, "No, I can't go with you. This is your quest. Only you can go and claim your heart back for yourself." He smiled like a well-wishing grandparent, then raised his hand in a farewell salute. "See ya later, good old buddy!"

"Wait, Lazaro! I want to know something before you go! Who is the real Striker in the land of Shook? Is my dream girl from the dream world The Striker? You know I did see you go behind the set of golden doors and you changed into The Striker yourself!"

Lazaro smiled and nodded, then answered the Spirit Man by saying, "We are all created in the image and likeness of The Almighty Striker. Lord Striker is the God of Hearts and he rules this dream world with an iron fist!"

With tears coming to his eyes, Michael began to beg Lazaro, "Tell me who my dream girl from the dream world is! I want to know! Damn it to hell and back again, Lazaro, why don't you want to tell me who she is?"

"Many a cruel game, by many a cruel name. Be brave, Spirit Man, be brave!" Lazaro told him as he vanished into thin air. Feeling quite sad and lonely once again in a strange new world, Michael began to walk on the narrow path that went through the green meadow. He followed the narrow path through the dream world, heading toward the seven mountains in the far distance or wherever it might take him.

He walked day and night, and it seemed weeks had passed. On another hot afternoon just like the day he started, when Michael was feeling very hungry and weak, he had a vision. He was still walking along the same narrow path in the green meadow that went through the dream world when he saw Captain Shapolsky and his soldiers, drunk as hell and partying their stupid fat asses off! When they saw him walking past, they hooted and laughed at him, "Spirit Man, oh yeah! Why don't you come over here and kiss my spirit ass!" One soldier bent over, pulled down his pants, and mooned Michael, to the delight of the others.

"You ain't got balls big enough to face Lord Striker, you scudzy putz," one soldier yelled. "What would you do, whine and ask him for your little farty heart back, Spirit Weenie?"

"Ooooh," crooned another, "he wants his little farty hearty. Here's a heart for you." Captain Shapolsky's thugs jumped up and grabbed bloody hearts out of the back of their trucks and jeeps. They had big piles of them, hundreds of them, all slopped together, and they threw the bloody hearts at Michael who was standing all alone in the middle of the green meadow. Michael had to raise his arms to cover his head as he was pelted with dozens of savagely-butchered hearts. The entire sky turned red as blood as the bleeding hearts came flying through the air. Michael stood up straight as blood splattered all over his face. He screamed out loud at them, saying, "There is nothing here that I fear! Nothing! Now go away and leave me alone in peace! Now!"

In the blink of an eye, the horrible vision that Michael was seeing of Captain Shapolsky and his men disappeared and the sky became a deep blue once again. Michael turned around and saw the huge black wall in the distance several miles away from where he was. He felt deep within himself a strange unexplainable fear at the sight of it. He knew he never wanted to see the black wall ever again, and he began to run as fast as he could all the way across the green meadow. "Who could have built that terrible thing and what could it be for?" he wondered as he ran.

Then he saw a cluster of running shadows come out of the depths of the black wall and they ran across the green meadow chasing after Michael in this part of the green dream world. Some of these shadow runners were over ten feet tall and completely black in color. They had no facial features at all and they ran as fast as the wind itself. They chased Michael for several miles ducking in and out of the shadows. But when the sunlight struck them with a flash, it vaporized the black shadows, and they began to just vanish into thin air as the sunlight hit them and destroyed their shapes and forms. Some of the shadow runners retreated back into the darkness that dwelt within the black wall.

Having run like hell for miles fleeing the shadow runners, Michael was feeling very weak and sick to his stomach and he had a terrible pain in the back of his head. Fearing he would fall down again, he stopped and sagged to the ground, where he lay only half conscious. When he looked up, he was standing in front of a pile of gigantic red rocks which towered high into the sky. A dozen or more California Redwood trees grew at the base of these red rocks. He knew that this place was sacred to the clan of Dangerous Gods and that it was known as The Garden of the Dangerous Gods. As Michael stood before the red rocks, a golden staircase that went up to the sky magically appeared at his feet. The golden staircase disappeared up into a thick blanket of silver mist and rolling fog. Michael looked up at the magical stairs in the sky and he could see lightning flashing in the high clouds above him and he heard thunder rumbling in the far distance.

With one mighty burst of pure energy and awesome power, Spirit Man leaped through the air and ran up the solid gold steps into the sky. One hundred, two hundred, three hundred steps into the sky he ran at full speed, up the golden stairs, skipping two or three steps at a time.

As he ran up the flight of golden stairs, he only looked down once at the earth far below. It looked so far away that he thought it seemed a long time away too. He then looked up again from the earth far below him and kept running toward the clouds, the swirling, whirling clouds, where the lightning split the sky and the booming thunder shook the foundation of space itself.

When he arrived on the top of the golden stairs in the sky, it was very windy on top of a small square platform. He was thankful there was a railing so he could brace himself from being blown off. The wind howled all around his head so much it hurt his ears. Thunder rumbled in the distance and lightning flashed across the stormy skies all around him.

A deep voice spoke from within the clouds, saying, "Spirit Man, are you ready to be tested by the fire? Why you have come so far just to claim your heart back?"

Michael shouted back at the spirit of the wind, saying, "Because I got desire! I got the will power in me! I hate to lose! I play to win! I will never be defeated! Never!"

"Ha ha ha!" cried out the spirit of the wind in the clouds in roaring laughter. "I will destroy desire and fire in your belly, Spirit Man! All of it! Woooooo!" And with a howl and a moan, the spirit voice swept the clouds away from the sky above him. Michael looked up in utter awe as the sky itself opened up and peeled back, revealing a huge black hole in space above him. Then the hole began to grow smaller and smaller, and to rush down toward Michael, as though the sky had folded itself down to make a straw pointing right at him.

Then from the depths and darkness of the black hole, he heard a voice, a woman's voice, sweet and beautiful to his ears. "Michael," the voice called out, like someone with a message desperately trying to be heard.

"Ace?" Michael cried.

"If you would save you heart, you must look into the Mirror of Truth The Mirror of Truth will set you freeeeee." With a rush of wind, the voice was swept away.

Now, the most curious thing about black holes is that the rate of time changes when you are in one. In one instant he was sucked into the hole, and in the next instant he was popped right back out the other side, thinking and feeling exactly the same as he had when he popped in. But while he was in the hole, he went on another strange dream trip that took him years to complete, and led him on adventures that would fill a book.

Spirit Man found himself standing alone in the dazzling light of a new day on the shores of Terminal Island, surrounded by the Red Shake Sea, a place he immediately recognized, though he had never been there before. He stood looking up and down the shore, filled with hope that he would see Ace come running up to meet him. There was nothing, just another lonely landscape, another horizon, another path, another invitation to nowhere.

He wanted to give up and die, right then and there. But instead, he took a deep breath, threw back his shoulders, and took a careful look around the entire horizon. And there it was, not too far away, built like a white marble monument on the top of a wooded hill: the beautiful Tower of Views. It was a tall and graceful pyramid, narrow and sheer, with a golden cap like a gleaming eye at the very top. As though it had been made just for him, the path on which he stood led directly to it. "Am I on a quest, or am I being led by the path?" he wondered. "Is this a pilgrimage, or just my destiny? Is this a catechism to free the soul, or a cruel trap to imprison it?"

The Spirit Man stood and gazed at the path before him. "I guess in any case, no matter which of those answers I choose to believe, the way is there before me, and there is where I must go." He followed the narrow path up to The Tower of Views, where he found a wide and open entrance, before which was a small and elegant wooden plaque, mounted on an eight-foot replica of the tower itself. Michael read it, sighed softly, and smiled.

> "The Tower of Views
> Where we all wind up
> Eventually."

## Chapter Twenty-four

Michael stood before the great and magnificent Tower of Views. With a great rumbling, the sheer surface of the tower began to split wide open before him, revealing a pair of huge gold-trimmed glass doors. As they slid from side to side, there was a gush of cold wind, and the sound of chimes in the distance. Knowing the Tower had been waiting for him to arrive, Michael took a deep breath and stepped forward through the doors. Swirling snow flakes sparkling like diamonds wafted over the Spirit Man as he walked inside, and stood in the Great Hallway of the Tower of Views.

The Great Hallway was ten, maybe twenty stories high, its smooth walls rising to a lofty domed ceiling, all in a strange pearly gray color, as though the tower had not been built, but had grown like a shell. A wide path of gold-streaked white marble went all the way through The Great Hallway. On one side of the white marble path grew a rich green forest of oaks and tall pine trees and golden Aspens. Some were so old and tall that they almost touched the top of the dome, and Michael felt like a dwarf standing under them.

He had a strange feeling that he would encounter a grotto where vestal virgins performed pagan rituals somewhere in this forest under a dome of pearl. Thick black vines grew along the gray walls of the Great Hallway and they went all the way up to the top of the domed ceiling. Some of these vines also grew along the overhanging branches of the great oaks and tall pine trees and golden Aspens and they looked like long slender black snakes dangling from the huge branches above his head.

But on the other side of the white marble path, nothing grew at all. Everything looked like it had been dead for hundreds of years. It was black and burnt and looked very ghostly. "So, here is a scene of life and of death," he said to himself. "Strange and surreal, yet clear enough. I am standing in The Garden of Two Deaths."

# SPIRIT MAN

For a moment Michael felt the fear well up within him again, and he almost turned around to see if the door had closed behind him, and if he might better choose to run out and never continue his journey at all in this strange place. Then the Spirit Man took hold of himself and began to walk along the path once again. "There is nothing at all that I should fear. Nothing," he assured himself, observing both sides of the garden of life and death in this lost paradise world.

When he walked around a corner of the white marble path, he stopped dead in his tracks. He found himself confronting a huge glass jar filled with millions upon millions of bloody beating hearts. The glass jar was several stories high and it rested in a hollow in a moss-lined grotto, right in the middle of the living side of the green forest. As the initial shock passed him, he stood there for a very long time wondering. "How did the entire mass of the hearts of all humanity get here in this forsaken corner of the darkest tower in the dreadful wasteland of Shook?" he asked himself. "I know I have seen many weird and dreadful things, but this is the weirdest and the worst. One thing I know for sure, and that is I am very close to The Striker. This time the Mass Murderer has really outdone himself." He shook his head. "Bastard!" he cried out.

There was a sharp explosion and a crackling cloud of purple smoke appeared right in front of Michael. The explosion echoed ringing from the walls of gray pearl, and the sound vibrated throughout the long and winding dark chambers of The Tower of Views. In the center of the cloud the Spirit Man saw Lord Striker standing in front of him in his royal blue robe. Michael did not move an inch or twitch a muscle. The two great visionaries acknowledged each other's presence, one from Shook and the other from New Mexico, and they locked their eyes together upon each other like laser beams guiding missiles in flight toward their targets.

Striker spoke first. "So, looky who's here. You made it after all. Well, goody for you. Your long struggling and suffering have paid off, and you have found this secret place of mine, and you have found me. Welcome to the Tower of Views, where no man has ever been before. You are the first, the one and only Spirit Man!"

With a wave to follow him, Striker turned and began to walk along the wide marble path. "Come on," he said, "we're going to the Field of the Basket People." With a perplexed nod, Michael followed him down the wide marble path for hours in total silence. Lord Striker led the way as the Spirit Man walked right behind him through the living and dead forests on the sides of the white marble pathway. Along the way, Michael saw many more huge glass jars filled with the hearts of humanity in the Great Hallway of the Tower of Views. Michael noticed on the living side of the green forest there were many different kinds of birds and wild animals living in the trees and giant ferns. But on the other side of the white marble path where the blackened and dead forest lay, nothing lived or breathed at all.

Hours later, they finally came to the end of the white marble path. They stopped at the edge of a large circle of green grass, roughly the size of a football field. In the middle of it was a white Stone Altar. "This sacred place is known to the clan of Dangerous Gods as The Field of the Basket People," Lord Striker informed him.

In the middle of the green field there was a crowd of people, perhaps ten thousand or more, all huddled together. They were dressed in brown robes, had very long and unkempt hair, and their faces were dirty and sweaty. Some of the women and small children in the crowd were half naked, and seemed to be dying from hunger and disease. Each one had a light brown basket made from Yucca plants and all of their baskets were empty. Each had a black band tightly squeezed around his neck which, as far as Michael could tell, prevented the Basket People from speaking or muttering a word at all. They could not speak or even whisper except for uttering shrieks of agony and grief. When they did try to talk, they sounded like pigs screeching or dogs yelping.

Then a man wearing a white mask and a gold crown upon his head appeared, riding upon a white horse. He was dressed in a long and loosely fitting white robe which was flowing freely in the wind as he rode through the middle of the Field of the Basket People. "Who is that?" Michael asked.

"He is known as The Ultimate Counter-Striker, The Great Scott Freeman himself," Striker replied. The Ultimate rode around like a hero in his glory, and the people swarmed around him like a pack of beasts. On the sides of the horse were large saddlebags, from which he began to pull out long loaves of bread. He tore each one into pieces, and threw the pieces into the crowd. Then he took out two large smoked fish, and he began to tear them into pieces, and to throw pieces of the oily flesh to the people. Croaking and groaning, they held up their baskets, trying to catch a piece of bread or fish. "He comes each day to feed the thousands of hungry and poor Basket Ones," Striker told him.

Michael watched the rider with the white mask ride in, throw food in all directions, and then leave again, just as he had come. After the Striker rode off into the setting sun, the people looked into their baskets, and found them as empty as before.

Lord Striker then glided over to the white stone altar, continuing along the same white marble pathway that went all the way across the green field to the altar itself. Michael hesitated at the edge of the green field, but Striker motioned for him to follow. He was only a few yards away from the Stone Altar when his eyes popped wide open. He glued his bright blue eyes onto a small glass jar that was sitting on top of the Altar. "Michael's Heart" was written in large red letters across the front of the jar and he could see and hear Michael's heart, his own heart, pumping blood and beating alive at the bottom of it. His heart beat so loud that he could hear it over the shrieks and sick cries of the Basket People. His own heart started to race and pound inside his chest. And for the first time in a very long time, he was glad that he had never given up in his quest to get back Michael's heart.

"You are right, Spirit Man," Striker said. "Dreams should never be permitted to die. If you let your dreams die in you, then, the rest of the world will never get to see them become reality, and you will never experience or record your own personal vision for the world to marvel at." Striker walked around the Stone Altar and stood behind it. He pointed down at the glass jar with Michael's heart in it, then took off the gold collar around his neck, and wrapped it around the base of the glass jar on the altar. "You are standing in The Field of the Basket People. These people hold their empty baskets without any hope or dreams in them because they were not willing to believe they could come true. Look at them, Michael. Their baskets will remain empty forever."

A great groaning sound rose from the Basket People as Michael looked at them. "The human spirit is the most powerful weapon we have to fight against the powers of evil and darkness. You know better than anyone else in the entire universe, Spirit Man, that if a human being can demonstrate to the gods that he or she has the will to live and not just to exist, to live life to its fullest potential, to rise above the greatest odds, and to dare to dream the most daring dreams of all, even if it is an impossible dream, well then, that man or woman will get his or her wish and life back. Wherever there is life, there is going to be plenty of good things to come your way. As long as you are still breathing, you will have a chance to become somebody in the world and do something great for all of mankind to witness. You have proved to me that Michael Seymour wants to live, and to have his heart back, more than anything else in the whole wide universe, and for that reason, I must give you back your heart."

Lord Striker reached out with a long silver-tipped walking cane and tapped the big crystal decanter holding Michael's heart. It rang like a singing chime, and then opened like the petals of a big beautiful lily. Striker reached into the center of it and scooped up Michael's heart, and he just handed it to Michael. With a gasp, Michael grasped it, and held it in his hands. It seemed to pulse with life, and warmth, and it began to purr like a cat and snuggle up against him.

"I thought there would be, like, some kind of big contest, like a big challenge, and I would have to defeat you to get my heart back," Michael said, a bit confused.

"Nope," said Striker with a shrug. "You showed you had the courage, and the determination, to keep coming, to keep on coming until you win. That's courage, and courage means heart. So, congratulations. You have now got your heart back, and you can get on with your life. You are free to go now, Spirit Man. Your mission is done here in Shook."

As Michael reached forward and took his heart back from Lord Striker, there was a terrible earthquake in the land of Shook. It was so mighty in strength that it shook and rocked the foundation of The Tower of Views, and Terminal Island as well. Flashes of lightning and thunder boomed in Michael's ears as the great tower of this dream world swayed back and forth like a tender blade of grass in a fierce wind. At that moment the dome shaped ceiling cracked wide open and split in half, exposing the light of the day and the blue sky overhead.

For a brief moment which seemed to last for eternity to Michael, Ace appeared to him in a vision. Her beautiful face replaced Striker's white masked face for a brief second or two. Her lovely face appeared within the hood of Striker's royal blue uniform which surrounded his white painted face. Her sweet voice spoke to him as from a cloud, saying, "Remember, Michael! Life is full of broken dreams but if we quit, we will never win! If we never give up, we will overcome! Dream on, Michael, dream on, and remember that I will always love you, my beloved Spirit Man!"

He began to give himself to the emotion rushing up in him whenever he saw Ace, but then he made himself stop. "No, no, stop it," he yelled. "Enough with the pyrotechnic storm stuff. This isn't right."

The flashing storm, and the siren call of Ace's voice, faded away, and Michael stood there with Lord Striker, who seemed a bit impatient. "Yes, what is it?" Striker asked.

"This isn't right," Michael said. "It's just too damn easy."

"What's the problem?" Striker asked. "You've got your heart back, don't you? What the hell do you care?"

Michael frowned, as though he thought the question should mean a lot more to him. Striker was right. Why should he care about anything? He probably had all kinds of unreal expectations about what was going to happen when he got his heart back, and it might just not be such a big deal after all. He was learning his way around in the spirit world, and might even be able to start visiting places, like Paradisa, and the jovial manic world of Laszlo Hitchcock, in the constant companionship of Ace Bianca and Magellan Champs. He could simply accept the wonders and delights of being the greatest and most renowned celebrity in a hundred worlds as Spirit Man.

What's more, he had a destiny, back in New Mexico, to rise up miraculously healed, to rise above all his past failures and to let the brilliance of the enlightened Spirit Man shine so all of them back there would see he was so much more, and they would be inspired to rise up above their pathetic state, and to aspire to be something, as he was something. He would begin with a comeback on the racetrack, and he would soar past all others with power they could not even understand, and he would be worshipped. Everyone would know him, and everyone would talk about him, and everyone would love him, and everyone would care about him. Being so much to so many, why should he care about anything?

He stood holding his trembling heart in his hands. He had won. The prize was his. Why didn't it feel like a victory? Was he being deceived, and somehow foolishly leaving the real prize on the table? "What else of value might be at risk here," he asked himself.

Pleading to be embraced, his heart cried out to him, "What could be more valuable than I am?"

Then he heard again the last words he had heard Ace cry to him as she disappeared, "Look into the Mirror of Truth." Suddenly he understood. The place called the mirror of truth is in the heart, and he was standing right in the middle of it. When he looked into it, he instantly knew two things. The first was that Striker had not taken his heart, but only his pride, and his pursuit of that pride had led him away from his heart, not toward it. The second was that his heart was full of pain, and it was pain that he had caused to other people in his life.

He looked at the plump pink self-indulgent organ in his hands, and he looked at the glorious crystal decanter which had held it. Striker smiled, innocently, but Michael saw something in his eye, the tiniest twitch of one hoping another will overlook something.

"There," Michael said, pointing to something lying at the foot of the crystal chalice. "What is that, a dark little stoppered bottle? Should I presume that has someone's heart in it? Whose is it, Striker?"

Striker shrugged. "You know whose it is," he said. "You broke it."

Suddenly the gleaming, all-revealing walls of the mirror of truth came crashing down onto Michael, and in his heart he cried out in grief and pain. "Oh, God, what have I done? What can I do?" He collapsed in tears onto the ground, weeping like a broken child.

"Ah," said Lord Striker gently. "So now you do have your heart back."

"Please," Michael begged, "let me make you a trade. Take back my heart, and let me be as I was, and let me destroy myself again and again pursuing my pride, and let him have his heart back instead."

"Wouldn't it be nice if it were that easy?" said Striker with a little smirk. "The great tragedy is that no one can get anyone else's heart back. You would be surprised how many people have come to me in spirit begging for a way to buy back your heart, Michael."

"Can I help him?" Michael asked.

"Perhaps," Striker told him, "but you know of course right from the start that when he walks in the spirit world, the face he sees behind the Dark Lord's mask is yours. You are the source of all his pain, and the object of all his rage. You'll have to start from there."

He started to ask, "So who does that make you?" but right before his eyes, Lord Striker ascended up into the deep blue sky in a huge flash of blinding polychrome light.

## Chapter Twenty-Five

Michael felt himself being shaken awake. He looked up to see the face of a young waitress. "Sir? Sir, you'll have to wake up," she said. "We're closing now." He shook his head and rubbed his eyes, and noticed she wore a tag with the name Cindy.

"Oh, I'm sorry. I guess I fell asleep," he said. He looked around. "Where am I? Oh, I'm in Benson, and this is...?"

"Betty Lou's Cafe," she said with a smile.

"Did I come in alone?" he asked.

"Yes, Sir," she said. "You came in about two hours ago, bought a hamburger, and fell asleep without eating it. I'll bring you another, if you want it."

"No thanks," he said. "I feel like all I've been doing is eating, and....well, never mind. I have to get back to Las Cruces." He stood, then had to sit back down as a wave of weakness flooded over him. He took two deep breaths, then carefully tried again to stand. He fished into his pocket for a five dollar bill, handed it to Cindy, mumbling, "Keep it, thanks."

As he started to leave the little country diner, he was stopped by a newspaper on a rack, carrying the front-page banner, "Magellan Champs marries Senator."

"Oh, no," he said, picking up the paper.

"You say that like you know her," said the man standing beside him, with a friendly grin.

"I guess we all take Magellan kind of personally," he said, shaking his head and sighing. He frowned and looked at the nondescript middle-aged man leaning on his pushbroom. "Who are you? Have I met you before?"

"Oh, you never know. Name's Lohman, John Lohman. I'm the janitor."

"You mean, you work here at the Cafe?"

"I'm your janitor," Lohman said, slurping on a plastic cup of coffee. "I sort of follow you around cleaning up after you, picking up the pieces of you, every time your world falls apart. That kind of janitor."

"You mean, like a guardian angel?" Michael asked.

"Believe me, I'm no angel," he chuckled, "but here's an idea for you: how about a guardian demon?"

"Now what the hell is that supposed to mean?" Michael scoffed. "Somebody whose special job in the universe is giving me a bad time?"

"Yeah," said Lohman with a big smile. "Exactly. Somebody whose job is getting you into the trouble you need to learn to get out of."

"Are you trying to tell me my worst enemy in the world might really be my best friend?" Michael asked.

"Something like that, maybe," Lohman said. "You got to learn to follow your heart in such things. You better get on, now. You've got a future waiting for you back in New Mexico. Don't worry about me. I'll clean up here, and everything will be just fine."

He found his father's Bronco parked in the lot, and he cranked it up and turned toward the freeway entrance that would take him back down 10E to Las Cruces. Though he was not accustomed to picking up hitchhikers, his attention was caught by a man standing beside the road, waving a thumb at him. There was something familiar about the man, and he seemed to recognize him too. He was dark skinned, roughly dressed, just another highway mongrel, not at all the sort of person Michael would expect to want to talk with, or sit close to, or turn his back on. Yet, it was as though he knew the man, or if not, he should know him, or he was going to know him. With the greatest reluctance, Michael let himself put his foot on the brake, let himself turn the wheel, and let himself sit there smiling while the grotesque figure opened the door to the car, got in, and settled himself comfortably in the seat.

"Thanks, Bro," said the man, giving him a dirty broken-toothed grin. "I'm Joey Pachuco."

"I'm Michael Seymour. I'm only going as far as Las Cruces."

"Hey, right on, Bro," said the rider, reaching out to grasp Michael's hand finger-to-finger in the handshake of the brotherhood of the road. "That's where I'm going too. So what you gonna do in Las Cruces?"

Michael chuckled. "To tell you the truth, I ran away from a hospital, and now I am going back home to die with my family and my friends."

"Hey, that's cool, that's really cool, Bro," Joey said. "You figure you got an early ticket out of here, huh?"

"What?" Michael asked, perplexed.

"Come on, man, you've heard the saying — only the good die young," said Joey with a snicker. "You might have a lot more shit to go through before you get your final ticket out of this place."

"Oh, yeah? What makes you think so?" Michael asked.

"Are you still playing many a cruel game on the people you meet in your dreams?" he asked, and he gave Michael a sly sidelong grin.

Michael's eyes widened, and he began to smile, but he didn't look over at Joey. "Well, yes, I guess I am," he said, "many a cruel game indeed."

"Then you tell me, Spirit Man, are your lessons done?"

They both began to laugh.

## EPILOG

It might be very romantic to think that when Michael Seymour awakened after three weeks in and out of coma in the Mesilla Valley hospital, he remembered everything he had seen in the spirit worlds beyond the gate, and could thereafter conduct his affairs with the wisdom that would come of having such inside information. It wasn't so simple, of course. The lessons Michael the Spirit had learned, Michael the Man had to demonstrate. Like the great Norse hero Siegfried, like every man, he had to do it without knowledge of his true spiritual nature, without a secret source of the answers to all life's questions and challenges.

It is fair to say that Michael rose from that hospital bed a different man, however. "There was a point at which I wanted to die," he told people, "but I realized I was just feeling sorry for myself, as usual, and looking for an easy way out. Since I didn't die, I guess I must be here for something other than my own feelings. I'm not sure what that is yet, but I believe it's there, and I believe it matters. I guess that's what some people would call faith."

It might also be very romantic to think that when Michael left the hospital, and went back to his life and his classes, he made up with Wendy, and they fell in love as never before, and got married, and grew old together in a beautiful house, with Michael's trophies on the mantle. That did not happen. For brushing her off in public, and then making himself the most celebrated loser in the school's history, he had lost all that had attracted her to him in the first place. She was not at all attracted to the contrite and sincere new Michael, and made it clear she would rather be dragged through the streets in chains than to willingly appear with him in public.

Realizing the shallowness of her attraction in the first place, Michael was ashamed of himself, and saddened for her, but nonetheless relieved. When she became pregnant in her Junior year and married a star basketball player with oil property in the Permian Basin, he wished them well, and went on.

Deep down in some secret place in his heart, he had a vision of someone he knew he would meet someday, with tousled red hair, and just that right look in the flashing eyes to tell him he would someday be her champion, and she would be the champ's, the one and only.

Mark wouldn't talk to him. He was once reported to Michael as having said, "I'm in there with my eyes gouged out, and he falls off the rock and spends three weeks in a coma getting all the attention. It's always got to be about him, the grandstanding son of a bitch."

That was something Michael knew he would just have to deal with. Mark was always going to see him as the source of all his pain and the object of all his rage, with all the strikes against him, until he could find a way through that image to reach his heart, and the old friends could be reconciled.

Mark was released from the hospital just before Michael awakened, and after a few weeks of outpatient care at home, he moved to the New Mexico School For The Visually Handicapped, in the town of Alamogordo, seventy miles away. Michael didn't see him, but he kept close track of what he was doing, and he began to look for ways to help him secretly. Some kind of inner understanding, something deep within him, told Michael that nothing he could do would give Mark his heart back, but he could help Mark do what he had to do himself. Mark would have to face the darkness, to face the anger, to take on a challenge, and win.

The answer lay where the problem began, on the racetrack. Michael learned that Mark had met a young man in the school to whom he was a celebrity athlete, and that young man, Henry Martin, was one of the school's track team, and a long distance runner. Mark reported later that he had been introduced to Henry by the old night janitor John Lohman, whom several of the residents reported having known, but who was never around to be interviewed. When Henry showed Mark how blind runners use a partner with a lead tether, and got him to come out and run with the others, Mark found a new hope. Michael arranged for his own coach at the college to get in contact with the coach at Mark's school, and he began to act as Mark's secret agent.

Mark was a winner from the start. Thanks to Michael, somehow the local media just happened to come out in force any time Mark was running in a competition. Somehow an anonymous donor was always around just when Mark needed a way to get to a race. Somehow there would be sponsorship when Mark needed to be at the world Olympics for the Handicapped, to set one record after another.

Michael knew how the story would end, how it would have to end. One day he would have to go to Mark at the school, and confess the truth, that he had been secretly with him all the way, and now there was something that only he could do. As Mark had become a world-class blind runner, it had been Henry who had run with him as his leader. The problem was that Mark could run much faster than Henry could lead him. The day would come when Michael would have to go to Mark, and to say to him, "There is something very precious you have to win. Only you can do it, but you can't do it alone. You can be the first blind man to break the four-minute mile, Mark, maybe even to set the record for all runners. But I am the only man in the world who is fast enough to run as your leader."

Michael could see how it must be, how he would lead Mark around the track, and into the last straightaway, and then to tell him, "Go now, straight ahead, Mark, for the record, on your own, to win for yourself, and to win for me, and to win for all the broken hearts!" For Michael, for his team, for all of us, Mark would surge ahead of him, faster than anyone ever had, into the record books, and into the hearts of millions.

And no one's heart would be more fulfilled for having known him than that of Michael Seymour, known throughout many strange realms, as Spirit Man.

THE END

## THE AUTHORS

George Mendoza was raised by his mother in New York until as a promising teenage athlete, he lost his vision to a rare disease which left him not without the sensations of sight, but living in a bizarre and surreal world of blobs and flashes of color. At the New Mexico School For The Visually Handicapped, he became a champion blind runner, and he received medals in the Handicapped Olympics in New York and Holland in 1980 and 1984. He began writing in 1982, while working on the PBS-TV documentary about his life, hosted by Robert Duvall. Working with James and others, he began the projects that eventually became the screenplay and novel "A Vision Of Courage," the screenplay "W.I.S.H." and finally, "Spirit Man." Most recently, George has discovered he can use his distorted vision to create images on canvas which he says resemble the world as he sees it, and which also reflect something of his inner world as well. He has produced dozens of paintings which have been seen in numerous galleries on tour, earning him a growing reputation as an artist.

James Nathan Post was raised in New Mexico, the son of a rocket research engineer and an artist. Already a serious writer by high school, he studied physics in college, flew both jets and helicopters in military service, earning the Distinguished Flying Cross as a gunship pilot in Vietnam. While pursuing the life of a writer, he has worked as a Forest Service pilot, dinner singer, VISTA grantsman, editor for an occult publishing house, promoter and disciple to a fundamentalist prophet, airline pilot classroom instructor, member of a Las Vegas sports book gambling team, movie extra player, and other curious callings.

To see more by these authors:

www.postpubco.com
www.georgemendoza.com

# SPIRIT MAN

CPSIA information can be obtained
at www.ICGtesting.com
Printed in the USA
BVHW04s1933300718
523077BV00007B/243/P

9 781440 457524